PRAISE FOR ONE FINE DAY

A heart-warming romance, *One Fine Day* is a great way to spend a day and tease your sweet tooth. Now I need to head to my local bakery!

— T. I. LOWE, BESTSELLING AUTHOR OF *UNDER THE MAGNOLIAS*

One Fine Day reunites a determined pastry chef and a former pro athlete for a second chance at love. Settle in for a charming escape in this small-town romance that's sure to warm your heart!

— DENISE HUNTER, BESTSELLING AUTHOR OF THE RIVERBEND ROMANCE SERIES

ONE FINE DAY

A HEARTS BEND NOVEL

RACHEL HAUCK

CARRIE PADGETT

sunrise
PUBLISHING

A NOTE FROM RACHEL

Dear friends,

Down, set, hut, hut, hut! Welcome back to Hearts Bend, Tennessee, where magic seems to happen. Where a wedding chapel is the symbol of true love. Where a wedding shop comes back to life. Where a country super star finds his one and only. Where the disgraced hometown girl finds her handsome prince...literally.

When I created Hearts Bend, I knew it would be a place I'd want to visit over and over. I knew it was special. I hoped readers would feel the same.

So when the opportunity came to partner with a new author to tell stories in beloved Hearts Bend, I jumped at the chance.

In Carrie Padgett's charming *One Fine Day*, we meet another hometown boy, Sam Hardy, who's parlayed his athletic ability into football greatness. But none of us can make it through life unscathed, including Sam. At the height of his career, he faces challenges of the past and present.

Chloe LaRue left Hearts Bend to pursue her dream of

being a pastry chef in Paris. She landed her dream job, fell in love, and hoped to one day own a café of her own. But when tragedy foiled her dreams, she returns to home to rebuild her life.

Their lives become quickly intwined and well, you'll just have to keep reading to find out what magic awaits our hero and heroine in Hearts Bend.

Carrie Padgett is an author you'll come to love. She brings heart and soul to her stories. Her Sam and Chloe will become your Sam and Chloe. You'll long to hear more.

So dear reader, I present to you, *One Fine Day*, and the fabulous Carrie Padgett. Enjoy!

With affection,

Rachel Hauck

Dedicated to the memory of Elnora King.
You said it would happen. I doubted but you never did.

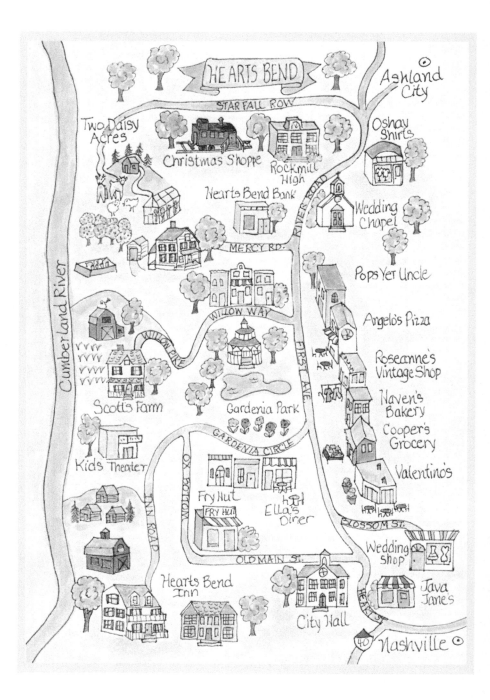

CHAPTER 1

$\mathcal{O}$f all the things Chloe LaRue had ever dreamed she'd be doing on a fine Monday afternoon in February, folding laundry in her old bedroom wasn't one of them.

Married to a handsome athlete of some kind? Maybe. Living in Paris? Oh, she'd hoped so. Making a name for herself as a pastry chef, maybe even owning her own café? Definitely.

She'd achieved most of these things, her dreams, until life kicked her to the curb.

Baking petit fours during the day and dancing in clubs with her gorgeous, extreme sports competitor husband all night, sure.

But thirty and widowed and moving back home to take care of her mother? Never saw that one coming.

She dropped the laundry basket on her bed and looked around. Mom hadn't changed much in here, other than replacing the ratty old carpet. The walls were still a loud purple, the bookcase stuffed with her old journals, and the Jimmy Eat World poster with curling and brown edges remained taped to the closet door.

Whoever said starting over, having a clean slate, was a good thing? Probably the same wise guy who said time heals all wounds. Because neither seemed to be happening for her.

She slid open the closet door and laughed softly. There were her Doc Martens, still on the floor in the exact spot she'd left them after graduating from Rock Mill High. Her studded belts still hung from the closet hooks, and her black emo clothes remained on the hangers.

If only she could go back and tell that lonely, angst-filled teenager to lighten up, to give herself—and others—a little grace. That girl who'd wanted to be different yet the same as everyone else had found herself in culinary school, and it was the best of both worlds. Her emo roots—the only Fall Out Boy fan in a school of Carrie Underwood wannabes—had given her the strength and fortitude for life in a fast-paced, high-pressure kitchen. For life as a pastry chef.

Chloe pulled a black hoodie off the hanger to make room for her red wool coat.

Oh Mom, you've changed so few things since I left. But why would she? Mom had lost so much. Chloe didn't blame her for hanging onto precious things. Like preserving her daughter's room. Chloe never dreamed she'd lose a second man she loved. That she'd end up widowed, just like Mom.

A week ago, she'd been spinning hot caramel into birds' nests to adorn cakes as the pastry chef at Bistro Gaspard, a small but highly regarded restaurant in the Bastille district of Paris. Then Mom called. "So...*I have a little bit of cancer.*" Chloe had dropped everything and returned to sleepy, slow, country-touristy Hearts Bend, Tennessee.

She'd lost her father when she was eight. Then her husband ten months ago, when she was twenty-nine. She flat refused to lose her mother. She'd will her to live, or—cue the irony and cliché—die trying.

A meow rustled the silence of the room and Chloe turned to see Honey, Mom's ginger cat, curled up on the bed. She stared at Chloe as if she understood her thoughts and spoke up to keep her from tumbling down into the familiar dark hole of pity and sadness.

"I'm working on it, Honey. I promise."

Honey narrowed her hazel-green eyes, waited a second, then seemingly satisfied, stretched and tucked her head into the crook of a leg.

A bit of light broke through the February clouds and leaked into the room, dripping over the window seat where Chloe used to read and dream about a life beyond her tiny hometown. Marriage. A pastry career. Maybe even her own café or bistro someday. She smiled, breathing easy, feeling free, at least for now, of the burdens she'd brought with her from France. The bare branches of the tree outside her second-story bedroom window allowed dim sunshine to puddle on the newly installed beige carpet.

But she didn't have time for pondering or the heart for any more painful memories, so she tipped over the laundry basket and settled down to folding as the sun retreated behind the clouds again. She snapped a cotton T-shirt and smoothed out the wrinkles. Coming home to help Mom didn't mean she was *moving* backward, right? Coming home allowed her to regroup, pass Go, collect her two hundred dollars, and—in a few months —get back in the pastry chef game.

Coming home meant she was looking *forward*.

Her earlier life, with its hopes and dreams, had ended so suddenly. She and Jean-Marc had talked of purchasing a café, had that odd, pointless argument about money, then she had found herself suddenly swallowed up by the dark pain of a graveside goodbye. The confusion of their emptied bank account and papers shoved at her to sign only solidified her feelings of loss and despair. The papers that her in-laws assured her were formalities needed to settle Jean-Marc's shares of the family business. When the whirlwind had settled, she'd faced the abrupt starkness of empty days without the man she loved.

Oh Jean-Marc, I'm sorry...so, so sorry.

Within weeks, the joy of blending flour, sugar, and butter into macarons, croissants, and èclairs had become a weight. Simple things like piping icing on a petit four became a laborious task. She battled a thick mental fog, and nothing seemed to nurse her broken heart. Getting out of bed felt like a chore. Chloe paced all night and slept all day, calling in sick to work often. Even when the sun was shining, her grief made it seem as though the whole world was cloudy. She thought she was going crazy. Often, she felt as though she was dying as well.

A colleague had recommended a grief support group, which she reluctantly joined. The leader assured her all she felt was normal. But if this was *normal*, she wanted out. What was the point of living when all her dreams—a café of their own and a cottage in the French countryside—were buried six feet in the ground with her husband?

Her breaking point had come last month, when she found herself lying on the couch of her cold apartment, calling Jean-Marc's phone just to hear his voicemail greeting. She would end up weeping and inhaling a faint trace of his scent in the threads of the old quilt. Then she'd remembered the good times, how he'd finally believed in her dream to own a café in Deux Jardins—and the grief started all over again.

When Mom called, it was as if life, fate, or perhaps God had taken pity on her and delivered her from the tomb of *Life and Love Lost*. Breast cancer, Mom said, trying to sound chipper. Chloe couldn't pack fast enough. She'd loaded suitcases and boxes with her rolling pins and cake pans, dishes, photos, one ridiculously expensive men's watch, clothes, and mementos of the life she'd built with Jean-Marc. She found herself buying a one-way ticket home.

Okay, Chloe, enough. No more dwelling on the past. Look to the future. However bleak and barren it may be.

For the next few minutes, she set up house in her old room, layering her old dresser drawers with her clean shirts, jeans and shorts, socks and undies, hanging up her coats and dresses—the remnants of her Paris life an odd juxtaposition to the girl she'd once been.

"Honey..." She held the laundry basket in her hand and smiled at the cat. "I'm leaving now. Keep my bed warm, okay?" Hand on the light switch, she was about to turn off the lamp when a glint of sunshine burst through the trees, bounced off the dresser mirror, and illuminated the row of pictures tucked into the mirror's edge. Chloe set the basket in the hallway, then crossed the room and leaned in for a closer look at the official photo of her high school cast and crew of *The Importance of Being Earnest*. Oh boy, that had been a fun production. She'd been in her "I'm a unique emo girl" element as a stagehand for the high school play, working behind the scenes, pulling the curtains, adjusting props.

JoJo Castle—Mathews, now—had played Gwendolen Fairfax. JoJo always won the female leads, but she had the talent and was always sweet to the crew, never stuck-up or snobby. Would she still be the same since she'd married Buck Mathews, the biggest artist in country music? Chloe imagined she'd find out since Buck and JoJo lived in Hearts Bend when he wasn't on tour. They were bound to run into each other in the town square.

Chloe replaced the picture in the mirror's brown, wooden frame and pulled out the next one—a photobooth strip taken at the fair that summer before their senior year. She and Sam Hardy made faces at the camera and each other. Sam...with his dark hair and deep brown eyes. Did he still have the stubborn curl that fell on his forehead? He'd done well, *really* well, as a first-round draft pick from University of Tennessee to the Titans. He'd been their franchise quarterback ever since.

Oooh, I had such a crush on you back in the day, Sammy.

She reached for the framed photo of Daddy on the dresser. How she'd love to feel his arms around her in one of his bear hugs, to bake his favorite pound cake for him one more time, to talk to him about Jean-Marc. She may have only known him for eight years, but Daddy had always made things better. He was her hero.

I miss you so much, Daddy. She ran a finger over the image of his hair, which was a tad too long for a hustling businessman, but he loved his ole '70s style. She smiled and tsked.

Now you're forever shaggy, Daddy.

A soft knock sounded at the door and Mom poked her head in. "Can I help with anything?" Her gaze drifted to Daddy's photo. "You remember when that was taken? At his last company picnic." She didn't speak the obvious. *A few weeks before he was killed.* "Twenty-two years and I still miss him."

Mom came the rest of the way into the room and picked up a different photo. One of Chloe and Jean-Marc at their wedding, coming down the aisle after the minister pronounced them husband and wife, their arms raised in victory. "I didn't know I'd left this here," Mom said softly. "I'll take it—"

"Mom, it's okay." Chloe set the gilded frame back on the dresser. She liked her expression in the photo. Would she ever smile that proudly, that excitedly again? "It's been almost a year since he died. I can see our picture without falling apart." But only recently. "Besides, I look really good here."

Mom laughed and after a second, Chloe joined her. Also only recently, she'd started to laugh again. Which seemed a sort of consolation prize for leaving Paris: her job, her memories, even her in-laws, whom she loved.

Being in Hearts Bend gave her a little window on life. Some semblance of home. Maybe she'd find the freedom to dream again.

"I have more photos with my things." Chloe glanced around the room toward her boxes, spied the one she wanted, and pulled out her favorite wedding photo, an image of her and Jean-Marc with their parents. "You looked beautiful, *Maman*, in your vintage Dior dress. Vivienne and Albert"—she gave the soft French pronunciation, Al-bare—"were so gracious and welcoming to us."

The five of them stood outside the old stone church near the LaRue family villa in Provence. Lavender fields behind them shimmered in the sun. In this photograph, Chloe smiled up at Jean-Marc while he gazed down at her with a tender expression. She remembered how his eyes had shone with love. They had been happy, so happy that day.

So how did it all end in a sudden death after a massive argument? There were moments when she couldn't really remember who had started the debate, or why. It had just seemed to snowball like an avalanche...

Chloe winced, a cold heartache pricking her moment of peace, and set the picture back in the box.

"Can we set this one out?" Mom retrieved it. "I think it will help you to grieve and recover if you remember the good times, darling."

"Y-yeah, sure." Mom knew some of the story of how Jean-Marc had died. But not all of it. Chloe peered in the box and, seeing Jean-Marc's watch, reached for it. This wretched thing had caused their first big fight, a few months after the wedding. She'd been furious when he told her what he'd paid for it.

"Why? You don't need it. A watch meant for scuba diving

with what, a chronograph and chronometer? You're a rock climber, Jean-Marc, a skier, not a scuba diver."

"Not yet, no. But I will be, chère cœur. Soon."

What a silly thing to fight about. If he wanted the watch so he could learn to scuba dive safely, he should have it. It was for his *safety*, after all. She set the watch on her dresser next to the photo. *Their* photo. Husband and wife. The couple who had stood in the chapel and pledged their love for as long as they lived.

An image flashed across her mind from Jean-Marc's grave-side service—which happened every time she wandered any distance down memory lane. A blonde woman speaking with her in-laws in hushed tones and how they'd quieted and glanced at one another dubiously when Chloe approached. But she'd caught the whispered "*affaire de cœur*" hanging in the air.

Affair of the heart.

"Chloe? Are you all right?" Mom roped her arm around Chloe's shoulder. "Are you glad to be home? Truly?"

"Yeah, um, I'm fine." Mom had been there that day as well, but she'd seen and heard nothing. If she had, she would've asked. That was Mom's way. "I'm truly glad to be home. I couldn't let you go through cancer treatment on your own. I'm where I need to be."

Mom's eyes glistened as she looked away. For her, Chloe knew, talking about the next months and year only made her diagnosis all too real. Too threatening.

"Did you see the rest of the pictures on the mirror?" Mom said, leaning in, hands clasped behind her back. "I've only dusted around them for the past decade." Mom motioned to the strip of Chloe and Sam. "I remember that summer. You and Sam spent hours in the Hardys' pool while I was learning his father's business, training to be his admin." Mom had been working for Frank Hardy, Sam's dad, ever since.

"Does Sam still call his dad Frank?" Until Chloe had seen the old stage crew picture and the photo strip, she'd not thought of her teenage friends in ages. Except Sam. Jean-Marc was a fan of American football and enjoyed telling his football-loving friends *his* wife had attended high school with the great Sam Hardy. Jean-Marc kept up with Sam via sports websites as well as the good ole *Hearts Bend Tribune*, which bragged about their hometown boy every chance they got. Jean-Marc recited details about Sam's successes, and they'd talked of a trip home last summer to see Mom, explore Chloe's childhood haunts, and of course, arrange an introduction to Sam.

"As far as I know he still does," Mom said. "Sam rarely comes home. Frank mentions him once in a while, but I'm sure he misses him, even if he's too proud to admit it."

"Sounds like they're both stubborn."

"In a word, yes." Mom laughed as she turned to peek into one of Chloe's boxes lined up along the wall. "Try working for one of them. Ooo, your teddy bear." Mom reached in for the trusty old stuffed animal, the one Chloe had moved halfway around the world—*twice*.

"For your bed," Mom said, her eyes glistening again.

She'd had the bear made from Dad's favorite flannel shirt, and Chloe liked to imagine his fragrance still resided in the threads. Maybe she'd have another made from Jean-Marc's dark blue thermal. Keep them both on her bed, make it a memorial. She shook her head, throwing off depressing thoughts.

"It's about dinner time," Mom said. "Are you hungry? We could run to Ella's Diner. Tina reinstated Monday night pie nights. If we go early, we can get a booth by the front window."

Chloe sighed and sat on the edge of the bed, a fresh batch of tears rising.

Mom placed a hand on Chloe's arm. "What is it, darling?"

She flopped backward onto the old soft quilt. "Just this... life. I don't mind being here, I want to be here, honest. But I can't get it out of my head entirely that this is not what I planned on doing when I was turning thirty. I've been a mess since Jean-Marc died. One minute I'm angry at him. The next, weeping and sobbing and missing him so much, it physically pains my chest. I feel like I'm having a heart attack."

Mom lay down next to her and Chloe rested her head on Mom's shoulder. "You know what I'm going to say, don't you?"

Chloe sat up. "Yes, so don't." She wasn't ready to hear —*again*—that she'd get over losing her husband, she'd go on with life, maybe even find a new love. Yada, yada. *Whatever.* Clearly Mom didn't practice what she preached. Twenty-two years after Daddy died, she was still alone.

Alone. Which was another reason why Chloe had left Paris to come home and help Maman.

"Why don't we bake tomorrow? That always cheered you up as a girl."

Chloe's eyes filled with tears. "MeMaw's vanilla cake?"

Mom kissed her forehead. "That's the one. Unless you've come up with some fancy French pastry that cures your blues."

"No way. MeMaw's cake is the *only* thing to soothe a sad soul."

"So, dinner?" Mom elbowed Chloe's side. "Ella's?"

Chloe surveyed the boxes stacked under the window seat— the ones she'd shipped at an exorbitant fee from France—and considered more unpacking. But where would she put the dishes or linens she'd acquired in her life as an ex-pat? The remnants of nearly eight years with Jean-Marc. She was here for now but not staying forever. This was just to get herself together and to see Mom through chemo and radiation.

Chloe drew a breath with a side glance at Mom. Now was as good a time as ever. "We've talked about Dad's death, Jean-

Marc, my return home, dinner, and vanilla cake, but not why I'm really here."

Mom got up and moved to the window. "You know why. I feel like if I talk about it, I'm feeding it. If I ignore it, maybe it will go away." She looked at Chloe. "Silly, I know."

"Not silly. I understand." Chloe slipped off the bed. "What time is your appointment in the morning?" The what-to-expect-during-treatment appointment would be Chloe's first opportunity to introduce herself to Mom's medical team. Chemo would start officially the next day.

"Nine o'clock. I hope you don't regret coming home from Paris to chauffeur me to the doctor or chemo clinic. I'm glad you're home, don't get me wrong, I just wish it wasn't to take care of me. What about your career?"

"You are more important than my career. At least death has taught me one good lesson. Besides, I wasn't in the right mind to make any more of my position at the bistro. This change to start over might spark something new, something different and good. Mostly I came home because you have cancer and need support. Mom, you were always there for me, now let me be there for you."

"I'm the mother. Of course, I was there for you. But you're supposed to be out living your life, having babies, buying a home, and becoming a world-famous pastry chef."

Chloe scoffed. "Well, life saw fit to do otherwise and there is no place I'd rather be. Fame, ah, it'll wait for me." She glanced toward the photo booth strip she'd taken with Sam Hardy. "I bet if you ask him, fame is way overrated anyway."

Mom turned away, brushing the back of her hand over her cheeks. "All this mush is making me hungry. I'll get my pocket-book and we can go."

"Sounds good." Chloe reached for her handmade leather bucket bag she and Jean-Marc had found at a custom shop in the

French countryside, and her favorite beret. She looked again at the boxes. Tomorrow. She would unpack tomorrow. If she'd learned anything from death, it was to not worry over the small things.

"Does Ella's still have fabulous milk shakes?" Chloe followed Mom down the stairs.

"You bet." At the coat rack, Mom and Chloe pulled on their winter coats before stepping into the Tennessee cold. "Let's walk. Ella's isn't far."

●●●

Their brisk walk was under a blue winter sky laced with the gold, red, and orange of the setting sun. Each step brought memories of running and playing down this lane with her friends. Riding her bike in the summer and throwing snowballs at the neighbor boy, Landon Martin, in the winter. She'd read in the latest Rock Mill High alumni newsletter he was a Wall Street mover and shaker now.

"Hearts Bend was a great place to grow up, Mom." Chloe slipped her arm through her mother's. "I have so many good memories."

"I'm glad. Hearts Bend is a great little town."

They turned off Red Oak Lane and headed down First Avenue. Across the way, Gardenia Park slept under a blanket of old snow. Mom's breath billowed about her head as she chattered and pointed out the new ice-cream flavors Pop's Yer Uncle Ice Cream Shop advertised in the window—Peppermint and Vanilla Sweetheart—as well as the pretty twinkle lights glowing inside Valentino's restaurant, the donut and muffin-shaped paper cutouts on the plate glass window, along with a placard propped on the sill of Haven's Bakery. Oh, she had a million memories of Saturday mornings at Haven's with Mom.

The more they walked, the more Chloe's memories surfaced, and she was awash with sentimentality. By the time they entered Ella's, she almost believed coming home was just the tonic she needed to shoo away the rags of death. Here she could ground herself in the truths that raised her.

Tina, Ella's pretty and peppy owner, approached with two menus and surprise in her eyes. "Chloe! My goodness, the famous French pastry chef graces my humble diner." Tina's hug felt like a warm drink on a cold, blustery day.

"Stop, I'm not famous. Not even close." Chloe slid into the second booth from the door and glanced out over Gardenia Circle, the park, and the slotted parking spaces filling up with folks coming to dine after a long workday. "But I do owe you for letting me bake and sell MeMaw's vanilla cake here. Remember that?"

"I sure do. Even back then you were a whiz in the kitchen. And darling, 'round here, anyone who makes it as the pastry chef in a Michelin-starred Paris restaurant is a big whomping deal." Tina handed Chloe and then Mom a menu. "Meredith, how you feeling? I've been praying for you."

"I'm fine, but I'll take all the prayers I can get."

"I'll be back with some waters, then y'all can order." Tina propped her hand on her hip. "Welcome home, Chloe."

The simple sentiment hit Chloe in the chest and her eyes flooded. Mom stretched her hands across the table and squeezed Chloe's arm but, like the wise woman she was, said nothing. Chloe reached for a tissue in her bag as Mom saw a couple across the way and went over to say hi, which led to her talking to the couple in another booth and the big, long table of what looked like town council members.

Look at you, Mom. She looked more like a council candidate than a woman battling a cancer diagnosis. But Chloe had seen the mammogram, read the biopsy report, talked to the oncologist while she was still in Paris.

"Fast growing, but caught early"—thank You, God—*"very treatable."*

So. Mom had cancer. People survived cancer all the time. Still, the thought stabbed icy fear into Chloe's heart. She took a deep breath and smiled as Mom's laugh echoed around the diner. She would be okay. She had to be.

Chloe dug in her bag for another tissue. Instead of the soft-pack that had taken up a recent permanent residence in there, her fingers brushed a stiff piece of paper, down at the bottom, wedged into the corner seam. With a gentle tug, it came free, and she smoothed it open on the table.

Oh my. She'd forgotten she'd stuck that list in her purse. How many months ago? Well over a year, it had to be. Our Goals for the Year, written in her neat script.

Jean-Marc's list focused on business: *Convince Papa to hire a social media manager. Research and contract with new microfiber vendor.* Hers covered both her job and her marriage: *Institute mentoring/coaching at restaurant. Weekly dates. Save 20% of our income for the café.*

A tear landed on the page, smudging the percentage sign. She remembered now. She had put the list in her purse to have it laminated, so it wouldn't curl and fade when she taped it to their bathroom mirror. But she'd forgotten about it. And then every time she had made a savings deposit, the balance was less than the last time. By the time she'd figured out Jean-Marc was making withdrawals, she'd been about to open a separate account to save for the café.

She crumpled up the list and stuffed it back into her bag as the waitress, Spicy, brought two glasses of water to the table. Chloe ordered a burger, fries, and a chocolate shake. Mom hurried over to say she'd have the same.

When Spicy left, Mom squared off with Chloe, that *mother* look in her eye. "You always tried to take care of me. It was cute when you were ten and endearing when you were sixteen. But now you're thirty and I do need some support. I admit it. We will get through this together, but darling daughter, I can't have you hovering and worrying. You'll drive me bonkers. So, here's an idea." Mom drew a deep breath and gave Chloe a tremulous smile. "Why don't you get a job?"

⬤⬤⬤

TITANS NEED A NEW FRANCHISE QB. ONE WITH TWO WORKING KNEES. @SAMHARDYQB15'S CAREER SEEMS TO BE FADING ALONG WITH HIS KNEES. SAVE THE $$ AND GIVE IT TO SOMEONE WHO CAN BRING HOME THE RING. #DUMP-SAMHARDY

– @NO. 1 TITANFAN ON TWITTER

ootball in the South was all *Friday Night Lights* and *The Blind Side*. Sam Hardy was determined to get back into the game no matter what. If he didn't play for the Tennessee Titans this season, he might never see the field again. He'd be sidelined. Listed as a has-been at thirty. And he wasn't ready to be anyone's "has been." He was a champion, and this was his year for a Super Bowl ring—and the Titans were his team.

"We don't have a choice, Sam." The tension in offensive Coach Jenson Ryder's tone could have shattered concrete. "Let's face the facts. You're just out of surgery from a torn ACL." He arched a brow at Sam who sat on the table in the Titans' Nashville training facility, his knee stretched out with an ice pack after physical therapy. "You know as well as I do, if you go out there without being a hundred percent, your career is over. So...you're on injured reserve. For the season."

He'd said it. Sam's most dreaded phrase. Injured reserve. Sam pinched the bridge of his nose and swallowed the anger threatening to paralyze his breathing. Who was he without football? Without the Titans? He'd been playing football since first grade when he started as a Tiny Mite in the Pop Warner league. Even earlier, if he counted throwing the ball with his father in the backyard when he was four. Without a team, he'd be immortalized in YouTube videos like *Greatest Game Winning Touchdowns*. Or exposés on the *Greatest Quarterbacks Who Almost But Never Won the Ring*. No, thank you.

"Bruce?" Sam looked over at his trainer who leaned against the wall, arms folded, his expression tight. "Got any ideas? Help a guy out here. There must be options."

"What do you want me to say?" The muscled man pushed away from the wall and made his way to the table. "The doc told you up front, torn ACLs take nearly a year to recover. And you're only three months out of surgery."

The cold, white tile walls in the otherwise empty training room reflected Sam's bleakness. Since the season had just ended, his teammates who were normally training—grunting and lifting—had cleaned out their lockers for the off-season.

Sam shook off the gloom of his situation with a fresh argument. "There are new methods and treatments. I read about them." He glanced between Bruce and Coach Ryder. So what if he sounded like a kid begging to get off restriction? He'd worked too hard to be sidelined. "Erickson was back in nine months and led the Vikings to the playoffs. I can beat that."

"He had a different injury. Never mind he's six years younger than you."

Thanks for the reminder, Coach. Only in football was a man of thirty an *old* man. Sam took a deep breath, tamping down his rising frustration as he searched for another option. He'd missed the last two months of the season and the team had tanked.

Because the coaches had officially listed Sam as "injured reserve," rumors swirled that the Titans were considering drafting the college national champion quarterback, Scott Fields, from Ohio State for the start of the next season. Just rumors, but still. What would Sam do with a year on the bench? He'd have way too much time to think. He could give more attention to his business ventures with his partner, Rick Moses. Some work with his charity foundation.

But when life got too quiet, when he wasn't consumed with football, Sam remembered the vacancies in his life. His thoughts drifted toward home, toward Hearts Bend and—

"Coach, what about Dr. Morgan?"

Sam gave a quick, hopefully invisible, fist pump when Bruce asked the question.

"She's just down the road in Hearts Bend and a sports medicine guru. Bruce, you sent North to her." Sam slipped off the table and hobbled toward Coach Ryder. "I want to make training camp in July."

"July?" Ryder said. "You won't be ready in five months." He and Bruce exchanged glances.

"Why not? By July, I'll have been recovering for nine months. Just like Erickson." Saying it out loud fed his hope. Made him believe this was doable.

"His injury was different than yours, Sam. We've talked about all of this," Coach said. "You knew this upcoming season was a long shot."

Yeah, they'd talked about Sam not playing but never about Dr. Morgan. Sam had been so sure he'd recover faster, beat the odds, come out stronger, that he hadn't considered the sports medicine specialist who just so happened to live in his home-town. He'd grown up with her sons, had eaten dinner at her house so many times he couldn't count.

"You're still pretty tender." Bruce motioned for Sam to get back on the table. "Not as far along as I'd like. Some of the simple exercises cause you pain."

"So that's it? You're going to stick me on IR without even calling Dr. Morgan?" He hobbled over to his gear to retrieve his phone. "I'll call her myself. I grew up eating peanut butter and jelly sandwiches at her kitchen counter with her kids."

And Hearts Bend was only thirty-five miles northwest of Nashville.

"She's always booked. We couldn't get Trevor North in to see her last year for six months."

Sam hobbled back to the training table and found Dr. Morgan's number in his contacts. She'd helped him with a small injury in college. *"Call me anytime,"* she'd said after declaring him healed and whole.

"Dr. Morgan, please," Sam said with a glance at his coach and trainer. "Sam Hardy calling."

He tried not to look all smug, because he didn't actually know if she'd come on the line, take his personal call. She had people upon people to manage her schedule. Her call-me-anytime invitation was what, ten years old? Since he only made it back to Hearts Bend occasionally—an Easter here, a Fourth of July there—he'd not seen the good doctor, or any of her kids, in years.

"Sam Hardy, is it really you?" Dr. Morgan's rich contralto voice bolstered Sam's hopes.

"Yes, ma'am, it is." Suddenly he was fifteen again, sitting in her kitchen with her son Seth and flirting with her only daughter, Haley.

"Are you calling about your torn ACL?"

"Yes, ma'am," he said again.

She was silent for a few seconds and Sam heard clicking in the background. "How's Thursday at two?"

"Yes, ma'am." He smirked at Coach and Bruce. "I'll be there." Today was Tuesday. She was squeezing him into her schedule in just two days. Hashtag miracle.

"Okay, Sam, listen, if you're my patient, you do what I say, when, where, why, and how. Otherwise, I'll toss you out." She paused, then continued with a bit of a laugh in her voice. "I may anyway, if you don't return your stepmom's calls."

Janice. She'd ratted him out to Dr. Morgan? What in the world? But what did he expect? Welcome to small-town life.

"She's my next call after we hang up," he said, trying to sound sincere. If he said it, he'd have to do it. Janice had been calling—*and calling*—about his father's sixtieth birthday party in a few weeks, wondering *when* he was coming, and *if* he was bringing a date. Well, he didn't know *if* he was going, let alone *when* he'd be arriving. And most definitely not bringing a date.

"Good. Now she owes me one. And Sam, tell Bruce to give me a call. We'll talk details."

Sam ended the call with a look at Bruce. "She says to call her." The expressions on Bruce and Coach Ryder's faces were priceless. "She'll see me Thursday." He should've called her before his surgery. She might have had alternate ideas. But he'd listened to the team's professional staff. He trusted them, which he didn't do lightly.

He'd learned a hard lesson about trust and integrity when he was fifteen. Since then, a person, a coach, or even a team had to move mountains to gain his trust and respect. But he gave a hundred percent to everything he did.

Except when it came to love. He'd made some *bad* moves on that playing field and had spent the last few years recovering from his playboy reputation. He was getting too old for that mess. Pieces of his party days still popped up now and then. While he wasn't signed up for the Lifelong Bachelors club, he couldn't see him trusting his heart to any woman. Ever.

"All right then," Bruce said. "Joann Morgan is the best, so you listen to her. Don't go getting cocky and overdoing it. No tossing the ball around to keep your arm in shape. If you injure that knee again, you're done. So slow down. Your long-term career is more important than one season."

"This is our year for a Super Bowl ring. We have all the magic. Me, Sparks, and the Brisket." Best in the league. "Our offensive line dominates the trenches. The D plays all out." Postseason told a different story. Without Sam, the team seemed to fall apart. "I want to be the captain of the ship who gets our guys their rings. That should have been us in the Super Bowl last week playing the Bears and *winning*."

Coach Ryder stepped up to the therapy table. "All right, see what Dr. Morgan has to say but, Sam, don't get your hopes up. She's good but so are our people. You'll have until July camp. I advise you to listen to Morgan, listen to Bruce. You're still our guy. We're invested in you but we're not taking unnecessary chances, and neither should you."

Yada, yada. Whatever. He had until July. Summer camp. He had hope. Sunlight broke through the picture window that looked out on the small patio next to the therapy room. Sam fastened the knee brace, gathered his gear, and headed to the door, keeping his limp in check.

A cold wind scattered gold, red, and brown leaves and an empty french fry envelope across his path. Fries. His favorites were from the Fry Hut back home. They'd sure hit the spot on a blustery day like today. After his appointment with Dr. Morgan, he might as well stop by his old high school haunt— where he had spent every Friday night after home games—and indulge. He could smell the fries now. Hot oil, crisp potato, salt. Maybe meet Jake? Nah. He'd call Cole and they could catch up.

And he'd better call Janice or hear about it from Dr. Morgan. Would she really kick him out of her program for not calling his stepmom? Yeah, better not risk it. The chill in the February day felt good as Sam walked toward his Range Rover, pulling out his phone. He so rarely called either his father or stepmother, it took him a minute to swipe through his recent calls to find her number.

"Janice, it's Sam. Sorry I've missed your calls."

❦❦❦

He'd just hung up with his stepmom, promising to possibly attend Frank's birthday party, when someone shouted his name across the parking lot.

"Hardy!"

Sam unlocked the passenger door and tossed his bag onto the seat, then turned to see built-like-a-monster-truck Marco Martelli stalking across the parking lot. He was young, twenty-three, and a second-year starter on the Titans brick-wall offensive line.

"What's the matter with you? Are you a complete jerk?" Marco stopped in front of Sam.

Good grief, he had a short fuse. "Not in the mood, Martelli." Sam limped to the driver's side door.

"Hardy, I said, what's the matter with you?"

Sam bit back a sigh and faced Martelli. Might as well get it over with. "Besides my knee? Not a thing. Why?"

"Carla."

"Carla who?"

"The girl you left Rankin's party with Friday night."

Her name was Carla? She had been so drunk he hadn't bothered to ask. He'd felt like he was rescuing a near-drowned cat. "The weepy blonde with too many margaritas on board? She was a mess. I gave her a ride home."

"She came to the party with me, Hardy. She's mine." Marco's eyes narrowed. "Stay away."

"She never said a word about you." Sam held up his hands,

took a step back, and eyed his Range Rover's door. If Martelli took a swing, Sam could dive for it but that would be a killer for his knee. "First off, I didn't know. I have a hard and fast rule about other players' girls. You know that." Everyone on the team knew Sam's code. At least what had been his code for the last few years. "She said she came alone. I drove her home and left her at the door."

"Not according to her Twitter feed." Marco brandished his phone like a badge giving him authority to arrest Sam for some perceived failure.

I MAYBE HAD A FEW TOO MANY TEQUILA SHOOTERS AT A TEAM PARTY LAST NIGHT, BUT SO WORTH IT TO WAKE UP WITH @SamHardyQB15's ARMS AROUND ME THIS MORNING. #SORRYNOTSORRY

@CurvyCarla ON TWITTER

Sam groaned. Would his past reputation ever die? Sure, there was a time when he had looked for women like Carla at parties—groupies, jersey chasers. Everyone knew how to play that game. But when he'd made the mistake of "sleeping over" and found his face, and a bit more, splashed all over the internet, he'd answered the wakeup call. Who was this man he'd become? Was this who he really wanted to be? It had been over three years since he'd been the kind of guy who partied too hard with the women that made it their life mission to hang around NFL players, offering "favors" in exchange for money, jewels, cars, and a good time.

"I don't care what she put on Twitter, TikTok, or wherever. I dropped her at her house. Didn't even unbuckle my seat belt to help her get out."

Marco gave him a long look, then skimmed Carla's social feed. He tucked his phone in his pocket, shoulders drooping, and stepped back toward the training facility.

"Marco." Sam stuck out his hand as the man turned around and waited agonizingly long seconds for Marco to take it. "Bro, stop going for these jersey chasers. They're trouble in more ways than one. Carla and girls like her are not the kind of girl you make a life with, trust me. Not the kind who will help you celebrate your career achievements or hang with you when in the valleys. If you want a relationship, go to church or join a club, maybe go back to your hometown and get reacquainted with an old friend. You're an NFL stud. Be a man, not a baby daddy. You're worth a good woman. Stop looking for the cheerleader and go for the scientist."

Marco laughed and wagged his finger at Sam. "Old man, you sound like my mama."

"Then listen to her if you won't listen to me."

Marco headed away and Sam climbed behind the wheel. As the engine roared to life, his phone rang. The screen showed his friend and business partner, Rick Moses, on the line. "Talk to me, dude."

"Hardy, how's the knee?" Rick's deep resonance untied some of the knots in Sam's shoulders over the whole IR business.

"I've got an appointment with the best sports medicine doctor in the business. I'll be on the field by July." God willing and the creek don't rise.

Meeting and partnering with Rick was one of the best things he'd done in his life besides making it to the league—which included some bit of luck. Rick taught him about finances, investing, preparing for life off the field. Even though a lot of the things he said were things Frank had been telling him his whole life.

"You've a knack for business, Sam. Invest wisely."

Except his father had completely discredited himself when he—

Rick interrupted his thought. Thank goodness. "I've got a property for us."

"Not another franchise?" Sam was always the face of whatever fast-food venture they bought. It was getting old.

He and Rick formed their investment partnership in the early days of Sam's pro career, right after they graduated from Tennessee. Besides the fast-food franchises, they owned a car dealership and a small start-up tech company Rick was sure would make Apple and Microsoft look like also-rans one day. Sam let him have his little fantasy. It didn't cost them much.

"Better than a franchise. It's a mom-and-pop business in a quaint, touristy small town. The owners are retiring..." Rick's pause made the hairs on the back of Sam's neck come to attention. What was he up to now? Whatever it was, Sam wasn't going to like it. "It's a bakery. There's just one little, tiny issue..." Rick trailed off again.

"Quit stalling and tell me."

"That quaint small town is Hearts Bend."

Sam's breath hitched. "Wait...a bakery? Are you talking about Haven's?" Sam heard the sound of papers ruffling in the background.

"Yeah, that's it. Bob and Donna Morton are retiring."

"Retiring? Wow..." He felt a wash of sentiment. One of his favorite, albeit buried, memories was Saturday morning trips to Haven's with his parents. Crullers and chocolate milk made him the man he was today. "I love Haven's, but Rick, I don't want to own anything in HB. I can see you calling me up and going, 'You need to run to Hearts Bend to check on something for me.'"

He'd put his hometown, and his memories tainted by his

25

parents' broken relationship, behind him when he left for college. Since he'd walked in on his father kissing Janice—who happened to be the mother of Sam's best friend—fifteen years ago, he'd not discussed much with Frank beyond the possibility of rain on the Fourth of July.

But Rick was still talking about Haven's. "Buddy, this is a good deal. We can't pass on it. The financials are solid. Bob was a smart businessman."

"You already made the deal, didn't you?"

"The staff has been there forever. Very experienced."

"Is one of them going to run the place? Who's going to do all the baking? Carry the vision?"

"Dude, you sound like we've never done this before. We'll do what we always do. Hire a baker, a savant, who can manage the place, cast the vision." Rick sounded pleased with himself.

"Yeah, yeah, okay. Say, is Ruby still there? She used to give me extra chocolate milk when my folks weren't looking." Sam grinned at the recollection of the cold goodness sliding down his throat, made sweeter by the secrecy.

"She's still there. Saw her name on the employee list. Been there thirty years. She'll be a wealth of knowledge to our new manager. I've got a headhunter looking for a baker now. I'd like to get on it fast."

Haven's without Bob and Donna. What would that even look like? No Bob with his Pillsbury belly and Santa laughs behind the register, no Donna singing along to the radio in the kitchen, her cheeks flushed from the heat, her nose dotted with flour. Life moved fast, didn't it?

Which was exactly why Sam had to play this fall. Why he had to secure his own Super Bowl ring. He'd just passed thirty. His father was turning sixty. Life moved on without guarantees. Then folks like the Mortons retired and took precious childhood memories with them. Sam's adult self might not care for Hearts Bend, but his child self couldn't have been raised in a better town.

"Sam? We good on this one?"

"My father's insurance agency is down the street from Haven's. Maybe we should pass on this one." If he and Rick owned a business on the same street as Hardy Insurance, what would come next? Exchanging May Day baskets and shaking hands at Chamber of Commerce mixers?

"You don't have to see him. He doesn't even have to know you own the bakery. HARDRICK LLC will own it." Rick could be persuasive when it came to their fiscal bottom line. "We should probably meet to hire a new bakery manager in person, but otherwise, if you don't want to be point on this one, I'll handle things from Atlanta. That's how we do everything else." It was like Rick read his mind. "Sam, believe it or not, this bakery is one of the best deals we've come across. Look up Hearts Bend tourism and revenue. Busting at the seams. If we don't get in now, it'll cost us double to get in later, if we manage to get in at all."

Sam stopped for a red light and drummed his fingers on the steering wheel. "You're right, I know it, but Frank and I—"

"You're a grown man, Sam. Act like it. When can you get to Hearts Bend to sign the papers? This week preferably."

Signing this week? So, Rick must've purchased the place when Sam was having surgery. Note to self: tell him not to do that again.

He hated when Rick played the older brother. Hated it even more when he was right.

"Fine. I've an appointment with Dr. Morgan in Hearts Bend Thursday. I can meet you then."

"Actually, that's perfect. Bob and Donna want us to interview some local woman for baker and manager. They say she's very good. Lots of experience."

"I thought you were using a headhunter."

"Yeah, but Bob asked if I'd interview this woman as a favor to a friend."

"Then why is she in Hearts Bend?"

"Family reason. Wrote it all down somewhere. We'll meet her on Thursday. By the way—" Rick paused with a hitch in his sigh.

"What?" Sam said.

"It's nothing, really, but weren't you giving up the love 'em and leave 'em lifestyle? What happened to wanting a real relationship? Commitment."

"Is this about Curvy Carla? I don't even know her, Rick."

"Never stopped you before."

Sam winced. He hated who he'd been three, four years ago. "She told me she was alone and wanted to go home. I should've known better. But I played the Good Samaritan and drove her home. Didn't even get out of the car, Rick. End of story. She's a groupie. Had her hooks in Martelli until she got bored."

"I believe you, but I had to check," Rick said. "Your private life is your business, but I notice we've had a lot more success since you changed your ways." He cleared his throat. "I would be remiss as your fiduciary partner and advisor if I didn't point that out."

"Find the right woman for me and I'll join you with the house and the picket fence with kids' toys on the front lawn." The words slid out even though Sam doubted their truth. He wasn't one to commit. At least he'd been telling himself that for years. But lately? He'd wondered if *maybe* there was someone out there for him.

Rick's laugh came easy. "Deal, brother. Deal."

Sam ended the call and turned onto Rosa Parks Boulevard. A fine day this had turned out to be. He'd gotten in with Dr. Morgan, but the therapy and follow-up visits would put him in

Hearts Bend every week. Then Janice had pleaded with him to attend his dad's sixtieth. Now he was about to own a Hearts Bend tradition, Haven's Bakery. If he didn't know better, he'd think this was some sort of celestial conspiracy.

Maybe it was time to be a man. Rick's words, not his. Time to face the pain of his past. He wasn't that fifteen-year-old anymore, watching his dad seduce another woman. Or watching his mom toss her suitcases into her car, declaring she was going to Charleston for some "me time."

"I'll be home soon, Sammy."

Fifteen years later, he was still waiting.

CHAPTER 3

"*A*re you sure you feel up to working this morning?" Chloe gathered her and Mom's dirty breakfast dishes and carried them to the sink. She'd had her first chemo session yesterday morning and still seemed rather knocked out by it.

"I'm fine, Chloe." Mom sounded uncharacteristically cranky. "I told you not to hover." Except she wasn't fine. She walked hunched over and her eyes were rimmed with dark circles.

"They told us you might be tired. There's no crime in staying home to rest." Chloe reached for her phone. "Let me call Frank Hardy and—"

Mom clapped her hand over Chloe's and lowered the phone. "What time is *your* interview?"

"I don't think I should go. I need to be here for you." On the way back from Ella's Monday evening, they had paused by Haven's and seen a sign in the window. *Baker and Manager Wanted.*

Mom called Bob and Donna while Chloe called the Atlanta area code to inquire. She talked to a headhunter who said she'd get back to her. So far, no call. Mom hung up with Bob saying the same. *"He'll call me back."* Which he did, ten minutes later as they walked into the house. *"Bob says the new owner will see you Thursday at two."*

"Chloe LaRue, you're going to that interview. I asked a favor of a dear friend, and you *will* keep your word.'

"And if I don't? You'll cut off my allowance?" Chloe forced amusement into her tone.

"Yes!" When Mom laughed, the gray pallor of her cheeks faded. "Chloe, I think this job will do you, and me, a world of good. I love having you near, but I'm used to living alone. You, my precious girl, must learn to get on with your life. Bob said the new owner is coming in to sign papers and it'd be nice to hire his new manager the same day. Now let me get ready for work." Mom paused at the kitchen door. "When you get the job, we can meet for lunch now and then. Frank's office is just down the street. At least until we move to the new building."

"I'd like that," Chloe said. Mom was planning ahead, thinking of a future. Chloe should take a page from her book.

Finishing the dishes, Chloe thought about the interview. She didn't have to take the job if they offered it to her. Maman was more important than glazing donuts for the good folks of Hearts Bend. Then again, Mom seemed adamant about having some space. Apparently it was easy to get used to living alone.

Chloe prepped a snack of tea and some crackers and cheese, along with apple slices, for Mom to take to work. Much like the snacks Mom used to make for her when she had play practice after school.

Mom had rented the rambling quasi-farmhouse positioned at the end of a city street when Chloe was fifteen. Before that, they'd lived with MeMaw and Pops for nearly seven years until Mom saved enough for them to move out. She'd been a sales-clerk at Cooper's Market, picking up every shift she could, and going to business school at night and online when she could. When Mom started working with Frank Hardy, they'd been able to move out. A few years later, Mom bought the house.

"I'm off." Mom stood at the door, slipping on her gloves. "What are you doing before your interview? Are you sure you don't need the car?"

"I thought I'd explore the town. I haven't been here in three years. I want to see what's new."

After Mom left, Chloe soaked in a long hot bath, dressed warm for her explorations, and spent sixty seconds scratching Honey behind the ears. Then she was off.

She wandered through Gardenia Park, sat on the bench under the large oak listening to the sounds of a small town, then strolled past Ella's to First Avenue where pink tinsel hearts still adorned the lampposts. The hearts would soon be replaced with green shamrocks. Hearts Bend sure did love its holidays. Hands in her pockets, the cold air on her cheeks, she strolled down the sidewalk past shoppers who called out to one another. She jumped sideways as a couple of joggers loped past toward the park, their breath misting about their heads.

In the familiar calm, she reflected on her life. She'd been moving on autopilot, living in the past, stuck in her final moments of life with Jean-Marc. Their arguments. His refusal to tell her why he was withdrawing large amounts from their joint bank account, from the savings they'd planned on to buy a café in the French countryside. His plea for her to go with him to Zermatt because the trip was more than just testing the new ski design. It was a family trip with his parents and brothers, the owners and executives of Sport de Qualité.

Except the chic brasserie where Chloe worked, Bistro Gaspard, in the up-and-coming Bastille neighborhood, was participating in the Moveable Feast. All the restaurants along the Rue de Charonne showcased their menu for five nights.

People came from all over France to dine on some of the best food in the country. It was an honor for Bistro Gaspard to participate. Chloe had enlisted her charming and very handsome husband to direct diners down the Rue Chanzy to the next stop.

Typically, they'd balanced their careers, supporting each other when an event or job demanded more of their time. On occasion, Jean-Marc deferred to his parents since it was a family-owned company. The Moveable Feast collided with the testing of Qualité's new skis.

"I can't, chère cœur. It is the test of our new design. I'm the one to ski."

"But you promised me. We're so excited to have you working with us. Besides, I hate when you test new skis on an unfamiliar trail. I have nightmares of you slamming into a tree or going over the side of a mountain."

"Ha, ha, ma chère amour, no tree or mountain can best me."

So he'd gone to Zermatt and left her behind to stew in her anger and resentment.

The chill in the Tennessee air nipped at her cheeks as she walked, retracing her and Mom's steps from Monday night. She stayed on First Avenue to Java Jane's, where she stood for a moment. A dusting of cold snow swept down the sidewalk and she felt it through her boots and wool socks, up into her still frozen heart. Her frozen heart that everyone assured her would begin to thaw after a year. It would be a year in two months and that particular organ seemed stubbornly focused on remaining hard and immobile.

As she opened the door to Java Jane's, a flier taped to the glass announcing the upcoming Spring Concert in the Park flapped and a voice called to her from the sidewalk.

"Chloe Beason, is that you?"

She turned to the voice behind her to see a pretty

blonde with a friendly smile. "Yes, it's Chloe LaRue. Umm..." Recognition flooded Chloe just as her pause became awkward. "Sophie Monroe? Hi." They'd been classmates and fellow sufferers in Mr. Ellison's chemistry class at Rock Mill High. She was also Sam Hardy's cousin.

"Wow, look at you!" Sophie grabbed her in a Hearts Bend hug. "I thought you were in France."

"I was but..." Chloe shrugged and dug her hands deeper into her coat pockets. "It was time to come home."

"Well, welcome back." Sophie shivered and reached for Java Jane's glass door. "Best get inside. Jane will kill us, heating up all of First Avenue." Sophie stepped aside for Chloe to enter.

Chloe inhaled the heady aromas of dark roast coffee and baked treats. The combination made her homesick for MeMaw's. Her kitchen had been Chloe's comfort after Dad died. MeMaw had taught her to bake. She didn't scold her for getting eggshells in the vanilla cake batter or for dribbling flour across the counter. MeMaw's kitchen was her happy, safe place. Papaw was her stability.

Perhaps those flavors and aromas could help thaw this grown-up heart too.

Sophie ordered a grande mocha and Chloe chose a small latte. "Do you have a sec?" Sophie pointed to a stand-up table. "I'd love to hear what you're up to these days." She pressed two fingers to her lips. "I'm an airhead. I'm so sorry. I know about Jean-Marc. Ugh."

Sophie had always been a kind friend. She'd included Chloe in her and Sam's high school clique of jocks and cheerleaders. It puzzled their friends and classmates, but they tolerated the awkward loner dressed in black. A testament to how well liked both Sam and Sophie were.

When Sophie touched her hand, Chloe's tears surfaced. Guess those wells weren't empty after all.

"Thank you," Chloe said in a whisper. "Ten months now. I'm still waiting to get used to it." She swallowed the swell of emotion in her chest. For the first six months, the grief had always caught her off guard, when she least expected it, coming in waves. Sometimes one giant tsunami, other times, sets of swells, battering her fragile shoals of strength and coping. Lately the storms came less often, but no less intense.

"I can't say I've experienced what you're going through, but I'm a good listener if you ever want to talk."

Chloe nodded. That's all she could manage. She sipped her latte and glanced around Java Jane's, willing the surge of emotion to die down. "So..." She cleared the fog from her voice. "W-what's new with you, Sophie?"

Sophie pointed out the side window toward the Book Nook. "I'm a business owner now. Bought it seven months back. It's touch and go some months but knock on wood—" She rapped the tabletop. "I'm in the black. Independent bookstores are making a comeback in this digital age."

"You own the Book Nook?" The news cheered Chloe. "I used to *love* hanging out there, breathing in the scent of the pages, picking out a book, curling up in a chair and reading until dinner time. Or the store closed."

"Me too. I lived in the mystery section." Sophie sipped her mocha with a glance at her watch. "You must come and hang out. If I could afford to hire you, I would."

Chloe laughed. "I'd accept. As a matter of fact, I'm interviewing at Haven's today."

"Girl, you'd be perfect. Though it's sad to lose Bob and Donna. I have so many memories of them from Saturday morning donuts at Haven's."

"Doesn't all of Hearts Bend?" Chloe smiled and the icy

shell that had formed around her heart when she'd gotten *the* call from Vivienne melted a bit more. "I think everyone in town spent Saturday mornings at Haven's."

"Chloe, we lost him. Jean-Marc...he—he's gone."

When Sophie glanced at her watch again, Chloe reached for her hand. "What's this?" A ginormous diamond sparkled from her ring finger.

"This little ole thing?" She beamed. "I'm engaged. His name's Eric, and he's amazing."

"Of course he is." Chloe smiled. She may have lost the love of her life, but she still loved hearing others had found their one and only. "Love is—well, love is worth it." Chloe nodded as if to assure Sophie, and herself, she meant it. Love *was* worth it. Even if it could also be painful.

"Thank you," Sophie said. "That means a lot coming from you."

They chatted a few more minutes until Sophie declared it was toddler story time at the Nook. "Which waits for no one."

Chloe promised to stop in soon then finished her latte alone at the table, thinking of her day and the job interview that awaited her. All she knew was baking, but could she still do it? Did she want to do it? Chloe closed her eyes and inhaled, almost smelling the butter, vanilla, and sugar blending together.

After tossing her cup in the trash, Chloe slipped on her gloves and stepped outside into the cold. Where to next? She glanced toward the Book Nook...yeah, she'd definitely pop in there later. She could go to Gardenia Park and across to the Kids Theater. She'd spent a few happy summers there, working backstage.

Work... She'd been working twelve-hour days, six—okay, seven—days a week for the last few months, burying herself in work, without sleep. Yet, she found that the harder she worked, the less relief she felt—and the more elusive the joy that baking had always brought her. The weight of Jean-Marc's death was so sudden, so unexpected, she lacked the ability to properly process it.

If she got the Haven's job, would it only bring it all up? Would baking keep her chained to the past instead of inching her toward her future?

Sophie's encouragement—"*Girl, you'd be perfect*"— soothed her a bit. She would be. The Bistro Gaspard was small, family run, but with a one-star Michelin rating. A well-earned accolade. Surely she could manage a small-town bakery like Haven's. Hearts Bend *was* home, and home was where she'd learned to love baking. Chloe rubbed her thumb over the indentation on her left ring finger. She was going to be fine, wouldn't she? Were there any other options?

She walked to the market to pick up a few groceries for Mom then took them home and put them away. She answered a few emails, talked to Honey, and ate a light lunch. At one-thirty, she once again started for downtown Hearts Bend.

Maybe this would be the beginning of a beautiful relationship.

☙☙☙

Sam parked in front of Haven's, the weak Thursday afternoon sun sparkling on the snowflakes falling on the town. The last few winters had been pretty mild, so he took a moment to enjoy the drifting and floating bits of frozen crystals. He stood on the curb, looked up and down First Avenue. Though he couldn't quite see Frank's office from here, Sam knew it was up the block all right, exactly forty-five squares of sidewalk concrete away. He'd walked the route often enough as a kid, careful to avoid the cracks and not break his mother's back.

Sticking his hands into his jacket pockets, he sighed as he

looked up the street again. Yeah, no, he couldn't do this. Couldn't own a Hearts Bend business that was literally a hop, skip, and a jump from the old man's office. Better get in there and tell Rick.

Sam climbed the four steps to the front door. The brace that kept his knee straight made him look like an awkward penguin, but he made it to the top and held the door open for a mom exiting with a squirming toddler. "Thanks," she said, barely looking up at him.

His meeting with Dr. Morgan had gone well. She'd examined him, giving him much of the same report the team doctor and trainer had. He'd have to be careful, do everything she told him, and be faithful to his therapy sessions, at-home exercises, and to rest.

"Rest is the most important thing, Sam. You want to be on the field in July? Rest."

Rest was such a weird word. He'd been working so hard to achieve his dream, rest felt like failure. He worked hard, played hard. Even his vacations were action oriented. Surfing at Malibu. Hiking the Grand Canyon. White water rafting in Colorado. Rest. Hmm. What would that be like?

Never mind that for now—he was inside the bakery with its amazing aromas. Ole Haven's was a time capsule, filled with the same chairs and tables, booths, decorations, and pictures as twenty years ago. For the first time in a long time, Sam felt a bit at home in Hearts Bend.

Standing in the doorway, he inhaled the aroma of baking bread and rich roasted coffee. Suddenly, he was a kid again sitting in the corner booth between his folks, scarfing down crullers and chocolate milk. Mom sipped coffee and read a paperback while Frank rattled newspaper pages. The same red vinyl bench seats in the booths. The same square, chipped Formica tables around the room. The same employees.

Wow, he really had stepped back in time.

"Oh, good gravy. Sam Hardy." Ruby's expression filled with surprise as she came around the counter to give him a big hug. "We ain't seen you in a month of Sundays."

Same ole Ruby. "I'm looking for Rick Moses. Is he here?"

"In the office with Bob and Donna." Ruby nodded toward the kitchen doors then stuck her hands on her hips. "So, we got us a quarterback for an owner." Ruby's voice rose above the voices and clattering dishes in the bakery's dining room. "Our own Sam Hardy."

"Shh, Ruby, no one needs to know." He pressed his finger to his lips.

"Don't shush me." She patted his back. "Get on in there. And Sam, don't know how you plan on keeping it quiet that the Titans' quarterback now owns Haven's."

She had a point. But he was going to try. He just didn't want his dad to know...and act all smug.

"Told you business was second nature to you."

Through the doors and into an industrial kitchen, which was much like the ones in the other restaurants HARDRICK LLC owned, Sam looked into the office, spotting Rick and the barrel-chested Bob Morton at a metal desk strewn with papers next to a computer monitor that had been considered high tech the decade Sam was born. Bob's wife, Donna, sat in a chair next to him, scrolling through pictures on her phone.

"Sam." Rick greeted him. "Glad you made it in time for the manager interview. Daughter of a friend of the Morton's but experienced. She should be here shortly."

Sam shook Bob's hand and gave Donna a hug. "Haven's won't be the same without you two, but we'll do our best." He took a seat on the small sofa.

"How was therapy?" Rick said.

"Dr. Morgan was more cautious than optimistic about

getting me on the field this season." She'd had a lot to say about his personal life too. Had slipped back into her role as his surrogate mom like he'd been fifteen again and hanging out with her son and crushing on her daughter. Lecturing him to forgive Frank and Janice for the affair that basically ruined his high school life. To let go of the grudge he'd been holding on to for over a decade.

Forgiving his father and his second wife for their affair, for destroying Sam's family, was something he still struggled with from time to time, and he was fully aware that bitterness and resentment would eat him alive. He didn't need "Mom" Morgan to tell him how emotions affected his body.

"That's good news, right?" Rick said. "That she's willing to work with you, at least."

Sam shrugged. "I have to come for therapy three days a week and do exercises at home, but yeah, my goal is to play." Dr. Morgan had sent him on his way with a month of appointments and an admonishment to at least try to like and trust his dad again.

"I'll see you at his sixtieth birthday party next month. Doctor's orders."

He'd agreed, because really, what choice did he have? He truly believed she'd drop him as a patient. So, he smiled and nodded and kept his mouth shut.

But when it came to owning HARDRICK businesses— Sam had a whole lot to say about that.

"Rick, I need to talk to you," he said.

❀❀❀

When Chloe reached Haven's, she paused by the front door. So this was it. The beginning of her new future. Back home in Hearts Bend, the quintessential opposite of her old Bastille neighborhood. Her pride battled the grief she'd carried for the last ten months. Look, this wasn't the last stop in her life. She wouldn't work here forever. This was just to stay out of Mom's hair and keep busy until Mom was cancer free. Besides, she could use the money since Jean-Marc had emptied their bank account.

Go in.

The bell swinging from the door rang as she entered the bakery. Chloe paused just past the threshold. The scent of coffee, baking bread, and cakes made her feel a bit more alive. This was her sweet place. No pun intended. A group of silver-haired women huddled around a table under the window overlooking First Avenue, coffee mugs and plates with sweet rolls in front of them, chittering like a flock of sparrows. They looked up but quickly returned to their conversation. Chloe did a double take. One of the women looked familiar. Probably a friend of Mom's.

She took a moment to gaze around. The daily special written on the chalkboard—vanilla cake—looked fresh and appealing, though it couldn't be as good as MeMaw's, she thought loyally. Lots of Hearts Bend's residents laid claim to the best vanilla cake in Tennessee, but only MeMaw had taken a blue ribbon at the state fair three years running. Rows of cinnamon buns, muffins, and donuts lined the trays, and stacked pink boxes waited to carry those treats home. A pair of swinging doors behind the counter led to the kitchen. The front part of the bakery held scattered tables and was lined with booths.

A low hum of conversation filled the room. Chloe tilted her head. Whether in French or with a Southern accent, conversations with a sweet pastry and coffee added something special to the day. The woman behind the counter wore her hair in a tall, gray wispy beehive hairdo underneath her hair net. She had a pencil tucked into one of the honeycombs of her hair. She wore bright pink lipstick and—

"I declare," Ruby said, looking over her half-glasses at Chloe. "I thought homecoming was in the fall. Chloe Beason, is that you?"

"Ruby? Hey, yes, it's me." Chloe melted into the woman's soft, bosomy embrace. She smelled like MeMaw. Of vanilla and sugar. "It's Chloe LaRue now." She hoped Ruby wouldn't break in with a plethora of questions such as, *"What have you been up to?"* or *"Tell me all about Paris."*

She'd have to know about Jean-Marc. His death notice ran in the *Hearts Bend Tribune*.

"I'm looking for Rick Moses," Chloe said. "We have a meeting."

"In the office, sugar. Through there." Ruby pointed to the double doors. "Welcome home, Chloe." Her voice...so much sympathy. So yes, she knew about Jean-Marc.

"Thanks, Ruby."

Through the doors, Chloe spotted the office in the back, but what really caught her eye was the young woman icing a cake on the prep table. Her baker's coat was covered in as much blue and yellow frosting as the cake, and even more colorful blobs layered the table. The area looked like a buttercream bomb had exploded. Yet the cake's frosting gleamed as smooth as the surface of Lac de Gravelle—Gravelle Lake in Paris. Flawless. Beautiful. But goodness, did Donna Morton allow such a disastrous workstation?

"Chloe LaRue?" A man stood at the office door. He was nice looking, very well dressed, his blondish hair perfectly styled and his cologne just strong enough to make her think of a walk in a French forest.

"Yes." She extended a hand. "Rick Moses? It's nice to meet you."

"Please have a seat." He motioned for her to come on in.

"Thank you for interviewing me." Chloe hugged Bob and Donna. "I can't believe you're retiring. And all the way to Florida."

"We're tired of the long days," Bob said. "We almost sold out five years ago to that Donut Heaven chain, after our boy didn't come home from Afghanistan. But we kept going. Now, though, it feels like the right time."

Chloe swallowed the sudden lump in her throat. She'd forgotten about Danny Morton.

Rick cleared his throat and indicated Chloe should take a seat in the wooden chair next to the desk.

She sat, vaguely aware of another man leaning against the wall behind her. As she twisted in the chair to acknowledge him, Rick spoke. "Chloe, I'd like you to meet my partner. He'll be co-owner of Haven's. Sam Hardy."

Chloe stood with such quickness, she knocked over her chair. "Sam? *The* Sam Hardy."

When her eyes met his, he smiled. "Chloe Beason. It's been a long time."

※ ※ ※

LOVE @SAMHARDYQB15'S NASHVILLE CONDO. JUST NEEDS SOME THROW PILLOWS! A WOMAN'S TOUCH. ;-) WE'RE SPENDING EVENINGS IN AS HIS KNEE IS STILL HEALING.

– @CURVYCARLA ON TWITTER

※ ※ ※

Thank you to everyone at the Grand Ole Opry for an excellent evening. We raised a million dollars for my foundation, SportsWorld. Every kid who wants to play, should be able to play.

– @SamHardyQB15 on Twitter

CHAPTER 4

"*C*hloe Beason," he said again. What was she doing here? Last he heard she was married to some sports company executive and living in France. But it was definitely her. Brown hair in a spiky cut, longer on top so she often clipped her bangs to the side. Eyes the color of sweet gum tree leaves in the summer. A nose that narrowed to a slight upturned tip.

"Sam?" She sounded as shocked as he felt.

"You two know each other?" Rick said.

Chloe's smile shot through him, so shy, so familiar, so beautiful. "If you define *know* as in a summer catching endless footballs from this doofus as he worked on throwing left handed."

"In return, this *doofus* taught you how to change a tire and the oil in your car. Pretty sure we're more than even."

"Yes, I earn millions changing my own flat tires and draining my oil." Her quip held the laughter he remembered.

"Aren't you on your way to becoming a famous pastry chef? Paris, I think?" Sam moved closer and perched against the desk, ignoring Rick's questioning glances. "Tell me what you're doing here."

"Interviewing for a job. I hear you need a manager." She glanced at Rick. "But it's Chloe LaRue now."

The interview had just started, and Sam was gleaning the latest details of Chloe's life when his phone buzzed. It was Briggs, his public relations manager. Sam had hired Briggs three years ago to help revamp his reputation. He was a brilliant strategist.

He pointed to his phone. "I've got to take this."

"Go," Rick said. "Chloe and I will keep chatting."

"Briggs," Sam said, moving into the kitchen. "Tell me we have good press from last night." The SportsWorld fundraiser at the Opry had been a huge success thanks to his friends Buck Mathews, Tracy Blue, and other country music greats.

"We do, but talk to me about Curvy Carla. What's going on?"

This again? Sam's jaw clenched and he rubbed a hand over his chin. "A groupie I drove home last week from a party. My bad. She was a Martelli groupie until she got bored or something. I dropped her off. Didn't even get out of the car." Dang, he sounded like a broken record. "Can we put out a press release or something?"

"We could but according to her Twitter feed, you two are an item. I got a call from *Entertainment Tonight* asking for details."

"Tell them we are not an item, and this is what Sam Hardy gets for trying to be a Boy Scout." Sam looked up to see Ruby staring at him, her finger pressed to her lips. *Keep it down.*

Right, right.

"I'll reach out to this Curvy Carla. In the meantime, I've got my team ramping up your social media feeds with your charity work. Last night's fundraiser is good copy. Also, give me details on your knee recovery. That news will spin nicely. Send me some pictures and deets when you can."

When he'd hung up with Briggs, Sam turned to see Ruby, wrapped in a white apron and drying her hands with a paper towel, watching him.

"Old habits die hard, Sammy?" she said.

"No, Ruby, old reputations."

"Stick with it. You'll turn things around."

Her tone and her confidence reminded him to believe it. She was right. It'd only been three years since he decided he needed a new way of living. He pushed out the kitchen's back door and paced up and down the alley. One direction led to Blossom Street, the other to Holly. He needed to cool off a moment, get his head back into business mode.

The day he'd decided to change his life remained at the forefront of his mind. He'd gone to a private party at a music mogul's home in Franklin and hooked up with a tall, lithe brunette. Since he never let women stay over at his place, he walked her to the door after the, well, deed was done. She'd been much sweeter than most girls who flirted with sports figures. It was then he'd realized she wasn't a groupie or jersey chaser, that she actually liked him and thought he was interesting. And he couldn't even remember her name.

That's when he knew he had to turn his life around. Or one day, when he did settle down with a wife and kids, he'd end up doing something like his father. And the last man he ever wanted to emulate was Frank Hardy. He wanted more. To build a life with a woman who made him laugh, who loved his heart but called him on his crap. A woman he could love, respect, raise babies with, and if he were lucky, grow old with. He wanted what his grandparents had, his aunts and uncles, what people referred to as *the white picket fence.*

He'd started to head back to the office and the interview

when a memory surfaced. Chloe making him watch a sappy romance movie one summer. Over and over. He'd teased her for all the corny love but now, he'd give anything for it. What was the movie? *The Notebook?* Yeah, that was it.

"I think we have our manager." Rick addressed Sam as he returned to the office. "Chloe LaRue. When can you start?"

"As soon as you want me." Chloe stood, glancing between Rick and Sam. She was smiling but he saw something in her eyes. A bit of insecurity.

"Chloe, are you sure?" Sam said. "Don't you have a life in France? What are you doing here?"

"I guess you don't keep up with Hearts Bend news? My husband was killed ten months ago, and I came home now to help Mom with..." She hesitated. "A few things. We thought that me getting a job would keep us from killing each other."

"She was a pastry chef at Bistro Gaspard in Paris." Rick handed Sam Chloe's résumé. "I've hired her already so don't bother protesting."

"I'm not protesting." Sam scanned the details. She'd trained at The Culinary Institute of America. Lived and worked in Paris for ten years. "I'm sorry about your husband." He returned the résumé to the desk. "I hope Haven's proves to be a place of healing for you."

Her eyes glistened as she nodded. "It's good to see you, Sam."

She and Rick settled on a start date—Friday next week—and when Sam was alone with Rick, Rick drilled him for details. Who was she? How long had he known her? Was it his imagination or was there a spark between them?

"She's a friend, was a friend, Rick, all right? Don't make more out of it than necessary. Besides, she's a grieving widow." But she'd been an important friend. One who had gotten him through the toughest season of his life. They'd had a crush on each other but at fifteen, he'd been too shy to do anything about it.

Walking back out to his car to head home, Sam wondered at Chloe's return to Hearts Bend. Would she, once again, be in his orbit? He was, perhaps, on the verge of another tough season in his life and could use an important friend once again.

❦❦❦

The next week passed with a few appointments for Mom, more unpacking, and a visit to Sophie at the Book Nook. Finally, Friday morning, Chloe stood in the bakery office and smoothed the hem of her white chef's jacket. It felt good to be back at work, running a kitchen.

She'd set her alarm for two a.m., tiptoed down the stairs so she didn't disturb Mom, and slipped out the front door. At three a.m., she inserted her first loaves of bread into the oven and blessed Ruby for starting the dough the night before. Soon the kitchen was filled with the greatest aroma on earth. When Laura Kate, the white-blonde cake decorator with the disastrous workstation, arrived at four, she began the process of making the donuts. By six a.m., when Haven's opened, the cases were lined with fresh baked goods, the coffees were brewing, and Ruby had boxed up all the standing orders for cinnamon rolls, crullers, donuts, breads, cakes, and assortments of cookies and other bakery items.

Chloe was in the flow. Every doubt she'd harbored during a restless night of sleep—battling a crack in her confidence—had vanished. The first hours after opening had gone smoothly, better than Chloe had expected. Laura Kate proved to be more competent than her messy workstation indicated, and she followed Chloe's directions with ease and knowledge. Ruby handled the front of the shop with her gregarious hospitality.

Chloe had yet to meet the third employee, a young woman named Robin, who was part-time and also attended the local community college.

Just after lunch, when things slowed down, Chloe called for a brief staff meeting. She was about to clap her hands for attention, just like at Bistro Gaspard, but the only two she needed were standing right in front of her.

"Well, we've had a good day so far. Thank you all so much for welcoming me. I just wanted to talk about the menu briefly. Do you—"

"Darling, here's our menu." Ruby jutted a printed paper menu at Chloe. "Been the same one for fifty years so best go slow with any new ideas. We're small-town Southerners. We like our traditions and our ways."

"Yes, well, thank you, Ruby, good to know. I do have a lot of experience with various pastries and—"

"Why did you leave Paris?" Laura Kate said. Apparently not letting a girl finish her thoughts was a new Southern tradition.

"To help my mom. She's having some medical treatments—"

"As any good daughter would. Family comes first." Ruby folded her arms and nodded her approval.

"I trained as a pastry chef in New York and Paris, where I lived with my husband until he died last year. I look forward to getting to know you both better and—" The back door flew open, and a young woman dashed in.

"Sorry I'm late." She shed a backpack, hung it on a hook near the door, and slipped an apron over her head as she turned toward them. "Oh. Hi."

"Robin, you couldn't be on time for the new boss's first day?" The exasperation in Ruby's voice was thick as fondant, but not nearly as sweet.

Robin flushed. "I had science labs to turn in. You're the one that's always on me not to neglect my studies."

"As I was saying, I want to learn about the bakery and its business." The double doors swung open, and Chloe turned to tell whoever it was they'd be right out to refill their coffee, but the words died on her lips.

Sam Hardy filled the kitchen with his broad, athletic presence.

"Well, butter my backside and call me a biscuit," Ruby said. "What are you doing here so soon, Sam? Or should I say Boss?"

"Came to check on my investment." His gaze landed on Chloe and stayed there. "Is it usual to have a bakery full of hungry customers and no one to sell them their afternoon crullers and donuts?"

"Seems if you don't want folks to know you're an owner, coming in every day and telling us how to run things isn't the best way to go about it." Ruby shook a finger at him. "Chloe, is your meeting over? We best get to work before Sam fires us all."

"I should get back to the muffins," Laura Kate said.

"Can I have a word?" Sam motioned to the office.

As much as she'd like nothing better than to sit and chat with Sam, she did notice the growing line out front. How had that happened so fast?

"I'd better help Ruby first."

It took a few minutes to get the line served and Chloe made a quick round of the bakery, topping off coffee mugs. As she replaced the pot on the warmer, she nodded to the same ladies with coffee and pastries at the table under the window overlooking First Avenue. She'd finally placed the familiar face in the group.

"Ruby, isn't that Octavia O'Shay?"

"Queen of O'Shay Shirts and of Hearts Bend? Yes, indeedy."

After fifteen minutes, the dining room was clear and Chloe saw Sam sitting in a back booth. He motioned for her to join him.

"How's it going?" he said. "Honestly."

"First day. It's fine, I think. Hard to tell." She thumbed her left ring finger. "By the way, Jean-Marc, my husband, loved American football. He was a big fan of yours. He wanted to meet you."

"I would've loved to have met him. Lucky man to catch you. I was sorry to hear about his accident." Sam leaned back in the booth.

"I think I'm still getting over the shock," she said. "But it's nice being home. Being here. Thank you for the job."

"Rick knows what he's doing." Sam smiled and she was once again the girl who'd loved him from afar in ninth grade all the way until she'd left for culinary school. But above all, he was Sam, her friend.

"So, my mom still works for your dad."

"Yeah, I get messages from her sometimes. In lieu of Frank." Sam nodded in the way one did when filtering through small talk. "Reminders of family gatherings at the holidays. I'm sure Frank puts her up to it."

"Things aren't better between you?" By Sam's expression, she knew the answer.

"A work in progress," he said. "No, not even that. But that's another story. Is your mom glad you're home? You said you're here to help her with something?"

"She's battling cancer." She'd not really told anyone until now. But that was Sam, getting the secrets out of her heart. "I want to be here for her. I lost my dad and my husband. I'm not going to lose my mother. Especially when I'm four thousand miles away."

"Chloe, I'm sorry. Anytime you need to take off to help her, do it. Even if you have to close the bakery."

Tears welled up and she blinked them away. When would she be able to handle her emotions better? "Thank you."

"Are you in your old room?"

Chloe laughed softly. "Yep. I think it makes both of us feel that life has stalled on us. Like, 'Really, I'm living with my mother?' Mom's like, 'Really, my daughter is back home?'"

"Give yourself a break, Chloe. Your husband died. That's not a failure or like you gave up and moved home to mooch off Mom. Besides, she needs you. She may not say it, but I bet she's glad to have you around."

"I think she likes living alone. She never remarried, let alone dated, after Dad died." Chloe leaned against the table, arms flat on the tabletop, hands crossed. "Do you talk to your mom ever?"

"My mom? We're talking about your mom, Chloe."

"Sam Hardy, you're avoiding a perfectly honest question."

"Yes, so let's move on. Remember when you dared me to jump from the roof into the pool? I about killed myself."

She laughed and allowed him to change the subject. They talked about his knee injury and his hope for rehab and getting back on the field in the fall. Then Ruby appeared with two mugs and a coffeepot.

"Y'all been sitting here for an hour. Coffee, Mr. Hardy? Chloe?"

"An hour? I should get back to work." She started to stand, but he motioned to her.

"We're catching up. Consider it part of your orientation for HARDRICK. Have some coffee. Please."

Chloe reached for a mug but asked for half a cup. She hadn't spent an hour chatting with a friend in—well, years. It felt good. Normal, even. She leaned back against the booth and inhaled the strong, rich brew.

"Ruby, call me Sam." He accepted a full mug. "You've known me since forever."

"It's true. I've served you more chocolate milk and crullers than there are ticks on a raccoon. But now you're my boss."

"Still, call me Sam."

"Okay, boss." Ruby glanced at the clock. "You'll be wanting to start the Friday afternoon cookies soon, Chloe."

"What cookies?" There'd been no cookie tradition when she was a girl.

Ruby put a hand on her hip. "Every Friday, Donna made Triple Chocolate Fudge Caramel cookies. Folks start lining up at two o'clock to get them warm from the oven."

"Okay. Can you have Laura Kate print out the recipe from the computer?"

"Computer? The only mouse Donna knows is one you set a trap for." Ruby arched her brow as if offering a challenge and turned for the O'Shay table to warm up their coffees.

Chloe glanced at Sam. "Did Donna leave her recipes?"

"With me? Are you crazy?" Sam looked at the door as the bell chimed. Five customers entered and hurried to the register. "Didn't she give them to you?"

"No one said a word about recipes."

He turned to Chloe. "You don't know how to make cookies?"

"Not just any cookie, Sam." Ruby was back. "The TCFC. Triple Chocolate Fudge Caramel. It's the new drug in town. I'm telling you, people go crazy over it." She pointed to the register line where Robin was scribbling on an order pad. "They're coming in now to get their orders in. Only two to a customer."

Chloe rode a wave of panic. "Ruby, call Donna."

"I'm on it." The woman was already dialing.

"Sam, we have to find that recipe."

He slid from the booth. "Come on, I'll help you find it."

❦ ❦ ❦

An hour later, after scouring the office, the bakery cabinets, the pantry, and the storage closet, Sam felt hot and sticky, grit clinging to his hands and face.

Ruby's call to Donna had gone straight to voicemail. The campy greeting said she and "...the Rodfather are out to sea and will return your call whenever the fish quit keepin' it reel."

Chloe was also covered in dust and oozed frustration. "How am I to make special cookies without the recipe? We're already late!" Emotion thickened her voice. "Ruby, you don't have the recipe? Or even an ingredient list? Laura Kate?"

"Donna never let me near her recipe box." Laura Kate looked up from slathering cream cheese frosting on apple nut muffins.

"So, I have cookies to bake without a map. My first day and I'm failing. With my boss standing right here."

"I feel as responsible as you, Chloe," Sam said, making his way to the sink to wash his hands. "Look, just make any cookie."

"Sam, do not blaspheme in this kitchen. You cannot sell just any cookie," Ruby said. "Folks want the Triple Chocolate Fudge Caramel, the TCFC Delight. I've already had a dozen calls to reserve their two."

"Oh my gosh, what am I going to do?" Chloe paced and Sam wondered if she felt like she was back in the Paris bistro, pressured by the intensity of an upscale, fast-paced restaurant. "Ruby, do you have a picture? Anything? Triple Chocolate

Fudge Caramel. I'll need chocolate, fudge, and caramel. What else?"

While Chloe labored over the unexpected, Sam wandered into the front of the bakery. He really didn't know why he was here today except he'd woken up in his Nashville loft over-looking the river and wanted to go home. He wanted to see Haven's. See Chloe, if he was being honest. After a few calls with the director of his charity, he'd driven over to HB.

Now, he was talking to a couple of customers, signing auto-graphs on Haven's napkins when the bakery door chimed as another customer entered. He heard a familiar gasp and steeled himself. "Have a good day," he said to the customer before turning to Janice, his stepmother.

"Sam?" Janice stepped forward to hug him then stopped short, self-consciously dropping her arms to her sides. "Why are you in town? Frank is so pleased you're coming to his party. He couldn't stop grinning when I told him you accepted."

"Don't make too much of it, Janice. Dr. Morgan pressured me into going." And there was the small matter of Frank not knowing he'd purchased Haven's. He'd like to keep it that way.

Her smile faded for a moment then she rebounded, raising her chin. "Well, Joann is a good friend. So...what are you doing here now?"

Really good question. "Dr. Morgan." It was mostly true. He was going to be in town more often to see her. Just not today.

"She's the best." Janice turned to the bakery case. "Ruby, do you have my cookies? Frank's *must-have* Friday night dessert."

"The Triple Chocolate Fudge Caramel?" Sam said.

"Yes, the TCFC. When Donna started making them about ten years ago, HB went nuts."

"We don't have the cookies, Janice." Ruby, in a very flat tone.

"Whyever not?"

"Well, Sam here—"

"Just overheard from the new manager that Donna didn't leave the recipes behind. Chloe's looked everywhere." He sighed and said something he couldn't take back. "I even helped her look."

"You helped Chloe? The new manager? Meredith's daughter?" Questions flickered in Janice's eyes. "Why in the world would you—"

As if she knew he needed rescuing, Chloe emerged from the kitchen and drew Janice's attention. "Hello, dear, your mom told me you were back from France." Janice glanced at the bakery counter then at Chloe. "I came for our TCFC order, but Sam here tells me you can't find the recipe."

"Donna didn't leave any recipes. At least not that we can find."

"Heaven help you, this town is going to go crazy on you. Frank and I will be fine, but best say your prayers. You'll have a hangry mob here any minute looking for their Friday afternoon fix."

The look on Chloe's face...sheer terror. "A hangry mob."

Nothing worse than angry, hungry people. Sam had seen that in some of his teammates.

"Ah, come on, darling," Janice said. "You're made of better stuff. Just tell the hangry folks you'll have the cookie next week. You've called Donna, right? See if you can't dig up the recipe. Now, as long as I'm here, I might as well order Frank's birthday cake. I was going to get it from a fancy place in Nashville, but I suppose a cake from an authentic French pastry chef would be a showstopper. You do have a cake recipe, don't you?"

"Yes, ma'am, cakes are my specialty."

Janice explained the '60s-themed party for Frank's sixtieth birthday while Sam flanked Chloe, hoping to provide a calming influence. What were they going to do about the cookies?

Sam gave Ruby a look that told her to call Donna again. Meanwhile, he pulled out his phone, texted Rick. *We need Donna's recipes. There's a special cookie everyone will want today!*

He returned to the booth he'd occupied earlier and waited for Rick's response. Meanwhile, Chloe talked about the cake order with Janice in another booth nearby.

"Give me a few days to come up with ideas. I'm just getting my bearings," Chloe said.

"Monday?"

"Perfect."

Janice stood to go. "Chloe, I know Meredith is happy you're home. She plays down her *issue*," Janice whispered the word, "but I know she's comforted by your presence. So, with Bob and Donna gone, who hired you? Who owns Haven's now? I've not heard a word and I'm on the town welcoming committee."

"Don't you know? The bakery was bought by—"

Sam scrambled from his booth and stood behind Janice. Waving his arms he mouthed, *No, no, no.* He'd told everyone that he didn't want Frank to know he was co-owner of Haven's. Perhaps he should.

"—um, a man out of Atlanta. Rick or Mick or something."

"Well, call me if and when he comes to town. I'd like to give him an official Hearts Bend greeting," Janice said. "Oh, one more thing for the cake. No fondant. Just buttercream frosting, please."

Sam followed Chloe to the office after Janice left. He received a text from Rick and held up his phone. "Rick is calling Bob and Donna to see about the recipes."

"Doesn't help me today."

"Just make a cookie. Give them away for free. I'll cover the cost and square it with Rick." His phone pinged a reminder. "I have to go. I'm on Zoom with SportsCenter in a couple of hours. Need to get home." He turned for the door. "Hey, if you want to fix up the place some, you can. We always set aside a few grand for updates, paint, and new supplies. I'll get our business manager to email you the details. And Janice kind of ambushed you. Thanks for agreeing to make Frank's cake."

"More like she ambushed you. Besides, a cake for Frank's party will be great for the bakery. People must wonder what it will be like around here without Bob and Donna. Especially now that we don't have the TCFC recipe."

"I have a feeling Haven's Bakery will be even better," Sam said. How could it not be with Chloe LaRue in the house?

Her smile eased some of the ache in his knee, the same smile he'd loved when they were fifteen and hanging out at his house around the pool. When she'd shared her recipe for lemon poppyseed bread with him. When she'd called his bluff with that dare to jump from the roof into the pool. They'd laughed a lot back then. She'd been the balm to the wound of his parents' divorce.

On his way home to Nashville, memory after memory surfaced of the shy, dark-headed girl, lost in a world of emo, and the summer he realized he wasn't as impervious to love as he had once believed.

CHAPTER 5

As the week passed without the famed Triple Chocolate Fudge Caramel cookie, Chloe tried every possible combination of chocolate, fudge, and caramel in her vast baker repertoire. And Rick had reported no luck at getting Bob to return his calls. Either the Mortons were out to sea for an extended fishing trip or when they'd retired and sold Haven's, they'd dusted the flour from their hands and not looked back.

Chloe had thrown herself at the challenge. When nothing was deemed good enough, she'd even called Gaspard Dupree, her old pastry mentor, for ideas. Everything he suggested earned a curled lip from Ruby.

"Darling, we're simple folks from Hearts Bend, Tennessee, not fancy, schmancy people from Paris, France."

Last Friday, Chloe gave away her version of chocolate chip cookies—which were amazing, if she could be so bold. They were well received, especially being free and all, but no one in Hearts Bend was calling to put a fresh batch on reserve. Fair enough. But what was she going to do this week? She'd quizzed

Ruby and Laura Kate, even a few customers, until Ruby threatened to strangle her, and Mrs. O'Shay's friends avoided Chloe and turned their backs to her. *"We don't know! Stop asking."*

Nevertheless, she was developing a special bond with the crew as they found themselves in a cookie crisis—complete with frustrated and clipped answers.

So now here she was on a Thursday morning, still with no recipe, fighting the urge to knock her head on her scarred wooden desk. Searching for this recipe was beginning to feel like she was trying to catch fireflies with oven mitts. Fruitless, pointless, and a little ridiculous.

"Are you going to try again?" Ruby leaned against the door, twisting a dish towel. "Tomorrow will be the second week without them cookies. I'm not saying for sure, but I thought I heard talk of an insurrection in the grocery checkout line last night."

"What?" Chloe sat bolt upright. "Please tell me you're joking."

"Of course I am...sort of...maybe...yeah, for sure I'm joking."

"Ruby, don't mess with me. Look, I'm shaking." She held up her quivering hand, which she tried to convince herself had nothing to do with the four cups of coffee she'd already swallowed. This cookie thing was robbing her of sleep. She'd called Donna after Sam texted the number to her only to learn she kept all the recipes in her head. Oh yes, there was a recipe box...somewhere...but she'd not used it since the Reagan administration.

"Okay, then just tell me what's in the cookie and roughly, if you could, the ingredient measurements."

Donna had laughed. *"A little of this, a little of that, sweetie. Flour, of course, and butter. Cocoa and, oh! The secret is my homemade caramel sauce. After ten years, I started to believe the*

darn things made themselves while I slept." Then Chloe heard
Bob in the background telling her it was time to go—the special
at the Golden Corral started in ten minutes.

So Chloe now spent each afternoon mixing up every
version of a caramel sauce she could think of to add to a chocolate fudge cookie base only to see the disappointed expressions
of her taste tasters—Ruby, Laura Kate, Mr. Petrella (who came
in every day for his coffee and donut), and the afternoon
counter girl, Robin, if she managed to clock in on time. (Hint:
She never did.) She even gave away free samples for honest
opinions. But not one recipe compared to Donna's.

Despite the devastation of the TCFC demise, the bakery
was doing well. Chloe was doing well. She'd made basic
versions of donuts and crullers, muffins and fritters. Laura Kate
told her the few Haven's secrets she knew for cakes and pies—a
little vanilla here, an extra dash of cinnamon or nutmeg there.
If Chloe didn't get it right, no one said anything. In fact, one
customer said, "Just like Donna's." That pinched just a bit if
Chloe was honest. Because...her skills were just a touch better
than Donna's.

In other news, Janice Hardy loved Chloe's '60s-themed
cake ideas: a classic Mustang, a Schwinn bike with a banana
seat, or an Etch-a-Sketch. But the woman had insisted on something reflecting her husband's favorite hobby. She'd chosen a
four-layer chocolate and vanilla golf-based cake that promised
to be a showstopper for Frank Hardy's sixtieth birthday party
in another couple of weeks.

*"Chloe, my goodness, you have a gift. I never tasted such
creamy icing."*

Chloe had designed a clever golf course made of frosting
and piping. She planned to teach Laura Kate some advanced
techniques when they did the actual decorating.

"Well, what're you going to do, shug?" Ruby said, interrupting her thoughts. "We might have to punt this one and invent a new Friday afternoon must-have."

"I'm not surrendering yet." Chloe rested her cheek against her hand and peered at Ruby, feeling more defeated than she cared to admit. "Let me think...keep working at it."

"Don't think too hard. Can't have that pretty forehead of yours all wrinkled," Ruby chuckled. "What would Sam say?"

Chloe gave her a look. Sam? "Why should he think anything about my forehead? He's a friend, Ruby. No, he's my boss."

"Whatever." Ruby waved off her comment and returned to the kitchen. Chloe was pretty sure Ruby didn't even hear her answer. Selective hearing, that Ruby.

Chloe had learned a lot about her staff's personalities this first full week—and fallen a little bit in love.

The staff ran like clockwork. Ruby, everyone's mother, grandmother, or dear old aunt, manned the front counter five mornings a week. Robin, the little sister who dashed in late three afternoons a week but was so sweet and eager to please that Chloe forgave her each time. And she was a hard worker. Robin manned the shop after school, but she also opened Saturday mornings and again on Sunday afternoons after church for a few hours.

Chloe took Donna's old time slot, arriving at three every morning to start the baking and opening the shop at six. Then there was Laura Kate, her assistant baker. Laura Kate closed up the two evenings Robin was off, and was in charge of the donuts and crullers, muffins and cookies, and simple decorating. She was also sweet, very focused, and *very* unorganized. But oh, Chloe saw genius in her work.

In fact, she could hear LK humming right now all the way from the kitchen as she smoothed icing on a Styrofoam round for one of the display cakes Chloe planned to put in the front window. Her first job in Paris had been a small bakery with over-the-top window displays, and since they did a cracking business, Chloe wanted to try the technique here.

Hopefully the display would expand the special-order department. Birthday cakes. Wedding cakes. Cakes for any and all occasions.

Chloe sat back in her chair and gazed toward the small office window. March had arrived two days ago and the sunshine already seemed brighter. But wow, this cookie recipe deal exhausted her. She was a trained chef. Surely she could figure out a simple chocolate fudge cookie. But homegrown bakers like Donna were tricky—they had recipes and tricks from their great-great-great-grannies that no one could imagine. A super-secret homemade caramel sauce should be easy.

Think, think, think...

Chloe reached for her hair clip—the one with pearly beads that had become her trademark in Paris—and reclipped her hair to include a loose strand. Might as well get to work. Office stuff today. She picked up the stack of envelopes and fliers from the corner of her desk. The mail consisted of bills and a magazine that promised articles on the prettiest Middle Tennessee hiking trails and the best diners serving banana pancakes. She set the stack on top of Donna's old leather scrapbook then nudged the computer mouse to wake up the machine.

Bob had managed to put all the accounting and ordering online in the last year, which made her job so much easier. But she found herself staring at the open accounting program. Besides the sideswipe of this cookie recipe, there was the issue of Sam Hardy. He'd popped in twice this week after therapy sessions at Dr. Morgan's office. Ruby had served him a cruller and chocolate milk—for old time's sake—as he chatted with the staff and customers. Before leaving, he'd stopped by the office and told Chloe she was doing a good job.

"Am I? It's only been a week and I've not figured out this famous cookie recipe."

"You'll come up with something. What about a new choco-late chip cookie?" He'd shrugged as if it was no big deal. But it was a huge deal. Of *insurrection proportions*, if Ruby was to be believed. Which she probably wasn't. *"What about a chocolate cookie with bacon?"*

"Oh sure, here's your box of cookies and a defibrillator, sir. Come back and see us when you get out of the hospital."

Sam's laugh—she could hear it now. So smooth and clean with some sort of deep echo that made her want to press replay.

He also had a killer wink, which he employed a lot when he was teasing. Or flirting? Was he flirting with her? No. Defi-nitely not. He was her boss. Yeah, of course, that was just him. The old playboy coming out. He'd winked at Ruby the other day and at Mrs. O'Shay. But she was a stunning eighty-some-thing-year-old.

Anyway, Chloe, gather yourself and get to work.

Back at the computer, she reviewed the accounts. Sam and Rick gave her a generous budget for updates and supplies. Tuesday afternoon she'd hired Cole Danner's company to strip the hardwood floors and replace the cracked vinyl benches out front. Cole promised to send a crew and get started next week.

The new sheet pans, muffin tins, and cake pans she'd ordered arrived yesterday. She and Ruby washed and stacked them on the shelves. There was a gorgeous vintage chandelier hanging in Roseanne's Vintage shop she had her eye on. She wanted to hang it over the display case, but since it was a tiny bit over-budget, she planned to save for it.

Eyeing the cracked leather scrapbook peeking out from under the mail, she reached for it. Donna had insisted on leaving it, saying it was part of Haven's history and should stay with the bakery. The first picture was a faded sepia, but she could see the pride on the man's face as he pointed to the Haven's sign over the door. *Hiram Conway, 1929.* Donna's grandfather. A browned news article from the *Hearts Bend Tribune* had been glued to the opposite page.

It told how Hiram purchased the former feed store with the intention of opening a bakery. He had a gas oven shipped from Chicago. The Depression hit, bringing lean times, so Hiram sold bread at cost, or gave it away if the customer, a fellow citizen, didn't have the change. When times got better, folks rewarded him with their loyalty, buying their weekly baked goods from Haven's.

Chloe flipped the pages, leaning forward when she came upon a wedding picture of Bob and Donna. 1975. On the opposite page was another *Hearts Bend Tribune* article. This one about Bob and Donna joining Hiram at Haven's. Bob's business mind expanded the bakery to deliveries around town —to Cooper's Market, Ella's Diner, the Hearts Bend Inn—and staked a claim at the Saturday Farmer's Market.

Chloe loved Haven's history and now she was a part of it. She would continue the history. The photobook even had blank pages where she would add her story.

Chloe's phone chirped a reminder about Mom's chemo appointment in the morning. She got up to tell Ruby she'd be out for a bit tomorrow.

As she walked by Laura Kate, Chloe picked a drooping piece of icing from her hair net. "Let me know when you're done. I'll come and show you some new decorating techniques."

"Sure thing." Laura Kate didn't even look up. Just hovered over her work with the tip of her tongue resting on the corner of her mouth.

Chloe watched for a second. Yeah, once she got the recipes straightened out and the supply ordering streamlined, she was going to teach Laura Kate the theory behind *mise en place*, having everything at hand, measured and in its place. Then the ever-important CAYG—clean as you go. Only then would she move on to more advanced baking and frosting techniques. But LK had some skill. Chloe wanted to learn her technique for the flower design she iced onto a batch of cupcakes.

Yeah, life was good at the bakery. Other than the missing cookie recipe. She hadn't realized how much she needed this job until she started waking at two a.m. to go to work every day. It gave her purpose. Which she desperately needed.

"Ruby?" Chloe found her in the dining area chatting with the same four ladies who came into Haven's on Friday afternoons for the famous and elusive cookies in addition to every Tuesday and Thursday morning at eight. The grand dame, Mrs. O'Shay, and her ladies in waiting. "I have to take Maman to her treatment tomorrow. I'll leave at ten and be back before noon."

"Darling, you take care of that mama of yours. I'll be here holding down the fort."

"Thank you." And she meant it. Having a solid team made the load so much lighter.

"Chloe."

She turned toward her name as Mrs. O'Shay stood. "I understand the TCFC recipe is missing."

"It's not missing so much as it never existed except in Donna's head. Nothing I've tried seems to work."

"Well, the annual O'Shay Shirts Employee Appreciation Day is next month, and the Triple Chocolate Fudge Cookie is tradition. And we love tradition at O'Shay Shirts. You must make them for us."

Despite all efforts, Chloe's cheer sank straight to her toes. "I'm doing my best to replicate it, Mrs. O'Shay."

"We do appreciate it. You know, we give Haven's a lot of business, well, all of our baked goods business."

"Yes, ma'am, and it's greatly appreciated."

She didn't say they'd take their business elsewhere, but Chloe heard the implication in her tone. Which made no sense. The new bakery that Mrs. O'Shay chose wouldn't have the TCFC recipe either.

She'd just returned to her office when her phone buzzed with a text from Mom.

Mom: *Don't forget the appointment tomorrow.*

Chloe: *On my calendar.*

Mom: *Eleanor said she could take me if you're busy.*

Chloe: *I'm not busy. I'm taking you.*

When Mom said Chloe didn't have to come home from Paris to help her, she wasn't kidding. Mom's friend Eleanor called last night to see if she needed a ride to the doctor.

"I'm not doing anything, and Chloe should be at work."

But Chloe insisted she would take Mom. She wanted to know how they were treating her, how to take care of her at home. She'd done well with her two treatments so far, save for being tired and weak.

Chloe began cleaning out a desk drawer. It looked like Bob hadn't purged his files in quite possibly forever. She pulled a stack onto her lap and looked through each folder before returning it to the drawer or tossing it in the trash.

Inventory May 1985. Trash.

Menus 1997. Keep. For the scrapbook if nothing else.

Donut Heaven. Trash. She didn't need a glossy brochure from the coffee and donut mega chain extolling the virtues of owning a franchise.

After finishing the accounting tasks and cleaning out one

file drawer, she headed back into the kitchen and reached for her chef's jacket.

"Laura Kate, finish what you're doing, because we're baking cookies."

"Yes, Chef. That's the last Styrofoam layer coated. What do you need?" The young woman tucked her hair into the net with her spatula, leaving a smear of icing across her temple, as she rolled the cart with the fake cakes into the walk-in.

Chloe smiled and shook her head. She couldn't help but love her assistant baker. Icing smeared all over her face didn't seem to bother her.

By early afternoon, they'd made three sample batches, none of which measured up to the elusive prized cookie. Chloe was cleaning up the mixer and utensils for another try when she noticed a small wooden box pushed against the wall on the lower shelf of the workstation.

"Laura Kate," she said, stooping over and pointing. "Grab that box, will you?"

Laura Kate reached under, pulled out the box, and set it on the table. "Do you think it's *the* box of recipes? How did we not see it before?"

"Great question. We practically took this place apart looking."

Chloe's heart thumped in anticipation as she lifted the lid and peered inside. Shoot. She slapped the lid closed and shoved it toward Laura Kate.

"No recipe?" Laura Kate looked inside and laughed. "Empty yeast envelopes. That's so Donna. She saved them for some unknown reason. Ruby and I found a trash bag full of them in the storage closet last fall."

Chloe instructed her to throw them out and to put the box on her desk. Might as well keep it as part of Haven's history.

"Chloe," Ruby said, peering through the kitchen doors. "Mrs. O'Shay would like a word."

"Tell her I still haven't discovered the TCFC."

"No, it's not about that...something else. But she didn't say what."

Mrs. O'Shay waited just beyond the kitchen doors. There was a good chance she heard Chloe's comment, but it was too late now.

"My granddaughter is coming home from Lauchtenland next week and I'd like a half dozen of those beautiful flower cupcakes." She pointed to the case at Laura Kate's oversized cupcakes decorated with dahlias and roses. "Scottie's coming with her sister-in-law. Gemma's visiting her parents."

"We'd be happy to make them." Cupcakes for a real-life princess. Local gal Gemma Stone had married the crown prince of Lauchtenland last year. Chloe had never made a pastry for a prince or princess while living in Paris. A duke, but not a prince. A check in the plus side for Hearts Bend.

"Also, I was a bit hard on you about the cookie. You know us small-town Southerners. Traditions die hard, which is why I give you my promise of support with the town council. Haven's is a Hearts Bend staple, a landmark, an artery in the heartbeat of this town and I'll not let the town council cater to the whims of modern chain restaurants and money grubbers." She ended her impassioned speech with a wave to her ladies-in-waiting and walked out the door.

Chloe stared at Ruby. "What was that about?"

"I have no idea. I didn't hear a word after she said the crown princess of Lauchtenland was coming to Hearts Bend next week."

❦ ❦ ❦

Love helping @SamHardyQB15 recover from knee surgery. ;-) #Everready

— @CurvyCarla on Twitter

🎃🎃🎃

Titans need a QB at 100%, not a washed-up has-been. #DumpSamHardy

— @No.1TitansFan on Twitter

🎃🎃🎃

Looking forward to getting back on the field! Knee feels great and #THISSEASONWILLBEAWESOME has a nice *ring* ☺ to it. My therapists are the best! Highly recommend @DrJMorganSportsMedicine in Hearts Bend.

— @SamHardyQB15 on Twitter

🎃🎃🎃

Sam finished his last set of foot slide exercises at his Thursday morning session at Dr. Morgan's clinic. As soon as his therapist, Jimbo, released him, Sam planned to head for the bakery.

He needed to check on his investment. See how the pretty, green-eyed baker was getting along with that stupid cookie recipe. Though he needed to be careful. Too many appearances in town beyond the doctor's office was bound to cause a stir, and Frank would find out.

People of all ages and fitness levels were scattered around

the therapy room, riding stationary bikes, doing leg presses, or other exercises. Some wore grimaces, some were sweating.

"Sam." Dr. Morgan appeared behind his therapist. "Jimbo says you're doing well." Dr. "Mom" Morgan leaned against the doorframe, arms folded, looking more like a tennis pro than a renowned sports doctor.

"I'm planning to be at the Organized Team Activities in two months. I know they're optional for me, but I always attend the OTAs, to set an example." Sam slipped gingerly from the table. His knee always throbbed after therapy. He'd swallow a Tylenol or two with his cruller and chocolate milk.

"Janice said you're coming to Frank's party." Dr. Mom, as he'd started calling her, handed Sam his knee brace.

"She cornered me at Haven's." He leaned against the therapy table to fasten the Velcro straps on the brace.

"Sam, I don't know what's between you and your father, but trust me, the body heals way faster when the heart is also whole."

He scowled at her. "What world do you live in, Doc? No one's heart is whole."

"Perhaps not, but they are healed. You can't get far with a wounded heart, Sam."

"My heart isn't wounded."

"I was there when your parents split up and—"

"That was fifteen years ago, Doc." He'd moved on. Way on.

"So that's not why you call your father Frank and refuse to see him except on the rarest of occasions?"

"I didn't know you'd earned your degree in psychology."

"It's my hobby and don't talk back to me." She gave him a *mom* smile and walked him to the door. "What about your mother? Do you talk to her much?"

Sam paused with his hand on the door. "I'll see you next week."

"You're at odds with your dad *and* your mom? I know you've not totally moved on. I know better, Sam Hardy. I'm a doctor and a mother."

"If you're so concerned, you talk to them. He cheated and she bolted. I was fifteen. What was I supposed to do, be the only adult?"

"I know the divorce sent you into a tailspin." Mom Morgan stood next to him, her gaze steady, yet compassionate.

"Frank and Janice's affair hit Mom like a ton of bricks. We were happy until then. They were happy." At least from what he could see from his seat as their son.

"Things are not always as they seem. You might talk to your dad some time."

"If he has something to say, he knows where to find me."

Sam's emotions churned as he exited the modern clinic on the east side of Hearts Bend. Why was it on him to make the past right? His parents were the ones who'd destroyed Sam's happy family.

They'd destroyed his faith in happily ever after.

Speaking of happily ever after... He paused at his car to check in with Briggs about Carla's tweets. So far, he'd not made any progress in stopping her lies. The woman was certifiable. He'd gone to a charity event last night and if Carla had been there, he'd planned to drag Briggs across the room to confront her. Man, he didn't need her as a complication and he held a secret hope that Chloe didn't see any of Carla's nonsense.

And about Chloe... To his surprise, he found himself thinking of her as much as crullers with chocolate milk. In fact, he wished he'd invited her to go with him last night. The band had played old standards and emo girl Chloe also loved the oldies. Frank. Dean. Nat. Sammy.

He got behind the wheel, pressed the start button, and pulled out of the clinic's lot, circling back to the other side of town. Turned out he didn't need any angst about owning a business down the street from Frank. He'd recently moved Hardy Insurance to a new building on the edge of town.

Sam stared at the glass and steel building as he passed. So like Frank, to construct a modern building out of step with the rest of quaint Hearts Bend. The downtown buildings were old red brick or white clapboard. But not Hardy Insurance. Ah well, one less issue for Sam to deal with if he wasn't worried about running into his dad on First Avenue.

His phone buzzed with a text. Meredith Beason. *Your dad would like to talk to you. Please call or stop by at your earliest convenience.*

Had his comment to Dr. Morgan about Dad getting in touch with him if he had something to say floated on the air to Hardy Insurance?

He was in a melancholy mood and wanted to explore his old football haunts. Sam passed the Rock Mill High athletic field, home to some of his favorite memories of cheering fans and adrenaline-fueled locker room celebrations. Did the football team still carry on their traditions? Chanting "Let's go, Rockets, Let's go!" as they marched from the locker room to the field. Kicking the large limestone rock near the entrance to the field as they passed it. Whoever made the last fumble in a game had to smear his hands with putty and carry the ball all day Monday.

He loved all Rock Mill's football traditions. He loved UT's tradition of running the T onto the field. He loved hearing "Titan-Up!" from fans on and off the field. Another reminder of why he had to get back on the field. It was where he belonged. His home. The field had been more of a home during the last year of high school and through college than the house where he'd slept.

Sam parked in front of Haven's, then wrote back to Meredith.

Sam: *Regarding?*

Meredith: *He said it's something to be discussed on the phone or in person.*

Sam: *I'll see him at his party.*

Then Briggs pinged back a message. *Still working on Carla. Stay tuned...*

This day wasn't going at all like he planned. The past kept knocking on his door. Was there a truth behind his parents' divorce he didn't know? Had he been on the wrong side of the argument all these years? But how? He knew what he saw that day...

His knee throbbed and Sam began to wonder, maybe, if the pain hadn't come all the way from his heart.

CHAPTER 6

*W*ell, that was new. A ceiling leak. Chloe stood by
the stainless-steel table in Haven's kitchen,
hands on her hips, and stared upward. A soggy patch, roughly
the size of a watermelon, stained the ceiling. March wind and
rain were not proving kind to the old bakery.

She'd planned yet one more Thursday to concoct another
TCFC iteration before starting the layers for Frank Hardy's
showstopper cake. Instead, she and Ruby worked a bucket
brigade. Ruby handed Chloe the bucket she'd just emptied in
the utility sink in the supply closet.

"The ceiling leaks every time it rains. Did Bob tell that to
Rick and Sam?"

Chloe placed the container under the drip. "My guess is no."

"It leaks in the snow too."

Chloe moaned. Fabulous. In the four weeks she'd been
managing Haven's, she'd spent all the money Sam gave her to
update the place. Cole Danner's team did a beautiful job on
the hardwood floors. The new bench seats in the booths were a

smooth warm brown, not torn and mended with red duct tape. Music played from newly installed speakers nestled in the corners of the bakery. And in the end, she'd been able to splurge on the vintage lighting fixture from Roseanne's.

No one had bothered to tell her the ceiling might fall in.

"I'll call Cole for an estimate." Chloe retreated to her office to make the call.

"I told Bob that patch job he did up there wouldn't last," Ruby hollered after her. "Cole's worth every penny. He does good work and he's reliable as my daddy's old coon hound."

Comparing Cole Danner to a loyal dog wasn't that far off. He'd shown up when he said he would, checking on his team, all while running other jobs. And with his dark brown hair and blue eyes, he did remind her a bit of the Great Dane puppy Vivienne and Albert adopted a couple years ago. In a good way of course.

In the last week, Vivienne had been messaging Chloe, saying they needed to talk. Something about unfinished business. What unfinished business? When Chloe left France, she'd firmly closed every door, every window, every avenue.

She settled at her desk, putting the LaRues out of her mind. The leaky roof was far more pressing. Chloe left a message for Cole, asking him to stop by and give her an estimate. Next, she needed to let Sam know.

Something in her smiled at the idea of talking to him. She liked how he popped into the bakery after his physical therapy treatments. He'd sit on the couch in her office, adjust the straps of his brace, loosening them, then tightening them.

Yes, she enjoyed seeing him in Haven's and in her office. But calling him for money? That was a different matter. That emphasized he was her boss, and she was his employee. Not his old friend. Not a possible romantic interest, if, you know, she was interested in romance. Which she wasn't. He certainly didn't seem inclined toward love.

Her phone pinged with a new text.

This is coming.

The unfamiliar number was local. Who was this? She opened the message to see a screenshot of a tweet.

Excited to bring Old-Fashioned donut goodness to Hearts Bend, Tennessee! Thanks to our local partners! Get ready for Heavenly treatment, HB. See you soon! #DonutHeavenIscoming

– @DonutHeaven

Chloe leaned back in her new chair, her heart pumping. Donut Heaven was coming to Hearts Bend? Since when? Was this the real reason Bob and Donna wanted out? That bright and glossy brochure from Donut Heaven she'd tossed out... Mrs. O'Shay...was this what she meant when she said she was behind Chloe? Who in the world would bring an impersonal mega-chain to quaint, homey HB? It was so wrong. So very wrong. On every level.

Never mind the donut giant was all over the country and boasted that they had the most popular coffee in the country. What about Java Jane's? What about Haven's? Chloe read the tweet again. *Local partners.* What did that mean? Hearts Bend folks? Who would want to harm the town's local business?

She stood, a bit of ire in her blood. This was downright criminal. Oh, she did not have time for this. Not on top of decorating Frank Hardy's birthday cake for tomorrow, a leaking roof, and those blasted cookies. At the computer, she searched the *Hearts Bend Tribune* for any hint of this news. Sure enough, there was an article from last year. Last year!

Oh Bob, you did know, didn't you?

Chloe skimmed the article.

The Reclaim Downtown committee has yet to approve Donut Heaven's application. "But it's in serious consideration," said committee member Drummond Branson.

If the committee gives the green light, Donut Heaven's bid moves to the town council.

"We'll take a good look at it but it's time for some more modern franchises in Hearts Bend. Tourists like to see shops and restaurants they are familiar with back home," said councilman Art Loamier.

"I beg to differ," said council member Octavia O'Shay. "Our home-grown businesses and shops are what make Hearts Bend so very special. Who wants to eat at the same old donut shop and coffee houses you see in every other city?"

The council plans to hear arguments in spring of next year.

Chloe printed the article then pushed from the desk. "Ruby, did you know about this?"

Ruby lowered her readers and squinted at the paper Chloe shoved under her nose. "Donut Heaven? Is that still a thing? Thought it died last fall."

"Apparently not. Someone just sent me a tweet with Donut Heaven announcing their arrival. Soon."

"Cue dramatic music." Ruby raised her glasses and carried a refilled tray of cookies to the front case. "How's that TCFC recipe coming?"

"Nowhere. I have leaky ceilings and a special birthday cake to make. Now I have a big market competitor coming to town."

"If you make that cookie, Donut Heaven won't stand a chance."

"The cookie for which I have no recipe?" She made a face.

"You'll get it." Ruby patted her shoulder, squeezed. "I know you will."

Back in the office, Chloe looked up the town council meeting agenda. Sure enough, the Benedict Arnold Reclaim Downtown committee had approved Donut Heaven's bid at their last meeting so the application was being formally presented at the town council's upcoming meeting. How in the world would a cold, impersonal chain donut and coffee shop help Hearts Bend *reclaim* its downtown?

Chloe scanned the committee's minutes, the ones the council would review. She wanted all the data at her fingertips before calling her bosses.

What a report it promised to be. A leaky roof, still no TCFC recipe and, last but by no means least, Donut Heaven threatening their livelihood. Her attention to detail used to drive Jean-Marc crazy. But how could she make a decision otherwise? And he loved her for it when they purchased their flat in the Bastille.

Reviewing all the minutes again, she caught a new detail. Someone on the town council was behind the invitation to Donut Heaven. Well, if that didn't stack the deck. Small towns like HB thrived on handshakes over dinner, a promise given in the church parking lot after a deacons' meeting.

But this really wasn't her fight, was it? No, this tangle belonged to Sam and Rick. Still, she couldn't—wouldn't—sit by and watch.

Ruby appeared at the door. "Had a thought. You should talk to the person who knows what's going on in this town more than anyone. Tina Danner over at Ella's Diner." Ruby nodded with a wink. "That gal knows where *all* the bodies are buried."

"Ruby, you're the best. Thank you." She could run over to Ella's real quick during the pre-lunch lull and get the scoop from Tina. Just as she reached for her phone, a new text came in from Vivienne. *Please, Chloe, we need to speak with you. It's important.*

Whatever Vivienne wanted could wait. Chloe grabbed her jacket and hat. "Ruby, I'll be back."

"Bring a list of folks we need to bribe with fresh fritters. Er, I mean, *remind* them of Haven's locally sourced, delicious baked goods. No franchise has our quality and personal touch."

"You're coming with me to the council meeting." Chloe stepped around the bucket. "If Cole comes by, tell him what's going on, then have him call me."

Chloe pushed through the swinging doors with a buzz in her chest, a certain determination to confront whoever was behind this Donut Heaven scheme. Not in her town. She'd had enough stolen from her: people that were precious to her, many of her personal things, her dreams. Haven's would not be next on her list of regrets and losses.

She strode through the doors. Bam! Right into the brick wall of Sam Hardy, smelling fresh and clean and looking better than any man had a right to.

"Oh, hey, what are you doing here?" She took a moment to compose herself, patted her warm cheek, tugged on her beret.

"Just finished therapy and thought I'd check in. Where are you going?"

"Um, to the—" Couldn't say the bank, she didn't have the deposit. Should she tell him? No, she'd gather her data and then tell him. She didn't want to spark drama for drama's sake. "Errand. Running an errand."

"Chloe, wait..."

She paused at the door.

"I was, um, wondering..." Sam closed the gap between them. "Are you free for dinner?"

What? Had he just asked her to dinner?

"Chloe?"

81

Ruby stepped between them, handing Sam the cruller and chocolate milk he had yet to order. "She'd love to go to dinner." She turned to Chloe. "He'll pick you up at six. Sam, you can sit over there and don't let this treat spoil your dinner. Chloe, go on and run your errand." Ruby pointed to the door.

Errand? Right. She started for the door then turned back to Sam. What just happened? She'd been so focused on the questions she wanted to ask Tina... What if Tina was in on the Donut Heaven deal? No, why would she be? It would compete with her business. Still...

"Chloe? Dinner?" Ruby said. "Law, what is going on with young folk today?"

"Yes, of course, dinner."

"See you at six then." He gave her one of his trademark grins, with one corner of his mouth tipped up, as he backed toward the newly reupholstered booth.

Chloe barely noticed the cold metal of the door or the four icy steps down to the sidewalk.

At the diner, Tina wasn't much help. She knew nothing more than last year's headline.

"Believe me, I wish I did know more. Whoever's behind this deal doesn't sit at my counter and drink coffee."

Shoot. Well, Tina promised to keep Chloe informed if she heard anything and Chloe promised the same.

In the time it had taken Chloe to walk to the diner, talk to Tina, and retrace her route, Vivienne had texted twice more. Chloe had other things to worry about at the moment, but she took a minute to type a message. *Hope you and Albert are well. I'm keeping busy in HB. Think of you often. Talk soon.*

When she walked back into the bakery kitchen, Ruby met her at the door.

"Cole said he'll stop by later. Anything from Tina?" Ruby

followed Chloe to the office, hands fisted in the pockets of her white uniform dress.

"All she knows is that someone big in town affairs, likely on the council, bought a Donut Heaven franchise and convinced the Reclaim Downtown committee to approve the business license."

"That's all we know too." Ruby sank onto the office's small couch. "The good Lord knows I can't imagine a town without Haven's or Java Jane's. Donut Heaven could put us both out of business. We don't have a drive-through or ninety-nine-cent donut sticks."

"Not sure if the Lord pays much attention to what's going on in Hearts Bend." Because as far as Chloe was concerned, He'd never paid much attention to her.

"Pshaw. The Lord cares about everything and everyone. He knows the number of hairs on your head, Chloe LaRue. He surely knows who is behind this Donut Heaven plot and what we should do to stop it right now."

"Then you talk to the good Lord, get His plan, and tell me."

Ruby slapped the couch arm. "That's a great idea. We'll call a prayer meeting, barnstorm heaven, and come up with some divine ideas." Ruby patted her '60s beehive hairdo. "I'll tell Laura Kate and Robin that we'll meet tomorrow morning at five. Course Robin won't make it, but we best invite her anyway. That girl ain't never seen five in the a.m."

"I'll be busy making the morning donuts and bread. Y'all pray without me."

"Nothing doing. You're the boss. The Lord is sure to hear you."

She seriously doubted it. He'd not heard her much in the last couple of decades. Not that she'd offered much to Him for response. But ever since Daddy had died, she'd wondered if He was a good God at all. How could he take her father and claim to be a good Father Himself?

🎃🎃🎃

Sam sat in front of the Beason house and checked email. Marco Martelli invited him to a party. Decline. Couldn't run the risk of running into @CurvyCarla. Besides, he'd rather hang with the married players these days than the single ones.

The next email, from his assistant Delia, asked if he wanted a plus-one for the banquet the Nashville Foundation was hosting at the Hotel TN in a couple weeks to honor him for his work with underserved youth through his SportsWorld organization.

Buck Mathews was also being thanked for his I Hate Cancer concerts that had raised a bazillion dollars for research. Well, maybe closer to a few million, but still. Mikayla Onofrio was the third honoree. The Hollywood actress lived part time in Nashville and used her name and status to raise funds for respite programs for Alzheimer's and dementia caregivers.

It promised to be a perfectly boring evening. Why would he subject another person to that?

Though it would serve @CurvyCarla right if he showed up with a real date. He sat up straight. Yeah, it totally would. Who would he bring? Chloe could make the night bearable, fun even. At last night's event, he'd remembered dancing with her back in the day. Maybe he should invite her to this shindig.

Delia attached a list of what had been donated for the swag bags. He gave a low whistle. They might need security guards to escort the guests to their cars. He scanned the rest of his inbox and told Delia to accept a podcast invitation.

Six o'clock on the dot, Sam climbed the steps to Meredith

Beason's front door, gripping the handrail. His knee still throbbed from therapy, but he trusted Dr. Morgan's process and prediction—he'd heal just fine. Though if she was right about his physical healing, did that mean she was right about his emotional healing? Sam shook off the thought and knocked on the door.

Chloe opened it and stood in the middle of the entry, backlit by a glow from the living room. She wore tight jeans, knee-high boots, a gauzy blouse, and a jeweled hair clip behind one ear. She was beautiful. Stunning.

"Wow," he said, feeling very underdressed. "You look great."

"Thanks. So do you, Hardy."

He scoffed. "Liar. I'm wearing what I wore to PT." He should've gone home to change but instead he had knocked around town, visited the Kids Theater, and run into his old friend, Luke Stebbins. They'd had coffee at Ella's until it was time for Sam to pick up Chloe. He'd brushed his teeth in the men's room before heading out. Smart men always carried a portable toothbrush and toothpaste.

"So where to, Hardy?"

"How about Angelo's?" He held the door for her as she stepped from the house into the night. "We can walk."

"Are you sure? What about your knee?"

"It's not far and walking will do me good. Just don't go too fast."

She offered her arm in an exaggerated move. "You can lean on me, Hardy."

The way her offer floated over him, he wanted to believe it. Really believe it. Dive in deep and drown himself in it.

They walked the short distance down Red Oak to First Avenue then to Angelo's, Sam waving at people who passed, gawking, whispering. *Is that really Sam Hardy?* A couple of cars honked as they passed. "Titan-up!" He waved to acknowledge the cheer and call to get in the game.

A man about a decade younger than Sam approached them at Angelo's front door. "Hi, Mr. Hardy. Kofi Smith. I'm a big fan." He stuck out his hand. Sam shook it with a blushing glance at Chloe.

"Thanks, keep watching. This is going to be a great season."

After a few more praises from Kofi, Sam reached for Angelo's door. "I didn't set that up, you know, to impress you."

She laughed, a sound he liked. Had always liked it. "I'm impressed you'd think you need to impress me."

He regarded her intently. "Don't I?"

"No," she said, so pure and simple. "Never have, never will."

He liked her more and more. Holding the door for her, they stepped into a warm, old-world Italian atmosphere with romantic candles flickering on the tables and soft classical music playing over the speakers.

The maître d' escorted them to a red-checked tablecloth booth in the corner. Sam ordered a bottle of wine to come out with their garlic knots.

"So...you didn't ask me to dinner to counterbalance the tweets from Curvy Carla, did you?"

She knew. Well, what did he expect? "No. She's making it all up. I saw her at a party, she was drunk, and I drove her home. Didn't even get out of my car." He should record this story and just play it for folks each time they asked. "She's an NFL groupie, hanging around one of the other players. I didn't know..." Sigh. "But given my past, my choice to drive her home was incredibly stupid."

Chloe stretched her arms across the table and took his hand in hers. "You're a nice man, Sam, and I mean that with the most admiration and regards. Not the cliché nice guy routine, but a genuinely nice man. A good man."

Darn if she wasn't making him choke up. He swallowed the sudden lump in his throat. "You remember the old Sam from high school."

"I know about your party life. Remember, Jean-Marc was a big fan. Also, the 'Sam from high school' wasn't always so nice."

"Oh, to the heart." He slapped his hand over his chest. "What did I do to you in high school?"

"That night at the fair with Missy Byrnes, Cole Danner, and Tammy Eason." She looked away. Now she looked embarrassed. "Never mind. It was a long time ago."

"According to Dr. Morgan, things from a long time ago can still hurt." He reached for her hands this time. "We'd gone to the Fry Hut together." She'd looked at him with this sparkle in her eyes, an anticipation of a fun evening, their first group date. Then he'd...been a jerk. What could he say?

"Here we are..." The server arrived with their wine and garlic knots and interrupted their conversation.

After a garlic knot and glass of wine, Sam had to return to the situation of Curvy Carla.

"She's just playing off who I was, Chloe. Curvy Carla."

"Is there a *but* coming?"

"No but. One day I woke up and—" He wasn't sure he wanted to confess everything here and now. That he wanted a real relationship, real love, a real woman. "And decided I didn't want to live like that anymore."

She tilted her head to one side, a serious expression on her beautiful face. "I'm proud of you then. It's hard to change your path, your direction."

The server came back for their order. Pepperoni and mushroom pizza with a Roma crust.

"Your turn now," Sam said. "Tell me about France. Do you miss it?"

She paused before answering. "I think I miss what it was more than anything." Chloe described pieces of her life in Paris. The restaurant where she worked, who trained her, how much she loved making delicious things.

Sam couldn't help it. He stopped listening and just watched her. The more she talked about making beautiful things to eat, the more her sadness of being a recent widow vanished and she was the Chloe he remembered. Vivacious and glowing with passion.

Their food arrived and the conversation gave way to large bites of hot, cheesy pizza and low moans of, "This is so good," and laughing as they pulled strings of melted cheese from their chins.

"Is it hard to talk about your husband?" He didn't exactly know the etiquette of what was okay to ask or talk about. How had she gotten through it? Being widowed and left alone so young.

She gave a wistful smile. "Not anymore."

"How did he die? I mean, I heard it was an accident, but—"

"A tree."

Sam froze mid bite. "A tree?"

Chloe dabbed her lips with her paper napkin, then set it beside her plate. "His family owns a large sporting goods company and Jean-Marc tested new equipment and designs. He was trying out a new ski design in Switzerland when he lost control and hit a tree square on. He lived a few minutes, but the crash was too severe."

"I'm so sorry, Chloe. I can't imagine."

"I dreamed about it afterwards for months. How he lost control, crashed into that tree. What he must have felt. Did he know he was dying? As his life ended, did he say anything to me? His parents were with him so if he did, they've not told me."

"Did you want him to say something to you?"

Chloe looked away and peered out the window. She watched the headlights as they streamed past the restaurant—illuminating the trees, the parked cars, the outside tables, and umbrellas—while she considered her answer.

"Yes." Her reply was simple and low, gravely with emotion. "We'd argued before he left. It was unresolved. Then I was so angry at him for dying, for leaving me. He didn't have to be the one testing the skis, but he insisted. He was supposed to be with me in Paris. I wanted to hear he was sorry."

"Sounds like he lived life to the fullest," Sam said, curious, though not jealous. Because who would be jealous of a dead man? "But I'm sorry about the circumstances before his death."

"Thank you. Believe it or not, it's a bit of a relief to talk about it, to talk about him." She drew a deep breath and smiled. "Jean-Marc was vibrant and full of life. A daredevil. The fun of doing something new was an addiction. He loved a challenge, loved the adrenaline rush. He loved being 'the first.' Hence the test run." She took an awkward bite of her pizza. "Which is why he loved you. Thought you were a daring quarterback. He was watching that day when you got sacked and had to miss the last few minutes of the game. I was trying to sleep and he's yelling at you to scramble or something. Then you didn't get up and missed the final drive and the team lost. He was worried you were concussed."

"So was I. That loss stung." Sam took another bite of pizza. "I'm sorry I never met him."

Her eyes glistened when she looked across the table and gave him her answer. "Me too."

"So, was Chloe—the former emo girl—a daredevil, going on adventures with her husband?"

"No," she said with a soft laugh. "The only chances I took were in my recipes. I hate heights, which I think was a bit of a disappointment to him. I would stand at the base of the mountain and watch." She sipped her wine and it seemed to him the conversation about Jean-Marc was over.

"Are you ready for Frank's big party tomorrow night?" Sam said.

"Cakes are frosted and partly decorated. I'm looking forward to it."

He restrained from any sort of negative response and rather welcomed it when the conversation fell into a civil and like-minded political discussion.

They polished off the pizza in style and ordered tiramisu for dessert—without hesitation.

A couple of fans shyly approached, and Sam signed his autograph for them, paid the check, then suggested a stroll through Gardenia Park.

When she looked up at him in agreement, his heart melted a little, despite the late winter chill in the air. *What are you doing to me, Chloe LaRue?*

🏈🏈🏈

Huge honor meeting @SamHardyQB15 at Angelo's in Hearts Bend. #GoTitans #TitanUp

— @KofiSBBaller on Twitter

CHAPTER 7

*C*hloe woke at two a.m. thinking about Sam, and somewhere between brushing her teeth and pinning her beloved beaded clip into her hair, guilt crept up her chest and filled her throat. She gripped the edge of the bathroom sink and stared at her reflection.

You cannot have feelings for him.

Jean-Marc hadn't been gone a year yet. Tears filled her eyes and she glared at herself. Jean-Marc loved her. She loved him. Madly. Was she ready to forget him? To forget everything they'd shared, what they'd meant to each other? But as she hurried to Haven's in that inky blackness that happens right before dawn, she felt his death more than ever. He was gone. Never to return. If he was still alive, they'd be together. It wasn't forgetting him to think about another man. Right?

With the kitchen lights blazing and the ovens warming up, Chloe started the bread rising, mixing dough for the crullers, and put Sam and their semi-romantic walk around Gardenia Park out of her mind. Mostly. She tried not to think about how their hands kept bumping and how easily the conversation flowed. How her heart felt, fluttering under her ribs, like it couldn't quite find its rhythm.

In honor of the approaching spring, they'd attempted to walk without being bundled up in scarves and hats and mittens. Not that she needed anything to keep her warm other than Sam's glances her way as they strolled and chatted.

After Ruby and Laura Kate arrived at five a.m., Ruby gathered them, as promised, for the barnstorming prayer meeting to figure out if God had any ideas about saving the town from Donut Heaven.

When Chloe suggested God might favor the competitor since Heaven was part of their name, Ruby scoffed and pooh-poohed her.

"God's a whole lot smarter than that, sister." Ruby prayed loud, rigorous prayers while Laura Kate sat in a solemn pose, her lips moving with whispers only she and God heard. Robin, to the surprise of them all, popped in at five-fifteen and offered a lovely, heartfelt prayer that moved Chloe to tears. So much so that she asked God to forgive her for every time she cursed when Robin was late.

After fifteen minutes, Laura Kate suggested opening Facebook, Instagram, and Twitter accounts. "I'll manage them," she said.

"We've been slowly introducing new baked items to the menu," Ruby said. "The fancy cupcakes and custard tarts are a big hit. But we *need* that cookie recipe."

Chloe nodded. "I'm working on it. Truly, I am." She snapped her fingers. "I could do Moon Pies. Solidify our Southern heritage."

"Oh, that's good. Customers around here love the old-school ways. Take that, Donut Heaven. Folks like ordering treats their grandparents bought for a nickel."

"What about savory pies and pastries on the menu, more of

a diner-type atmosphere for folks who come out at lunch time? Or they can take something home for dinner." Chloe could do pasties and quiche with meat.

"Let's see if that's not smacking Donut Heaven in the teeth," Ruby said. "I told you God would give us ideas."

"Don't get too carried away with the God stuff, Ruby," Chloe said. "We *are* intelligent women."

"Who got our brains from the Lord, don't you forget."

By the time the bakery opened, Chloe had a list of solid ideas to beef up Haven's reputation and position in the community, and hopefully increase sales. She might be ready to tell Sam what they faced. Then Laura Kate brought a bit of distressing news.

"The baguettes are overdone. The oven is too hot."

"What?" Chloe checked the gauge inside the oven, which read twenty degrees higher than the dial setting. Thank goodness they'd baked Frank Hardy's cake layers yesterday. "Ruby, who did Bob call for oven repairs?"

"Himself."

Chloe made a face. "Think he'd make the trip up from Florida?"

"Doubt it."

"Okay, I'll have to call an industrial oven repairman, which means he'll come from Nashville or Memphis."

The "fixer-upper" dollars started totaling up in her head. She could live with buckets of water from a leaky roof, but not with a broken oven. Now she was suddenly nervous and checked the cakes in the walk-in. All the layers were there, safe and sound.

"Laura Kate, let's put these on the worktable and I'll show you the finishing touches I want you to add."

The touted Frank Hardy sixtieth birthday bash was finally here. Tonight. She was nervous and excited to show off her and

Laura Kate's creation. And to see Sam. Something she'd confess to only herself.

Chloe had decorated the layers into the golf course she'd designed. She'd assemble it at the Hardy home later. Laura Kate quickly picked up the techniques Chloe showed her, piping a row of shells around the sand traps and long blades of grass by the water hazards.

"You're a natural, Laura Kate," Chloe said. "Though you need to unlearn a couple bad habits." She showed the younger woman how to hold the pastry bag in one hand and guide it with the other to get a smoother piped line.

"Oh, that's so much easier than my way of double-fisting it." Laura Kate exhaled, and her white-blonde bangs whiffled up.

"You learn quickly," Chloe said. "I don't understand how you can do such beautiful and delicate work when you and your station look like frosting exploded all over." Chloe didn't know whether to scold the girl, get an attorney on retainer for the inevitable unsafe workplace lawsuit, or offer her a pay raise.

"I know, I'm a mess." Laura Kate's hand was steady as she squeezed off the last shell. "I just get so caught up in what I'm doing."

Chloe remembered feeling like that when she'd first started out. She'd wonder why her back and arms ached, then realize she'd been crouched over a table, piping frosting, making gum paste flowers, or drizzling hot caramel into intricate patterns for three hours.

"That means you love what you're doing." Chloe patted Laura Kate's shoulder. "I can't fault you for that."

"I wanted to go to the Culinary Institute of America like you, but my daddy got sick, so I just hung around here and copied everything Donna did, watched YouTube, read books. Every gray hair on my parents' heads is because of me. I blew up our kitchen with flour, sugar, eggs, milk, and vanilla bombs so many times..."

"I'll be honest, you have more skill and talent than some of the highly educated and trained pastry chefs I worked with in Paris. Good for you."

More and more, Chloe loved this place. If she ever began to solidify plans of going back to France, maybe getting that little café she and Jean-Marc dreamed about, she was starting to believe that Haven's might just change her mind. Might.

By mid-morning, the bakery bustled with customers, both homegrown and tourists. It seemed impossible that they could lose their standing in Hearts Bend to a Donut Heaven. But DH had deep pockets. Chloe retreated to the office to balance the books and check on her inventory orders.

"I see you're finally out of your Sam daze." Ruby slapped the mail down on Chloe's desk.

"You exaggerate. I'm not in a Sam daze." She leafed through the bills, ads, and a magazine.

"Okay, a Sam stupor then."

"Not even close." But she had been in a bit of a—okay, a haze—continually pulling her mind back from the park last night.

"Whatever you say, boss lady." Ruby folded her arms and gave Chloe a steady gaze. "So, Art Loamer just came in for a fritter and coffee."

The name rang a bell, but a search through her memory drew a blank. "And that matters to me how?"

Ruby tutted and sighed. "He's on the town council. One from the pro-Donut Heaven camp. I held his coffee hostage until he'd tell me who's behind this stupid scheme."

"Did it work?"

"He left without coffee. Took his fritter and was gone. All he'd say was more of what he spouted in the paper. It'll be good for tourism, bring jobs, and help modernize the town." Ruby's disdainful expression made Chloe smile. "Same old claptrap."

"Thanks for trying." Chloe knew Ruby hated the thought of Donut Heaven coming to Hearts Bend and changing the town's hominess and quaintness as much as she did.

"What do you want us to do about Frank's cake? Laura Kate's finished that decorating."

"Let's start packing it up and loading it in the van." As part of the sale, Bob had left his windowless van for the transportation of baked goods around town. It drove like an old jalopy, but it did the job. Chloe had just tied on her apron to help Laura Kate box the layers when Sam poked his head into the kitchen.

"Come on in, Sam. Cruller and chocolate milk coming up."

"Ruby, you're going to make me fat."

"Fat chance." Ruby thought she was so funny.

Chloe smiled and gave him a short wave. *Oh, my.* He looked...amazing. Street casual Sam, dressed in jeans and a polo, his hair styled except for the stubborn dark curl flopping over his forehead. She didn't regret brushing on a touch of mascara before daybreak this morning.

"What's this?" He stood over the drip bucket, which needed to be dumped out back.

"Leak in the roof," Chloe said. "Cole Danner is giving me a bid."

"Go ahead and call a roofing contractor for a bid instead of Cole. Cole will just contract it out anyway." Sam's gaze went to the table. "Is this Frank's cake?" He looked genuinely impressed. "Wow."

"The prettiest decorations are Laura Kate's." Chloe felt so warm standing next to him. Like he belonged here, admiring her work, helping her with the bakery. Like they were...partners. "We'll load it up in a minute," she said, stepping away from him. "I'll drive it to the house and assemble it there."

"Can I help?"

"Sam Hardy, are you asking to help with your father's party?"

"I might. But don't tell anyone."

"See, you are a nice man."

He pressed a finger to his lips and leaned toward her. "Shush. Don't tell." He was so close she could breathe in the scent of his soap. Her hands trembled slightly under his watchful eye. *Say something!*

"Hey, Sam, is there a reason you don't want Frank and Janice to know you bought Haven's?"

He shifted his position and glanced at Frank's cake. "I don't know. I—I guess Haven's holds my best memories from before the divorce. When I thought our family was something special. I'm not ready to share it with Frank and Janice. Besides, Dad might step in and start telling me how to run the place and— yeah, no thanks."

"I get it. I remember the afternoon you found out about your father's affair. Then later when your mom packed up and drove off."

"Sorry you had to witness it all."

She touched his arm. "I was glad to be there for you...honestly."

He clapped his hand over hers and the tenderness between them lingered. Then he broke away, saying, "I had a good time at dinner last night."

"Me too. Thank you."

"Did you tell him?" Ruby said as she walked back into the kitchen.

"Tell him what?" Sam said.

"Donut Heaven is opening a store in Hearts Bend." Ruby, the Town Crier.

"You're kidding. Donut Heaven? In Hearts Bend? Are you

sure?"

Chloe gave him the details. The whispers from Octavia O'Shay, the old newspaper headline, the recon at Tina's, and Art Loamier leaving the shop without his coffee.

"Apparently, the Reclaim Downtown committee already approved them. Now we're waiting for the town council. There's a meeting in a few weeks."

"Then we have to be there." Sam pulled out his phone and started a text to Rick. "I can help out some," he said, almost to himself.

"Help out?" Chloe said. "Here?"

"Sure. I can work the counter. Start some buzz."

Chloe gave him a dubious look. "That will cause a stir. Your dad and Janice will know you own this place for sure if you do that."

Sam grinned. "It's the price I have to pay to save my business. First things first, we'll fix the roof and find out who's behind this Donut Heaven venture. See if we can't influence things our way, Hearts Bend's way." Sam stuck out his hand. "You with me?"

"I'm with you." Chloe slapped her hand on top of Sam's. Then Ruby joined the huddle followed by Laura Kate.

"On three, Haven's up," Sam said.

"1-2-3, Haven's up!"

She felt the words all the way through her soul. She was on a team with Sam Hardy—and for the first time since Jean-Marc died, her life seemed to be moving forward.

🍩🍩🍩

Sam parked his SUV in front of his childhood home, the Craftsman-style bungalow with stacked-stone porch pillars. It had been a warm, inviting place as a kid. Mom always did it up for holidays and birthdays. She had so many traditions.

After she moved out, the house turned cold and lonely. Just a couple of sad bachelors under the high-pitched roof. Then Janice moved in a few months later. The house smelled better and felt warmer, and Frank certainly cheered up. But Sam remained on the outside, lonely, disconnected, and confused.

Then he and Chloe started hanging out regularly and all of that changed. She was warm and bright and liked to do things up for Christmas and birthdays.

Sam chuckled at the memory of her bringing a Charlie Brown Christmas tree into his room, insisting he decorate it and put presents underneath. He plugged the thing in every night. Slept with the lights flashing around his bedroom walls. He hadn't taken them down until mid-February, when the last needle dropped from the skinny limbs.

When he was with her, he had felt...carefree. In fact, she *still* made him feel carefree. Like he could tackle whatever life sent his way.

What was this? Feelings for his old friend? But she was a recent widow. Her husband hadn't even been dead for a year. And he was still recovering from his ribald reputation. To be honest, sometimes he wasn't sure he could really be a stand-up man and go the distance.

Sam paused at the bottom of the porch steps—did every building in this town have steps to test his knee?—to adjust his tuxedo tie, making sure the ends were even. Janice was serious about this vintage 1960s theme. A Ford Mustang had been parked in the circular driveway. A '64, the first year of production, if he had to guess. He chuckled and shook his head as he climbed the front steps of his old house and rang the doorbell, tentatively bending his knee to gauge the pain before peering through the side window to peek inside.

The place looked amazing, decorated with glitz and glam, the china and crystal set out on a long table. He'd seen the bakery's van parked out back. Chloe must be in the kitchen with the cake. Black-tie caterers and servers hustled about, fine-tuning the last-minute details. A band was setting up in the corner of the large stone-and-wood den. He could hear someone playing a scale on a keyboard.

Why was he early? He should've arrived an hour late. He turned to go back to the Range Rover when Janice, in a form-fitting sequined gown, swung open the door.

"Sam, I thought that was you. Come in."

Why did he feel awkward walking into his childhood home? Because it wasn't his anymore, was it? There was nothing of his life with Mom and Frank here anymore.

"Your father will be down in a minute," Janice said, smiling, her hands clasped at her waist. "He's excited to have you here."

"The old man only turns sixty once."

Janice's countenance brightened. "I guess that's true, yes."

Through the living and dining rooms, he caught sight of Chloe carrying in a portion of the cake.

He limped over to help her. "Here, let me." He took the layer. "Is this it or is there more in the van?"

"The rest is in the kitchen. Laura Kate is assembling them, making sure everything looks good."

"I hope you're charging Janice enough," Sam whispered in Chloe's ear. "This is a high-class party."

"I charged her the price in the book."

"Oh...wow. Let's go over the prices next week."

Sam grudgingly admired the remodeled kitchen as he entered the room to watch Chloe and Laura Kate. He liked the idea of working at Haven's, of being around Chloe.

Chloe and Laura Kate set to work assembling the cake and adding the golf decorations. The final addition was a miniature figure of a man dressed in plaid knickers, argyle socks, and a matching sweater, leaning on a golf club. Chloe set him on the bottom layer and gave Sam a look as she stepped back to survey the finished product. "My attempt at a '60s golf cake."

"It's beautiful." Sam gave her a side hug and when she relaxed against him, he wanted to never let go.

The kitchen door swung open. "Sam?"

Chloe stiffened again, pulling away just as his cousin Sophie appeared in a slim skirt, heels, and with her honey blonde hair clipped behind one ear. A tall man followed behind her. "There you are!" She threw her arms around Sam and hugged him. "I'm so happy you're here. This is Eric."

Eric was Ichabod Crane-thin and gangly with a benign expression as he shook Sam's hand. Sophie greeted Chloe, then gasped at the cake. "This is amazing! Does it taste half as good as it looks? Do you design wedding cakes?"

Chloe assured her she did, and Sophie launched into fast-paced wedding cake chatter. Chloe offered her a Haven's business card—with Bob's and Donna's names scratched out—and told her to call and schedule a taste test. Sam made a mental note to get new business cards for the bakery and for Chloe.

Sam watched as she and Laura Kate carried the cake out to the dessert table for the final assembly. Pride flickered through him. *Chloe, way to go.* She'd come a long way from the shy girl dressed in black who had introduced him to Red Jumpsuit Apparatus and Fall Out Boy music.

A man entered the room and Sam tensed.

"Jake!" Janice swooped and wrapped him in a hug. Janice's son, Sam's former best friend, and now his stepbrother.

"Sam." Jake extended his hand, which Sam shook, the familiar ache squeezing his chest.

Once upon a time they'd been closer than brothers—until

they actually became brothers. Thanks to Frank, that rift never mended.

Jake turned to Chloe and his face lit with appreciation. "Um..."

"Chloe Beason. Now LaRue. Rock Mill High School."

"Emo Girl?" He grinned. "Always scribbling in a journal with your earphones in."

"That was me," Chloe said with a laugh.

"I think it's past time we caught up. What's it been, ten years? More?" Jake crooked his arm toward Chloe, but Sam stepped in.

"She's working, Jake. Besides, I think I have the first dance."

Chloe glanced between them then down at her work clothes. "Afraid I'm not dressed for a party or a dance, boys." She and Laura Kate disappeared back into the kitchen as more and more people arrived. The place filled up with family, long-time friends, and town leaders.

A couple of Frank's old Rock Mill High buddies slapped Sam on the back and greeted him, launching into football talk before he could say, "I'm fine. How are you?"

Then Janice announced, *He's coming*, and the guests surged forward as the man of the hour descended the staircase with the air that he was the king of his castle.

"Happy birthday, Frank!"

Someone started a rendition of "For He's a Jolly Good Fellow," which Sam could not sing. He loved his father. But he did not like him.

Frank made the rounds shaking hands, clapping shoulders, you-ole-dogging the high school football buddies—they still met once a month for poker and beer. Then he saw Sam. For a moment, it seemed as though his dad's eyes glistened, but Sam was sure it was just his imagination.

"Happy birthday." Sam extended his own hand.

"Thank you, son. Thank you for coming." His father shook his hand, then pulled him close and clapped him on the back. "H-how's your knee?"

"Getting there. I'm hopeful for the season."

"Good, good. We've got our season tickets. We'll be there no matter what."

The confession struck a deep chord in Sam. One he'd thought he had completely walled off from his father's reach. Frank had always been his number one football fan. He also loved the Titans. When they drafted Sam nine years ago, Frank was with him and his agent in Indianapolis. The image of Frank's face when the Titans called his name in the first round would forever live in Sam's memory. Pride. Frank had been proud.

But that changed nothing about what Frank had done to their family. To Mom.

"Hey, I want to talk to you about something," Frank said. "You got a minute?"

"Now? Frank, this is your big birthday party. We'll talk later." Sam gestured to the crowd as Janice made her way toward them.

She slipped her hand through Frank's arm, and together they worked the room.

Sam leaned against the wall, watching, wondering if Chloe and Laura Kate had snuck away. In spite of the group surrounding him, it seemed lonely without her nearby.

Snatches of conversations floated to him. "...tourism on the uptick..." "...Top 40 and movie soundtrack..." "...filing process..." Frank's voice and laughter stood out above everyone else's.

Finally, Janice led Frank to the cake table. "We're going to sing "Happy Birthday"—where's Buck Mathews?" The country music star strolled out of the kitchen with his guitar and a mini sandwich. "Buck, you raided the food already?"

"I told you, Janice, I sing for food."

The guests erupted with laughter. Sam caught Buck's eye and they chin nodded each other.

"Well, then I'll just cancel my check." Janice winked. "Listen, y'all, we'll sing, cut the cake, and then you can load up your plates. We've got tables inside and out, with a fire blazing in every possible place and pit to keep y'all warm." The guests laughed and Sam had to admit Janice was charming. "Buck?"

Buck strummed his guitar and launched into "Happy Birthday." Harmonies and melodies intermingled as the mix of seventy friends, family, and colleagues honored Frank Hardy.

Why couldn't Sam do the same? He cleared his throat and joined in on the last two lines. If he was going to prove to Dr. Morgan that he'd forgiven his father for the past, he'd best sing him a happy birthday song.

But he wasn't over it, was he? Not entirely. Pain shot from his knee up his thigh. Sam leaned hard against the wall.

"Look at this gorgeous cake." Janice handed Frank the cutter. "From Haven's. Meredith's daughter, Chloe LaRue, made it."

Sam glanced around to see Meredith smiling from the fringes of the party. He inched through the crowd to say hello and wish her well with her health.

"Love this cake. Howard, grab your nine iron. We'll shoot a few rounds." Frank took a bite of the slice on his plate. "Edible golf? I've died and gone to heaven." The guests rewarded his quip with a hearty laugh.

Janice instructed everyone to grab a plate, and Sam made his way around the room to head outside.

Someone tugged on his sleeve. "Sam." Chloe looked at him

with trust and confidence. "Janice said she'd pay us tonight. But should I just leave and get it next week?"

"Let's ask her. If she said she'd pay today, then make her do it."

Chloe made a face like *You sure?* then followed him inside. "I'll ask her, all right? Since you're keeping your stake in Haven's a secret."

"For now, until I start working there."

"Here I go..." Chloe started across the grand room with high ceilings and expensive art on the wall. "Janice," she said. "We're off but I wondered if you wanted to pay us tonight or—"

"Oh, darling, of course, but aren't you staying?" Janice withdrew an envelope from a nearby drawer.

"Staying?" Chloe said with an over-the-shoulder look at Sam.

"For the party?" Janice glanced at Meredith. "Didn't you tell your daughter to stay?"

"Thank you, but I can't." Chloe regarded her mother and then Sam. "I'm Cinderella, not dressed for the ball."

"Well, then I'm your fairy godmother." Janice grabbed Chloe by the hand and even if she tried to wrestle her to the ground, Chloe wasn't getting free of that grip. "I've a million gowns. What size are you? I have a four and sixes from my WW days, but that ship has sailed," she whispered conspiratorially.

Chloe leaned toward Sam as Janice led her toward the broad staircase. "If I'm not back in fifteen, rescue me."

Rescue you? Anytime, Chloe, anywhere.

🦋🦋🦋

Janice wasn't lying—she had a dressing room full of cocktail dresses and gowns. From the outside, the Hardy bungalow looked like a small, old-time family home with three beds and a bath, but no, this place never ended. Five bedrooms at least, five bathrooms, a to-die-for gourmet kitchen, and a media room that could be classified as a small theater.

"Try this one. I only wore it once and then somehow, who knows, I gained ten pounds."

"That usually comes from someone adding butter to your food when you aren't looking." Chloe accepted the ice-blue organza gown with the halter neck and beaded embellishments at the waist. "Janice, this is too much. Are you sure?"

She'd gone to some fancy balls and banquets in Paris with Jean-Marc. Her in-laws were connected to the French nobility, after all, but she'd rented gowns for those occasions. What would a pastry chef who worked elbows deep in dough do with a closetful of designer gowns? Though she did have a few nicer dresses she'd bought at resale and consignment shops to wear when Jean-Marc took her to dinner for their anniversary or her birthday.

"I think these shoes will work." Janice set a pair of red-soled Louboutin heels at Chloe's feet. "I'll fetch my stylist. She'll fix your hair and makeup." Janice paused at the door. "If you want, that is. Am I pushing you? It's just, well, Sam seems more relaxed when you're around and I remember how he was with you when you were teens."

"We're just friends, Janice."

"Right, of course, but shall I get her? My stylist?"

Chloe looked at her image in the mirror and saw the spark of life she'd felt in recent days reflected back at her. No didn't seem like an option.

"Send her up. I need all the help I can get."

"Chloe." Janice hesitated at the door. "About Sam—speak well of his father, would you?"

"Janice, really, this is none of my business. It's between you and Frank and Sam. All I know about your relationship with Frank back then is that you were his secretary before my mom. If your invitation comes with conditions, then I should just go home."

"It doesn't. You'll look stunning in that gown. Please stay. But Chloe, there are lots of details Sam doesn't know either." Janice headed out of the room.

While she waited for the stylist, Chloe tucked Janice's payment into her purse then texted Laura Kate to take the van back to the bakery and lock up everything. *Thank you and see you in the morning!*

Twenty minutes later, Chloe was tucked and zipped into the ice-blue organza confection with a crossover neckline that bared her shoulders and a good deal of her back. A large burn on her forearm, a regular occurrence for someone continually reaching into hot ovens, made her self-conscious. She stood in front of the mirror, one hand over the angry welt in an attempt to hide it.

"Here." Francie, the stylist, daubed on some concealer and rubbed gently. "It barely shows."

Francie gave her a sophisticated makeover with subtle spring colors. Not much could be done with her pixie cut, but instead of Chloe's usual spiky do, Francie brushed her hair flat and managed to make her look sleek and sophisticated. Chloe had one of her sparkly hair clips in her purse that she swapped out for the beaded one. That made the finishing touch.

Francie handed over a disposable toothbrush. "Can't really be complete without fresh teeth."

"You're an all-service stylist."

Francie laughed. "When you work with artists and actors like I do, you learn to come prepared."

Teeth brushed, lipstick reapplied, Chloe left Janice's dressing room and started toward the stairs. Dang, she was shaking. Like a princess making her debut. This was Frank's party, not hers. She was just a guest. *Relax, act casual, pretend you're wearing street clothes.* But as she made her way down the stairs, every head turned and the voices faded. Everyone watched her.

Chloe held onto the railing, sure she'd trip and tumble down to the bottom. As she hit the third step from the bottom, Sam parted the crowd to stand in front of her. It was like a moment in a movie that a girl always dreamed about but never really happened. His eyes, his expression, told her she was beautiful, and for the first time since Jean-Marc had left for Zermatt, she honestly believed it.

"Chloe, wow." He offered her a hand down the last two steps.

"Stop," she whispered, the slight tremble in her voice giving her away. "You're embarrassing me."

"You're gorgeous. Easily the most beautiful woman in the room." He took her in his arms as the band began to play, then swept her through the crowd and out to the lighted dance floor overlooking the pool and the vast Hardy grounds.

Was this happening? Being swept up in Sam Hardy's arms to melodies from the '60s? He wasn't a skinny teen with lean muscles anymore, dreaming of playing for the league. He was tall and broad, his body sculpted by years of training. He was kind and smart, funny and an achiever of the impossible.

She needed him tonight. His strength and the ability to believe she'd emerge from the shadow of death into a new and wonderful life. One song bled into the next. "Summer Wind" to "Moon River" to "Everybody Loves Somebody"—a veritable array of '60s jukebox hits. She spied Mom beaming at her from the arms of Pastor Robinson from Community Church.

When the band took a break, they made their way to the buffet line, filling their plates with barbecue chicken, potato salad, coleslaw, deviled eggs, and more of Frank's favorites. Sam led her down the steps to the pool deck where they sat at a linen-covered table, just the two of them, talking, laughing, reminiscing.

Sam took a bite of his pimento-cheese-stuffed celery stick, chewed, and swallowed. "What are you doing in a few weeks?"

"A few weeks? Rather vague, Hardy."

He laughed. "I forget the exact date, but the Nashville Foundation is honoring a few people for their charitable work. Buck Mathews, Mikayla Onofrio, and myself. I feel like I'll be more convincing if I walk into the banquet hall with a friend. Wanna go?" He gave her a broad smile, his full lips tugging up a smidge higher on the right side.

"If you really want me to go, then yes. Am I to help change the narrative away from Curvy Carla?" Chloe reached for her napkin and wiped thick barbecue sauce from her fingers.

"No. I just think we'd have a lovely night together. I'd be proud to be with you. If it shuts up Curvy Carla, so be it."

"So, I'm more than just a PR stunt." She narrowed her gaze but softened it with a smile.

"Chloe, I'd never do that to you."

"Sam." She laughed and touched his arm. "I'm teasing. I'd love to go. And I'd love to shut up Curvy Carla." It had been eight—nine?—years since she'd been asked on a date. Maybe she'd forgotten what it felt like. She examined her heart. No guilt or regret hovered, ready to pounce. Just a flutter of antici-pation. "Sounds fun."

"It's black tie." His warm gaze made her insides feel all buzzy. What was going on? His eyes caressed her, nearly as softly as when he'd run his hands over her arms during their dance.

"Maybe Janice will let me borrow this dress again."

"Good, then it's a date."

"Is this honor for work in your foundation? What sort of charity work do you do?"

"The Sam Hardy SportsWorld Foundation supports youth sports programs, provides scholarships to kids who want to try for elite schools and sports programs. We also provide bikes and sports equipment to underprivileged neighborhoods. We do job training, tutoring, and life skill courses."

"I'm impressed." She looked at him longer than she intended. "My nice guy declaration is proving to be truer than I imagined."

"Hush, you'll ruin my already sullied reputation."

"Good. That'll shut up Curvy Carla for good."

When the music started again, Sam stood and made a motion that included Chloe and the dance floor. When she stood, he took her in his arms and she followed him to the dance floor without hesitation.

"Sam," she whispered as they moved across the floor to the band singer crooning Elvis's "It's Now or Never." "What are we...? I mean..."

"What are we doing? Becoming more than friends?"

"Are we?"

The singer smoothly shifted to "Sealed with a Kiss."

He drew her close and echoed in her ear. "Aren't we?"

She spoke into his shoulder. "Are you trying to make me fall in love with you?"

"I'm not sure. Is that where we're headed?"

"Sam, you're not thinking. You're my boss."

"Well then, Chloe, you're fired."

She laughed, a little freer from the ribbons of sadness that had bound her the last ten months. "Let's not get hasty."

"I get it. I'm a former bad boy with a rep, but I think we could have something between us. I don't want to rush you away from Jean-Marc, and I know he'll always be with you, but—"

"It's not him, well, not entirely. But Sam...I have to be honest." She pulled out of his arms and walked from the dance floor to the wraparound porch. Fewer people. Quieter. Maybe she could catch her breath, organize her thoughts.

She stopped by the railing, one hand at her neck, feeling her pulse race. Sam came up behind her, touched her elbow. She turned to him. "Don't you know, the men I love die? Daddy, Jean-Marc—"

"Come on, you don't really believe that, do you?"

"It's the reality."

"Well then." He leaned over her shoulder and whispered in her ear, his words settling like a warm blanket on her cold, stale soul. "I'll take my chances, Chloe LaRue."

"Sam—" When she turned, she stood just inches away from the man who made her feel alive again. Their gazes locked and he tipped her chin up and lowered his lips to hers. Her pulse pounded as warmth flared and ignited inside of her. His kiss was full and hungry, but giving and searching, and she could do nothing but respond to him.

The music faded until it seemed as though they were the only two people on the porch, everyone and everything a distant buzz.

The kiss she'd yearned for fifteen years ago had arrived. And it was everything she'd dreamed it would be.

CHAPTER 8

*H*e could've danced all night. But like all good things, the evening ended, and he drove home in a schoolboy-crush daze.

Now, slumped in his favorite chair, the Saturday morning scene beyond his downtown Nashville loft held scattered clouds and blue sky. Sam could still feel Chloe against his chest and smell the scent of her skin.

However, he'd done his knee no favors. With a moaning wince, he leaned forward to adjust the ice pack resting on his knee. He'd hardly noticed his wounded joint while dancing with Chloe last night. Today, however, his knee was in agony.

The more he thought about it, the more he realized he didn't care. He'd held Chloe in his arms. He'd kissed her. Kissed Chloe Beason LaRue. Something he'd wanted to do for a long, *long* time.

She was tender and passionate, soft and supple, kissing him back with her heart as well as her body. He thought his heart might explode for the wanting of her. The band had changed up the music. The cacophony brought them both back into the present and suddenly she pulled away and grabbed his hand. The next thing he knew, they were on the dance floor in a twist contest. She put some flip and flair into her hips as they *twisted the night away.*

It was right about then he'd caught Dr. Morgan's eye and thought, *Uh-oh.* He knew that she would bust him at his next appointment, but nothing mattered except Chloe and having fun. What Super Bowl ring? In truth, it felt good to let go of that dream for an hour or two. Sometimes the dream ended up owning the man.

Dad, rather, *Frank*, won the twist contest. He and Janice cut a mean rug, so he deserved to win, and not just because he was the birthday boy. As much as he hated to admit it, Sam had seen a different side of his father last night. The one from his youth, the one before his hypocrisy and cheating tore their family apart.

Sinking further into the chair, he closed his eyes and willed his knee to settle down. Could he run down to see Chloe today? Or would that be rushing things? He wanted to give her time. She'd seemed hesitant about moving beyond friendship. But if it was only a matter of him being her boss, he'd quit HARDRICK and let Rick manage the bakery.

He'd dropped her off at her mom's house and walked her to the door. Their goodnight kiss was more sweet than passionate, but he was okay with the various movements of their relationship. They were still figuring it out. He'd give her time.

They'd decided he would work a shift on Monday afternoon after he finished physical therapy. See if they could gain some momentum against Donut Heaven. But with the town council meeting in a few weeks, they didn't have a lot of time to build support.

His phone buzzed with a text from Frank. *Thanks for*

coming to the party, son. If you have a few minutes, I'd like to discuss something with you.

Sam started to reply then tossed his phone aside. He'd call him later. For now, more ice and painkillers.

He'd just dozed off when his phone rang. Ah, Bruno Endicott, agent extraordinaire.

"Bruno, tell me something good."

"You're still my favorite client." Bruno laughed at the joke. It was one he and Sam started years ago. "How's the knee?"

"Good. Healing." No need to mention last night's dancing. "What's up? You don't normally call on a Saturday."

"Sam, um, I just—" Bruno paused. Too long.

"What's up, Bruno? Tell me." Sam's knee throbbed.

"The Titans' front office called. They're going for a new franchise QB in the first round."

Sam shoved the ice off his knee and tried to stand. But the thought of putting weight on his knee kept him poised on the front of the chair. "I'm out? Is this their way of giving me the boot? Ryder never hinted he was thinking of a change."

"We're in contract negotiations and you're not cheap."

"Hey, they offered the money. I just accepted."

"No one doubts your worth. It's your knee that's the question mark—"

"But it's not, Bruno."

"They think it is, Sam. You're an amazing quarterback. But sometimes the clock runs out with a certain team, and body parts just don't heal like they used to."

Sam slouched back into his chair. "So that's it? I give nine years of my life to this team and after one injury they're giving up on me?" He should've taken the sack instead of trying to scramble. But he'd just seen Bennett break open as the defensive end bore down on him.

"I just got off the phone with the Raiders' front office. They are very interested. Very. Do you trust me?"

"Of course I do, Bruno. You're the best in the business. But the Raiders?" Sam did not want to live in Vegas. Too many memories of too many wild nights in that town. Regretful memories. And if he were honest, too much temptation for his weak flesh.

"Rumor is Schnetzler's retiring next year. You could lead the team the next ten years."

"Bruno." Sam's voice broke with surprised emotion. "I love Nashville, I love the Titans, and maybe, I'm not sure, I might have met the girl I want to marry. So tell the front office I'll be ready for summer camp. No ifs, ands, or buts."

"Marry?" Bruno's laugh quickly faded. "I've never heard you use that word before."

"Yeah, me neither." The confession surprised Sam as much as Bruno. Yet Chloe made him think about commitment and forever.

"Tell you what. I'll call the Titans Monday and keep pressing until I have an answer."

"Thank you. I mean it."

"You really want that ring with the Titans, don't you?"

"More than anything." They were his family, his brothers.

After disconnecting, Sam pushed up from his chair, harder this time, until he could hobble to the fridge for a fresh ice pack from the freezer. He slapped it on his knee with invigorated resolve. He'd be ready for summer camp, no question about it, no doubts, no maybes.

His career officially came first.

❦❦❦

HAVEN'S HAS DELICIOUS CAKES FOR ALL YOUR SPECIAL OCCASIONS! COME BY AND TASTE TEST.

– @HavensBakeryHBTN on Twitter

❦ ❦ ❦

Chloe tossed her beret and keys on the entry table and listened. Everything was quiet. Too quiet? Mom could be lying down, recovering from the excitement of Frank's party last night.

"Mom?" Chloe made her way into the kitchen. She'd stopped at Cooper's deli on the way home from the bakery and ordered two thick ham and cheese sandwiches. "I brought lunch."

Robin was actually on time for her shift, shock and awe, so Chloe was able to leave a little after one to get some rest. And some space to remember last night. The way Sam had kissed her. The way he'd looked at her...

She shivered as she reached in the cupboard for two plates. She had thought Jean-Marc was the only man who would ever look at her like she was beautiful. Then Sam had given her a slow up and down, his smile in his eyes when he'd looked at her face.

She loved dancing with him, leaning against his firm chest, hearing his heartbeat. Then his kiss. Another involuntary shiver ran through her. She felt treasured with that kiss, not just wanted. And Sam behaved himself all night, not one inappropriate touch, not one word out of line.

"Mom? Lunch from Cooper's. The ham on this sandwich is two inches thick. Do you want milk, water, or soda?" She went to the kitchen door. *"Bonjour, Maman. Es-tu réveillé?"*

She'd been exhausted after Frank's party. She'd insisted on

staying all night even when Chloe had noticed her wilting in a chair, head back, eyes closed.

"You don't have to prove anything by staying until the end, Mom. Frank knows you're going through treatment. I'll drive you home."

"No, you're having so much fun and you need some fun in your life." Mom had touched Chloe's cheek and smiled. *"It's doing my mama's heart good."*

Honey appeared and curled around Chloe's ankle.

"Where is our *maman, chatte?*" She peeked into Mom's room. The covers were thrown back, but the bed was empty.

"Mom?"

A soft moan came from the attached bathroom.

"Mom!" Chloe pushed into the room.

Mom sat by the toilet in a stained nightgown, a distinct green pallor on her face, and no wig or turban to cover her thinning hair.

"What happened?" Chloe crouched down.

Mom gave a wan smile. "I seem to have picked up a stomach bug."

"We're going to the ER." Chloe helped Mom to her feet. She ignored her mom's protests, and helped her clean herself up, get dressed, and get out the door.

Time dragged at the hospital. No one seemed to be in a hurry. *Hello, sick woman undergoing cancer treatment here.* After what seemed like an eternity, they were led into an exam room where an efficient doctor diagnosed Mom with a stomach virus.

"Chemo can affect the immune system. You should be over it in a day or two. Get rest and plenty of liquids." He wrote out a script for a stronger anti-nausea medication and off they went to have it filled at the pharmacy.

Chloe carefully tended to her mom. Once they got home,

Chloe set Mom up on the sofa. She propped her up with pillows and a blanket, then made sure that Mom had everything within easy reach: TV remote, medications, tissues, water, and some herbal tea. Throughout all of this, her phone pinged and buzzed—all of which Chloe ignored. Nothing mattered more than Mom.

She'd let work distract her from Jean-Marc and her marriage—she'd not let the bakery or Sam or anyone distract her from Mom's care.

"Are you good? Need anything? A book?"

Mom's smile was sweet. It was so like her to always try to smile, even amid the pain of Daddy's death. "You're taking good care of me. I'm fine." Honey jumped up with a purr and curled on Mom's lap. "Pardon me, *now* I'm fine."

"I think I'll run to the market, get a roasted chicken, and make some soup. I can get a loaf of bread from the bakery." Winter still held on to the March day and the forecast predicted a solid temperature drop tonight. "We can curl up, watch an old movie, and dip our bread slathered in butter into a rich, brothy soup."

"If my stomach can handle it, sweetie. Sounds perfect."

Right. Take it slow. She would heal in time.

Heading back out into the blustery day, Chloe checked her phone as she walked toward the shops. A slew of messages from Robin, asking multiple questions and then a final text saying to ignore her as she'd found the answer.

Another text from her mother-in-law. *Please, Chloe, we must speak with you.*

She sighed. This was the third or fourth time Vivienne had reached out. Chloe might as well answer her.

She was about to respond when a text came in from Sam. At once, the chill in the air warmed and she felt invigorated and more determined to move on with her life.

France was her past. Hearts Bend was her future.

Outside of Cooper's, she paused, smiling, to read his message.

Sam: *Afternoon.*

Hmm, that felt rather formal.

Sam: *I had a great time last night but I've been thinking, we should take it slow. Not get ahead of ourselves. I really like you but need to focus on my career, get my knee healed.*

She fell against the brick storefront, rereading the message through the sting of tears. Then through a wave of ire. Was he actually sending a we-don't-have-a-relationship-yet-but-I-want-to-break-up text?

Another text came in as she typed out a sarcastic reply.

Sam: *I'll still help out at the bakery. Just don't want things awkward between us.*

Chloe: *All for the best. I need to focus on Mom. I was going to text you about it.*

Sam: *Oh, good, well, I guess we're on the same page.*

Well, they were now. She started a response but then closed the app. What else could she say? Cuss him out? In French. She'd love to but then the words would be out there, and she hated things she couldn't undo. Like death.

She could tell him the truth. *Last night, for the first time in ten months, I felt hope. I started falling in love with you. I thought you were falling in love with me.*

But she couldn't be that vulnerable to him. Not now.

Batting away her tears, she shoved her phone in her coat pocket and pushed inside Cooper's. She had chicken soup to make. A life to build with Maman.

Sam Hardy was history once again.

❦❦❦

A fire blazed in Mom's fireplace, the light was warm and cozy, and *Pride and Prejudice* was paused on the TV, ready for viewing. Chloe set a bowl of soup on Mom's tray.

"Think you can take a bite?"

"I hope so. It smells good." Mom blew on the hot surface then took a sip. "Oh Chloe, it's delicious."

"Want some bread? It was just coming out of the oven when I got to the bakery. We've been having trouble with the oven temperature, but Laura Kate kept an eagle eye on it."

Chloe went back to the kitchen where she fixed her own soup bowl. She buttered up several slices of warm bread, gathered two large glasses of water, and carried everything on a tray back to the living room. Then she settled on the couch next to Mom, and they ate in a peaceful silence, neither one reaching for the remote.

The wind blew against the house and a splash of cold rain battered the windows. Chloe sank even deeper into the overstuffed couch cushions. She was home. Safe. Loved. At least she could feel the love from her mom, especially after the text brush off from Sam. A wave of sadness caused her to sigh.

"What was that?" Mom said.

"Yeah, sorry..." Chloe shook her head and made a face. "I don't know."

"Something the matter?"

"No, well..." She didn't want to talk about Sam, so she went with her first thought. "Vivienne has texted me quite a bit this month. More than when I was in Paris. She said they need to talk to me but, Mom, I want to move on. What could they possibly have to say?"

"You won't know until you talk to them. Chloe, they love you. You were married to their son for eight years. See what she has to say."

"I'm afraid she just wants to reminisce about Jean-Marc. I'd love to...someday, because I loved him with my whole heart. But not now. Not when I finally thought—" Scratch that. She'd not tell Mom she'd finally thought she was ready to fall in love again. "Well, not when I'm here, with a new job, helping you."

"Why do I have the feeling you left something out?" The screen saver flashed on the television. "Is it Sam? You two seemed very *engaged* with one another."

"I thought maybe we were, but, well, I was wrong. He's fixed on healing and getting back on the field." She kept the disappointment from her voice with a struggle. Mom wouldn't let that pass.

"Jean-Marc would want you to move on, Chloe." Mom touched her arm. "Sam is an amazing man. A bit troubled, but with someone like you, he'll find his way."

"Maybe in football but not with me, Maman. He texted today that whatever started between us last night couldn't go on." She aimed the remote at the television. "Shall we watch the movie?"

"He texted you." Mom's voice held disbelief.

"Yes." Chloe stirred her soup without taking a bite.

"He's scared," Mom said, so tender, so wise. "Be patient."

"We're all scared, Mom." Chloe took a sip of her soup then let her spoon clank against the side of the bowl. "How did you do it, Mom? Go on after Daddy died? There were days I barely got out of bed after Jean-Marc's funeral. If it wasn't for my job, I'd have never left the house. Heaven help me if I'd had a child to take care of."

"That's how. You. My child." Mom stilled, and a beat passed before she went on. "I had to keep myself together and get us through it."

"But how? I think I'm moving on, over the grief, when suddenly a wave hits me out of nowhere. Last night, when I was with Sam on the dance floor and when he kissed me, I felt like the sun had finally burst through my clouds. Then he texted."

"Grief isn't the enemy. Denying it is. You lost the man you were to grow old with and now you have to start over, in your teenage bedroom no less, living with your old mom."

Chloe laughed softly. "Being here is more healing than I imagined."

"Grief comes in waves and stages. I had waves of grief for years, Chloe. I embraced them, processed them, and moved on." Mom sipped her soup and took a bite of bread.

Chloe knew the truth of that. "So then what's the point, if we just end up alone? Daddy left and never came back. His work was more important than us, than me, than our vacation to Disney World."

"Oh, sweetheart. That's not true." Mom set her soup on the TV tray and looked at Chloe.

"He went on that business trip and postponed our Disney vacation." She'd been so hurt, but Daddy promised to reschedule it as soon as he returned.

"He went on the trip because his boss promised him a commission and a bonus. We were using the money to stay at one of the Disney World hotels instead of the Peppermint Inn across town. You weren't more important than his work. He worked because you were important to him."

"Why didn't you tell me that?"

"I didn't know you thought your father loved his work more than you. He adored you." Mom stroked the back of Chloe's hand. "I'm sorry, honey. I should have made sure you knew why he postponed our trip."

Chloe swallowed the lump in her throat and nodded. So, everything she'd believed for over twenty years about Daddy choosing work over his family—over her—had been wrong? "I—that's a lot to take in. I'm glad he—wow, well, Daddy, I'm so sorry." She brushed the wash of tears from under her eyes. "You know what I said to Sam last night? That he couldn't love me because the men I love die. Daddy. Jean-Marc."

"You know that's a lie. Don't give in to it." Mom handed her a tissue from the box on the coffee table. "Chloe, you're the bravest woman I know. Packing up and moving to France to study, then trying to heal from your husband's death. I am so proud of you. Coming home was equally brave. But be kind to yourself. Let time help you heal. You healed from Daddy dying."

"Because of you." Chloe slipped her hand in her mother's. "And now you're helping me heal again."

"I had one thing that you didn't, Chloe. Faith. A strong relationship with Jesus. There were many nights I cried and talked to Him, pleading for help and understanding, asking for peace."

"Did it work?"

"Every time. Sure, I didn't understand everything, like why we lost Daddy, but I knew that God was watching over us, taking care of us. My job with Frank was a real gift from God. He gave me a generous salary and about every quarter, I find a bonus check on my desk. He's been doing that for twelve, thirteen years. I've almost paid off the house."

"I'm not sure I can make the leap to trusting God, just like that. I've never felt God with me. Not the way you do."

"Have you ever tried? Remember our quarrels every Sunday morning?"

Chloe covered her embarrassment with a laugh. "How could I forget?"

"You want to know what I did to get through those dark days after Daddy died? I grabbed hold of the hand the Lord offered me and never let go."

"Just like that? Reached up and grabbed God's hand?"

Chloe stuck her hand in the air and "felt" around. "God, hello, Chloe LaRue here. I'm grabbing your—" She inhaled and pulled back as her fingers grazed something large and firm, yet soft and warm. "Hand. What was that?"

When she looked at her mother, she was grinning "Well, smart aleck, I think it was the hand of God."

CHAPTER 9

*T*his was a risk.

It could be argued that it may be the biggest one he'd ever taken, including the wild throw that had caused him to blow out his knee. Here he was, standing at the Beason front door at six o'clock on a Sunday night, unannounced, about to ring the doorbell.

If Chloe opened and punched him in the nose then slammed the door in his face, he'd deserve it. In a way, he sort of hoped she did.

So ring the bell, smart guy.

Sam took a deep breath and pressed the button, the pretty chime muffled inside the walls of the house. At first, he didn't hear anything, then steps sounded over hardwood floors. The porch light flipped on, and the door swung open.

Chloe stood across the threshold in a pair of yoga pants and a T-shirt, her hair pulled back from her face with one of her shiny clips. She cocked her right hip and leaned against the doorjamb. "Can I help you?"

"Yes, could you punch me in the nose?" Sam leaned toward her, pointing to the middle of his face.

"Gladly, but that would make me petty and small. Like you."

"Good point." He righted himself. "Can this jerk come in?"

"Are you here in an official capacity? As my boss?"

"No, I'm here as the guy who sent you a stupid text."

"Stupid? More like honest. But whatever, best to know things between us wouldn't work before we even left the gate."

"That's what I want to talk about. Chloe, look—"

"Sam, we've said our piece. Let's just move on, forget Friday night." She wrapped up in her arms as a cold blast blew across the porch. "See you at work."

"Come to dinner with me. Valentino's. I took the liberty of making a reservation. They were booked but I did some name-dropping. See, that's how much I want you to come out with me."

"I don't think so, Sam. Let's just—"

"Sam, hello." Mrs. Beason appeared from the kitchen down the hall, a bowl of popcorn in her hands. "Come in, come in. Chloe, you're letting out all the warm air."

Chloe made a face and stepped aside. "Sam was just leaving, Mom."

"Leaving? He just got here." She tugged on the belt of her robe. "Sit. I'll make some hot chocolate. I was sick yesterday, but Chloe's chicken soup last night fixed me right up. I'm feeling so much better."

"I'm glad to hear that." He paused. "And actually, Mrs. B, I made reservations at Valentino's. I'd like Chloe to join me."

"She'd love to join you."

"I'm busy." Chloe pointed to the television in the living room and bowls of popcorn.

"Not really," Mom said. "We haven't even started the movie yet. Sam, she'll be ready in a few minutes."

"Hold on, don't I have a say? You and Ruby have got to stop answering for me."

"Go on up and get changed, darling. I'll keep Sam company."

"Mom, I really don't think—"

"Good, thinking is so overrated." Mrs. B turned Chloe for the stairs and with a pat on the back, sent her on her way. "Wear your LBD, the one from Christian someone?"

"I don't have a Christian Siriano little black dress."

"Yes, you do. I saw it in the back of your closet when I was hanging up your laundry."

Sam checked his grin as Chloe's mumbled complaint echoed in the stairwell. But she obeyed her mom, climbing up.

"LBD, can't make me... Dinner with Sam after he... Why am I doing this?" Her footsteps hammered her displeasure across the downstairs ceiling as she stomped into her bedroom.

Sam winced and sat in the chair next to Mrs. Beason. "Guess she told you about my text."

"She did. But don't worry, she'll come around. If you do a bit of wooing."

"A bit of wooing, eh?"

"Yes, and while you're here, did you call your father?"

Dad. Right. Frank. "No, not yet."

"Please, Sam, do. He's eager to talk to you."

"Can't imagine why."

Mrs. B gave him a look. "Then try. He's proud of you, Sam. Talks about you all the time."

"He's a fan of the Titans."

"He's a fan of *you*. On and off the field."

"I'm ready." Chloe came down wearing a fitted black dress with a flared skirt. She'd spiked her hair, adding a gold clip with flowers formed out of little pearls. She wore a touch of makeup, and her effort made him feel a little bit forgiven. "But I don't know why I'm doing this."

"Because you're a nicer woman than I am a man." Sam moved to help her with her coat.

"Well, it's a reason. I'll take it."

"I'll have her home early, Mrs. B."

"I trust you, Sam." Three simple words and he felt them all the way through. This woman, this mother, trusted him with her daughter. Two, three years ago, no mother should've trusted him with her daughter.

But Mrs. B saw something he wondered if anyone would see. That he was trying.

"Thank you. That means a lot. And I'm cheering for you to beat this cancer."

In the meantime, Chloe was out the door and down the sidewalk without him.

"My car's back here, Chloe."

"Okay. I'll meet you there."

"Chloe, wait." Sam hobbled after her. "Look, I'm sorry. I shouldn't have sent that text. Especially since I didn't mean it. I'd just gotten off the phone with my agent who announced I might be looking for a new team this year and—" He dashed in front of her and walked backward. "Please forgive me. Forget what I said."

"You're forgiven, Sam. To be honest, I wasn't really surprised by your text. You did this to me before."

"When? I never."

"You ditched me at the county fair to go make out with Missy Byrnes in the Fun House."

He forced a laugh. So she did remember. "I was fifteen."

"You still abandoned me. I had to follow Cole Danner and Tammy Eason around like a bumpy third wheel. Unwelcome, I might add, but Tammy refused to abandon me. She couldn't believe you ditched me."

"Excuse me, but I don't recall you going as my date?"

"I *thought* I was your date. You invited me. You picked me up." Chloe set off again toward Valentino's. "I'm hungry."

"As I recall, you hardly spoke to me before I snuck off with Missy." He stretched to match her quick stride. "By the way, Cole didn't speak to me for a month after."

"Good for him. I felt like a fool. Obviously, I wasn't good enough for you and your friends. I don't even know why you invited me."

Valentino's came into view with its string of twinkle lights under the awning, so he tabled the conversation.

The maître d' bowed and smiled when Sam entered, calling him Mr. Hardy, and led them to a romantic table in the back. Immediately, he motioned to one of the servers who hustled away and returned with a bottle of wine.

"On the house, we insist."

The silence felt steely as they looked over the menu.

"I'll have the lasagna." Chloe set her menu on the table.

"Looks good. Me too." Sam closed his and stacked it with Chloe's. "Look, you want the truth—" He sat back as the server set a basket of bread on the table and two antipasto salads.

Next, he poured the wine, then took their order, smiling like a crazy man the whole time. Sam itched to get back to the conversation. A couple at the table across the way waved, trying to catch his eye. He gave a wry smile and waved back.

Please, leave us alone.

"The salad is good," Chloe said, digging into hers, shoving lettuce and tomato into her mouth like she was on a fifteen-minute break.

"Chloe, the truth is, I had a mad crush on you." He

adjusted his knee brace, loose after their fast pace down First Avenue.

She scoffed and shoved in another forkful of lettuce. "You're such a liar. I was the emo girl. You were the cool, popular guy, a jock with jock friends and cheerleaders shouting your praises every Friday night of the season. Batting their eyes at you in the hallway and class too."

"Maybe...but Chloe, all my friends thought you were hot. And fun. That summer we hung out at my pool, after my folks split up, we all had crushes on you. But no one dared ask you out."

"Right. Because I was so *scary*."

He chuckled. "Yeah, if you must know, sitting on the edge of the deck in your black bikini—very sexy, by the way." He finally elicited a smile from her. "Scowling at all of us through narrowed eyes and this 'I'll kick your butt' look on your face."

"Because all of you were judging me."

"No one judged you. We wanted you there. Even the girls. When you stopped walking around with your proverbial dukes up, you were cool. Funny, smart, and you were always baking something. Between the black bikini and your sugar cookies? All the guys were in love."

"I heard you all laughing behind my back."

"When? Who?"

"That day some of the seniors from the football team came, and they wanted to know what I was doing there, said I was weird. You said, 'She's doing the best she can.'"

"Well, weren't you?"

"That's how you defended me? 'She's doing the best she can?' You were my best friend. I almost didn't let you in again. Only to get your texts yesterday." Chloe sat up straight and saluted. "Aye, aye, Captain. You and I, we'll never be a thing. I get it. I'm not cool enough for your football world."

"Now you sound like a twelve-year-old. I invited you to my upcoming honors banquet, didn't I? You're more than cool enough."

"Let's face it, we're still from two different worlds. We're too different." She gulped her wine, then scooted from the table. "I'm sorry, I'm really not hungry after all and I have to get up in"—she glanced at her phone—"seven hours, so I need to get to bed." She fished around in her handbag for her wallet and dropped a couple of twenties on the table. "Will this cover my half?"

He reached for her arm. "Chloe, come on, stop. That was fifteen years ago."

"And yet, it was also yesterday."

He followed her as she retrieved her coat and exited the restaurant.

"Look, Sam, I know you didn't mean to hurt me. I do forgive you. But it did hurt. I thought maybe I was finally moving on from grief and death. Maybe I should just stay in my lane a little longer."

"Sir, Mr. Hardy, your dinner?" The maître d' came after them. "Your dinner?"

"Box it up for us." Sam handed his credit card to the man. "If you have a basket, put it in there, please. Chloe—"

"See you at work, boss."

She strode down the street while he waited for his credit card and his basket. He'd walk dinner back to the Beason house, then leave them alone. He'd known tonight was a risk, a long shot.

Still, her confession from fifteen years ago surprised him. Had he meant that much to her? Were they on a date that night? How many sincere women had he hurt over the years with his love 'em and leave 'em lifestyle—like the night with the woman whose sincerity had opened his eyes to his selfish ways?

The server returned with a basket full of fresh bread, disposable wine glasses, napkins, a plastic tablecloth, and their lasagna in boxes. Overkill, but he'd take it. The server also handed Sam the re-corked bottle of wine, which he tucked in the basket before heading out.

First Avenue remained quiet, typical for a Hearts Bend Sunday evening. The wind was brisk and as he started toward Red Oak Lane, a light snow began to fall. Sam paused to flip up his coat collar and peered toward the park where the snow appeared like falling stars through the park's lights.

A dark form sat on the bench under the grand oak. Chloe. He knew it without seeing her face.

⚫⚫⚫

"Kind of cold to be sitting outside."

Chloe scooted toward the other end of the bench as Sam took a seat next to her, a basket in his hands.

"I had them box it up. You can take it home." He shoved something into her coat pocket. Her forty dollars, most likely. "I'm sorry, Chloe. About everything. I never knew..."

"I was just sitting here feeling like a fool. I'm sorry, Sam. I *was* acting like a twelve-year-old." She looked at him through the light and shadows of the park lamps. "I never told you how I felt, so why am I bringing it up now? Stupid."

"Does it have to do with what you said to me the other night? That all the men you love die? So did my stupid text trigger you to be mad at me for something that happened years ago?"

She laughed into the cold. "That's deep, Hardy. I'll have to think about it. Maybe. I don't know."

"Why didn't you ever tell me how you felt when we were teenagers?"

"How? When? I was too embarrassed. I didn't want you to look down on me any more than you already did."

"I never, ever looked down on you." His voice was forceful, like he truly meant it.

"Maybe, but you never looked *at* me either. You wanted girls like Missy. I was so embarrassed in that black bikini, but I wanted you to see me."

"I saw you all right." He laughed, sitting forward with his arms on his legs, the basket swinging between his hands. "I told the guys if they touched you, or tugged on one of your bikini strings, I'd pummel them."

"Really?"

"Really."

"So you were my defender, my brother, not a potential boyfriend."

"A little of all three. To be honest, I remember being scared to death that if I asked you for a date, you'd bite my head off."

"Bite your head off?" She scoffed. "Please, we hung out all the time that summer. We had a blast. Why would I bite your head off?" Perceptions were so deceiving. "Can you believe we're having this conversation? 'You hurt my feelings when I was fifteen,'" she said in a sing-song voice.

"I thought you hated jocks, except maybe me. That you most certainly didn't want to be seen dating one."

"I didn't hate you, that's for sure." She tugged her coat collar around her neck. "What an honest conversation would've accomplished back then."

"To be honest, Chloe, you wouldn't have wanted to be with me, even when I was fifteen. After my folks split, I couldn't see or think straight. Jake and I had a massive fist fight, both blaming the other's parent for the breakup of our families. I was so angry and bitter."

"I remember."

"I did whatever I wanted when I wanted. I wasn't a nice guy at all, despite what you claim to see in me now. I got worse in college, then in the league."

"Then I'm proud of you, Sam, for your effort to be a different man. I guess it's true, we don't really know each other as we are now, as adults with lives, with a past." Her stomach rumbled as she looked over at him. "I'm starving."

"Me too. Want to take this to your mom's and—"

"It's beautiful tonight and I love the snow. I'm getting used to the cold again. Why not eat here, in the park?" She helped him set the basket on the bench. "Get to know one another."

The tension between them melted and Sam spread the tablecloth over their laps. He passed out the lasagna, filled the plastic wine cups, and tucked a napkin in Chloe's collar, then his own.

Chloe took a bite of lasagna and sighed. It was rich and savory, the right blend of spices, meat, cheese, and pasta. "Oh, this is so good," she said. "Th-thank you."

They ate for a bit, passing bread, refilling wine, and discovering two containers of chocolate layer cake in the bottom of the basket. Sam collected their lasagna cartons when they'd finished and carried them to the nearby trash can. The snow swirled in large flakes and began to accumulate on the park grass. Sam refilled their wine and set the bottle on the ground.

"So, what's next?"

"I think that maybe you're right. We should take it slow and see how things go. I'm probably not ready to get involved anyway, and who knows what the future holds—"

"My head says you're right. That we'd be smart to back off and just be friends and focus on healing—me physically, you emotionally. But my heart says, 'Go for it.' You need to know, I don't usually listen to my heart and I'm starting to wonder if I should give it a chance. I like you. I feel at home with you."

"I know, and I feel we might have something special, but sometimes the timing is wrong. Sometimes we can't escape the past."

"What hope is there if we can't escape the past? Chloe, I want to try."

"Then start with Frank. Do you know what Janice said to me Friday night? She said you don't know the whole story. She wanted me to speak well of Frank to you." She swirled her wine and sipped. "You can't escape the past as long as you're mad at him. Can't really escape your bad boy ways because they're rooted in your anger at Frank. Maybe even your mom. I can't really go on in a relationship until I'm convinced the next man I marry won't die a young and untimely death."

"Your mom told me tonight how proud Frank is of me and not just because of football."

"Wouldn't it make everything easier if you stopped holding the divorce against Frank? I've been married and trust me, it takes two. Jean-Marc and I had a horrible fight before he went on the trip that killed him. And I can't take it back. I can't fix it. Now his parents are texting me, wanting to talk. About what?"

"You've not responded to them?" He lifted a brow and she laughed at the irony.

"Okay, I'll respond if you respond to your dad. There's stuff he's not told you. Even if it was all his fault, isn't it time to let it go? What's it gained you to be so cold toward him?" Was that a sheen of emotion in Sam's eyes?

"You might be right, but if I have to let go of the idea the divorce was all Frank's fault, you have to give up the notion that all the men you love die."

"Ha, that's a tough one. I have pretty convincing proof."

Sam took her cup from her and pulled her into his warm embrace. "Chloe, your dad died in an accident. Jean-Marc died in an accident. I don't know why, but I bet you've reached your quota. Besides, I'm too dang arrogant to die. I spit in death's eye." He said the last line in a pirate voice.

She laughed, but quieted again. "You're still my boss. I don't want to lose my job. I love Haven's. I also don't want to lose you as my friend."

"All right, we'll make a deal. If the romance doesn't last, then we'll work on being friends again. You stay on at the bakery and I'll let Rick handle things until, you know, the friendship kicks back in."

"Just like that?"

"Yeah, just like that." He hooked his finger under her chin and drew her face closer to his, searched her eyes, then slowly touched his lips to hers.

She shivered as the warmth of his kisses permeated her heart, and everything from the past thirty hours faded away. Suddenly, they were back to Friday night when she was maybe falling a little bit in love with Sam Hardy.

CHAPTER 10

*M*arch slipped into April and the snow gave way to spring showers. It'd been two weeks since Chloe and Sam dined in the snow in Gardenia Park. Two weeks since they'd agreed to give their relationship a chance. Also, two weeks of rain that melted the late winter snow and pelted the nascent buds and blossoms eager to emerge.

It was raining again this Monday morning as Chloe shook the drops from her umbrella and entered Haven's from the alley door. She gazed toward the rain bucket in the middle of the kitchen floor. Water had reached the brim and threatened to spill over. Carefully she carried it to the door and tossed the water into the alley. The contractor had been about to start the new roof when the spring rains began and put a stop to the whole project.

Chloe clicked on the kitchen lights and tuned the radio to the local country station. Then she fired up the ovens, which, after she'd called the technician, seemed to suddenly be working again, thankfully. She hadn't canceled the repairman, who was due this week.

Ruby claimed the ovens worked because she'd prayed for them, but when Chloe had asked how Ruby knew that God cared about Chloe or her ovens, Ruby'd said she had to go wait on a customer. Chloe had campaigned for new ovens with Sam, who talked to Rick, but the budget was tight for HARDRICK LLC's newest business.

"I can live with a leak, Sam, but not with faulty ovens. How can we compete with Donut Heaven if our bread is burned on the outside and doughy on the inside?"

"Unless the roof caves in—then where are you?"

"Why do you have to go all logical on me?"

She was getting used to being a girlfriend again. Though she still wondered at the idea of being Sam Hardy's girlfriend. They were keeping things quiet, staying off social media, spending their evenings at Mom's, watching movies. Mom offered to let him stay in the downstairs guest room, but he declined.

"I want to do this right, Chloe. If I'm in the same house with you—"

She fell a little bit more in love with him.

But doing it "right" sparked a discussion on what exactly was "right," which developed into a conversation about faith. Both believed in God, but as a rather distant, cold deity. Occasionally, when Chloe was alone in the office or her bedroom, she'd hold up her hand. "Okay, God, are You there?" Usually nothing happened, but one time, she again felt that warm, firm hand that had reached out to her that night with Mom. Goosebumps rose on her arms whenever she thought about gripping God's hand.

She was starting to see what Mom meant, about being blessed by God. Even felt it a little bit. The sharp, cutting grief morphed into a dull ache. She'd told Sam about the blonde at Jean-Marc's memorial and how it had sparked fears of an affair.

"I trusted him. Truly. He wasn't the cheating kind. But who was she?" She had to trust Jean-Marc. She had no other evidence really.

"You never know what a man will do if he really wants something." Sam's honest, reflexive comment ignited a few anxieties. Jean-Marc wasn't the cheating sort. He was the workaholic sort. But Sam Hardy? He knew how to play the field, how to get what he wanted. And plenty of women wanted him.

Yes, he'd changed his ways. At least so he claimed. But could she trust him with her heart for a lifetime? She thought of all these things in the early mornings, when she was alone with the flour and eggs, sugar and spices, and the aroma of bread baking. Haven's was becoming her haven.

If only she could find that cookie recipe. She'd stayed late every night last week, trying different variations of fudge and caramel, but nothing was right. Everyone was pitching in, but that cookie remained as elusive as Bigfoot in the Smokies. And people were *still* asking for it.

"Did she figure out the recipe yet? My kid's birthday party is coming up."

The *Hearts Bend Tribune* even ran an editorial about it. Good grief. Though the press might help when they attended the town council meeting in a few weeks. Chloe just hated feeling like she was letting down the town.

Laura Kate came in at five to start the donuts and fritters, the crullers, and every other assortment of sweet treats. At half past five, Ruby arrived to make the coffee, fill the display cases, the empty napkin holders, the stir stick dispensers, and whatever else a customer needed for the perfect cup of morning Joe. She also checked inventory and left a list for Chloe.

At six, Chloe opened the shop and Ruby greeted every customer with, *"Darling, come on in, get 'em while they're hot."*

Around ten when the house products were done and the morning rush slowed, Laura Kate started special orders—cakes and pies—while Chloe ran errands, did the banking, and ordered supplies.

Laura Kate was turning into a genius with dough, with frosting and decorating, with just about everything—except cleaning her station. Last week Chloe found her in a puddle of bright red ooze. For a nano second, she thought the girl had cut herself royally. But how? Turned out it was only cherry pie filling. She and Ruby were still laughing at Chloe about that one. Even got Robin in on the joke.

The plan to raise Haven's profile seemed to be working. Robin took over the social media accounts from Laura Kate—who kept forgetting to post, no surprise—and caught the attention of local teens who started stopping in after school for coffee and treats, even doing a bit of homework. The Rock Mill High football team quickly figured out Sam was there on Mondays and filled the place, which sent Chloe looking online for outdoor tables. If she found a set that worked, she'd file for a permit from the town. Her plan to add savory items like quiches and hand pies was going over well. However, the French pastry offerings were taking a bit longer to implement. Managing the bakery didn't leave her much time to create.

At home, Mom's chemo continued, and she seemed to settle in, no more tired than after the first treatment. She still went to the office though Frank offered to let her work a bit more from home. She thought she'd give it a try next week.

Every Monday, Tuesday, and Thursday, sometimes on Saturday, Chloe's handsome, hunky, football-playing quarterback boyfriend walked through the alley door, and well, she felt like ganache being poured over a fresh cake. Warm and liquid and gooey. With a side glance at Ruby, he'd grab Chloe and hurry her into the office for a kiss or two.

"I see what you're doing. Got eyes in the back of my head." Trust Ruby not to let them get away with a stolen moment alone.

Then he'd wrap an apron around himself and work the counter, charming all of the customers. He'd clean the dining room, refill dispensers, make coffee, and pull dough from the proofer. Last week, when the rain let up, Sam tossed the football, careful of his knee, in the alley with some of the Rock Mill High team. And, when he could, stole a few more kisses from Chloe.

Every Friday afternoon, Chloe walked to Hearts Bend Bank where she deposited a healthy amount, which made her a bit proud. While Jean-Marc was her number one fan, he'd expressed doubt when she confessed her dream of owning their own café.

"Chère cœur," he'd said in his French way that gave her shivers. *"You're a genius with your pastries, oui, but to manage books, counting coins and euros, you will be bored, no?"* To prove her seriousness, she'd signed up and aced an online accounting class. She'd had her husband's attention then. That's when they'd started truly talking...

Never mind. It was the past. For the present, she had to think about the upcoming town council meeting.

"Uh-oh, you're frowning." Sam entered the office and perched on the edge of the desk. "Everything okay?"

"Yeah, hey..." Chloe rose to kiss him. "I was just thinking about this place and how much I love it. Jean-Marc and I dreamed about opening a country café before he died. And now, here I am, managing a small-town bakery. We can't let Donut Heaven win."

Sam pulled her close, wrapping his strong arms around her. "I know it's not the same as owning a café in the French countryside with your husband, but I'm glad you're running Haven's, Chloe. With this man, who loves you."

She pushed out of his arms, gaped at him. He did *not* just use the L word. "What?"

He pressed his fist to his lips, grinning. "Yeah, I've been meaning to tell you, but—"

"Love? It's only been a few weeks." Trembling, she turned to the office door, ready to make her escape.

"—Rick's in love with you, Chloe. Yeah, that's what I wanted to tell you. It's Rick—"

She whirled around, frowning at his laugh, swatting at him. "That's not funny." She couldn't help but smile, though quickly grew serious again. "Sam, are you really in love with me?"

"I think I am." He pulled her close. "Have I scared you?"

"Um, no, never mind all my trembling."

The bakery phone jangled on the wall outside the office door. "Ruby," she called, "can you get that?" Chloe wrapped her arms around Sam's waist, tucked her head under his chin. "Where were we?"

"Look, babe." Babe? He called her babe. "I still want to go slow, but I've never felt this way before. Ever. I feel like I've been waiting my whole life for this day. For our fifteen-year-old selves to grow up."

"Wow, I'm—I don't know, I mean…" She made a face. "That didn't sound good. Sam, I am so ready to move on with my life. I know, for the first time since Jean-Marc died, that I have a future." She brushed her hand over his chest. "I'd love it to be with you. It's just—it feels quick. I still have feelings to deal with. Feelings about—"

"Your husband." Sam kissed her, quick and light as a hummingbird flutter. "It's okay. I'm not jealous. And take your time about falling in love with me. I'm not going anywhere." He pressed his lips to hers, more firmly this time, and a fire ignited down low in her belly, sending a warmth through her veins.

As Chloe deepened the kiss, Ruby charged into the office. "That was the oven repairman. He won't be here for another week."

Chloe pulled away from Sam but leaned against him. "Well, according to you, your prayers have healed it. We're doing okay, right?"

Ruby looked away, ran her fingers along the waistband of her apron.

Foreboding skittered up Chloe's back. "What now, Ruby?"

"God said *not no more*. The oven done gone and died. Robin is playing taps."

● ● ●

Sam smoothed his apron. Ruby's news about the oven had put a damper on his and Chloe's flirty banter and kisses. He enjoyed teasing Chloe too much, seeing her at a loss for words. "Once we sell out of product, we'll close, right? Then we need to talk about the town council meeting in a couple weeks."

"I'll let you and Ruby cover the front of the store and I'll call the repair company," Chloe said. "Next week won't work."

"Go get 'em, babe. We'll take care of everything out there."

As he strode through the kitchen, he caught a glimpse of Laura Kate, the tip of her tongue just visible as she slathered white frosting on what looked like carrot cake—or maybe apple spice—muffins. She had a glob of the frosting hanging from a strand of hair that had come untucked from her hairnet.

Sam stuck his head back into Chloe's office and cleared his throat so she looked up from the phone. He tilted his head toward Laura Kate and spoke in a low tone. "Do we need extra insurance to cover her? Or cover potential lawsuits?"

Chloe threw a pencil at him. "She's a work in progress. Leave it to me."

Sam got busy pouring coffee and plating donuts and crullers. A guy in khakis and a blue polo shirt took his mug and donut to a booth and watched Sam pulling espresso shots and serving pastries like it was high entertainment.

Mason Delroy. A sports columnist in Nashville. With any luck, he was writing about players and their businesses in the off-season. Maybe a story would remind Titans' management Sam was healthy and able to work. Able to start the season. That's the kind of news he wanted to see his name in. Not tweets about partying all night. An article also wouldn't hurt if it appeared just before the town council meeting.

"Ruby, can you cover the counter?" Sam said.

She waved and nodded.

Sam carried the coffeepot to Mason's table. "Looking for a story?"

"I got one." Mason held out his mug for the refill. "Talk to me about the banquet this Friday."

"I'll make it an exclusive if you include Haven's fight against Donut Heaven."

Chloe emerged from the kitchen with a tray of tarts, each topped with a swirl of caramel threads. She caught his eye and shook her head. No luck getting the oven repairman out. After moving the tarts to the display case, she brought two to the booth where he sat with Mason.

"How's it going out here?" If the tart crusts were baked earlier, she'd probably made the custard on the stove top, he was guessing. It wasn't like he knew what they could make without an oven.

"Mason, this is Chloe LaRue. She's the manager of Haven's Bakery, newly arrived pâtissière from Paris."

Mason cut off a hunk of tart, forked it into his mouth, then leaned back and moaned. "This may be the best thing I've eaten all year."

"She *is* the best and can you believe it? A Donut Heaven is coming to town with their frozen pastries and coffee pods. Wouldn't it be heartbreaking for them to put Haven's out of business?"

"A tragedy."

"Besides the best pastries and baked goods in a hundred-mile radius, Haven's—" Sam gave Chloe a wide-eyed look. He'd thought of this while serving the high school kids and young moms but hadn't had a chance to run it by her. "—is open early on Saturday mornings for families on their way to Pop Warner or Little League or soccer games." Panic crossed her face. Probably wondering how they'd be serving those families when they didn't have an oven. But that was a temporary problem.

Mason pressed the last of the crust crumbs into the back of his fork, licked it, then appraised Sam across the table. "What's your stake in this?"

"I'm a silent partner in Haven's. You'll write the story?"

"Maybe." Mason swiped at his phone. "Okay if I record this? I'm here to do an article about the Nashville Foundation's banquet this Friday night." He placed the phone on the table. Mason asked questions, Sam answered. He was honored to be honored. He was proud of the Sam Hardy SportsWorld Foundation's work.

"What happens if you become a free agent? Will your foundation stay here or go with you?"

"My foundation will stay here. And I'll start a chapter wherever I go, but, Mason, write this down in blood. I'm not leaving the Titans. We will win this season's Super Bowl."

"Write it down in blood, eh?" Mason took notes while his phone continued to record.

"Now about Haven's," Sam said. "We're David fighting

Goliath. We want to preserve the charm of Hearts Bend and keep Donut Heaven from bringing in mass-produced goods with no heart or soul. That's a story dying to be told."

Mason smirked and pocketed his phone. "I'll think about it."

⊛⊛⊛

DUE TO UNFORESEEN CIRCUMSTANCES, HAVEN'S WILL BE CLOSED THIS WEEK.

– @HAVENSBAKERYHBTN ON TWITTER

CHAPTER 11

Sam stared out the window of his downtown loft, listening to Bruno try to sell him the high points of a possible move to the Raiders. Friday morning, spring sunshine glinted off the Cumberland River and draped a golden ribbon over the south end zone of the Titans' stadium. An end zone he'd be throwing to this fall if God cared at all for him.

Emotions warred inside him as Bruno kept talking, extolling the pluses of Las Vegas and the Raiders. Yeah, he got how great it was to be wanted. But Bruno didn't seem to be listening to him. Sam wanted to stay in Nashville. Although Bruno had one good point. Why would Sam campaign to stay where he wasn't wanted? If the Titans were serious about the Ohio State kid, fine. But he'd have to earn his spot. And Sam was a great competitor.

If he went to Las Vegas, would Chloe go with him? Even as he had the thought, he knew the chance of that was slim. She'd come to Hearts Bend because her mom was sick. She wouldn't leave, at least not until Mrs. B had a clean bill of health. While he'd expressed his growing love, Chloe was still coming around.

She was still falling in love. Sam was pretty sure he'd hit rock bottom.

He paused his call with Bruno to take the incoming call from the oven repair company. He'd taken over the job from Chloe since she had enough on her plate managing the roof and ceiling repair. She'd made a deal with Valentino's to use their ovens until their chefs came in at ten a.m. She and Laura Kate started baking down the street when Valentino's closed at midnight and then worked a full day at Haven's as well. On Sundays, thank goodness, they sold day-old bread, donuts, cakes, and cookies. But even those were delicious.

"Look, I need a repairman today. Yes, this is really Sam Hardy, the quarterback. Now do I have my technician or not?" One more day and he'd pull the plug and buy a new oven. He'd pay for it himself if Rick couldn't find funds in the budget. Right now, he'd do anything for Chloe. He sighed and ran a hand over his head. Man, he was in deep, wasn't he? The company promised to have someone there by lunchtime, and Sam clicked back over.

"Bruno, sorry, I'm back. Bakery business."

"What about football business? Sam, don't let your injury cause you to lose focus. We have a real chance here to resurrect your career."

"But Vegas, Bruno?" No, he wanted Tennessee. Hearts Bend. Chloe. "What's going on with your new guy?" He'd just change the subject, get Bruno on to something else. "Ellis out of Georgia Tech? Fastest forty at the Combine." He gave a low whistle. "That'll get him some attention."

"I know what you're doing, Hardy. I'm focused on you too. But, yeah, Ellis is a hot prospect. We're expecting he'll be first round in the draft. Now, back to you. Ryder's concerned you're going to push your recovery and not heal, then blow the knee again mid-season. Besides, they want Fields.

They've been drooling over him since his first game at Ohio State."

"Okay, then what's the plan?" He hated this, the uncertainty, the feeling of betrayal. But it was the NFL. That's how the game was really played.

"The Raiders."

Sam closed his eyes, fighting to keep his tone calm. "I told you. I don't want to move to Vegas."

"They're keen on you. I also talked to Phoenix and Seattle."

"I'd rather be on the East Coast."

"I'll make some more calls. But the Falcons just named their new franchise quarterback and Jacksonville is happy with..." Bruno's voice faded into yada, yada. The man was trying. He was on Sam's team, but just like that, Sam was looking at a career he was no longer sure he even wanted. He'd gone most of his football life without a serious injury. When the odds had finally caught up with him, they'd dealt a death blow.

Vegas. Was God testing him? Was He trying to see how Sam would handle temptation now?

"You're the next Peyton Manning. Released after an injury, you'll take a season to recover, then come back better than ever, with a winning season and a Super Bowl ring." Bruno knew the right song to sing, Sam had to give him that.

"Yeah, okay, I'll think about it. I have to go. The Nashville Foundation event is tonight. You can keep me posted."

"I need your word if I make this deal with the Raiders, you'll give it your best."

"I never do anything less." How ironic. Nashville honoring him just as he might be leaving. The city he'd poured his heart and soul into, as well as hundreds of thousands of dollars. Apparently, football, business, and charity work were all different animals and about as compatible as kittens, hyenas, and badgers. He reached for the phone again. He needed to let Chloe know the repairman would be there soon and to confirm the limo bringing her to his loft for the banquet tonight.

Later that afternoon, Chloe texted him from the limo that the repairman still hadn't arrived by the time the driver picked her up. Ruby had sent her away with a promise to wait until the tech showed.

Sam pulled the dry-cleaning plastic off his tux. As he hung it in the closet, the doorbell chimed, and he hurried downstairs. Even in jeans and sneakers, Chloe took his breath away. The moment she stepped into his place, it felt warmer, homier, even classier.

He rolled the loft's barn-style door closed behind her and took her bag. "I'll show you around and put this in the guest room where you can get ready." He led her down the short hallway into the open living-dining-kitchen area. The aroma of his lemon poppyseed bread baking filled the room.

"Wow."

He looked around, seeing the place through her eyes. An expanse of windows looked over The District and the Cumberland River, with the Titans' stadium visible across the river. Exposed brick walls, dark beams, a spacious kitchen with a subway tile backsplash, a long bar counter with high stools, and a wooden dining table between the counter and the living area. A big-screen television over the electric fireplace with a couple of leather recliners. He thought of it as masculine without being all about football or looking like a British lord's library, which every decorator he'd consulted seemed intent on pushing.

"Do you want something to drink? I have soda and water in the fridge. Beer and wine too," he said, moving to the kitchen. The lemon poppyseed loaf should be done. "Coffee? Are you exhausted? You've been up all night baking at Valentino's, then working all day at Haven's."

"I grabbed a nap in the back of the limo. I'm fine. I just want to stand here and look at your amazing view." She moved to the French doors, opened one and stepped out onto the balcony, as he pulled the bread from the oven and set it to cool on a rack. "You're a real live superstar, aren't you? This amazing loft, a banquet honoring you...and I've got you serving coffee and crullers three afternoons a week."

But those afternoons were the best. He didn't worry about the younger players wanting to knock him—literally—off the field. He didn't think about his knee. He didn't wonder how Chloe or Laura Kate would let him down.

"I like serving coffee," was all he said, though. "I should let you start getting ready." Alone in his room, he sank on the bed. Chloe was digging her way deeper and deeper into his heart. He didn't want to be without her. He changed into his tux as quickly as possible and then paced in the living room.

A soft click signaled her emergence from the room, then footsteps and a swishing sound. If she took his breath away the night of Frank's party, the sight of Chloe Beason LaRue in his condo wearing a light pink dress that showed all her curves nearly dropped him to his knees.

"Wow."

"Like it?" She gave a twirl and the skirt flared out. "I bought it at my favorite resale shop in the Batignolles, an area in Paris with cute and quirky shops."

"It's amazing." He reached for her hand and pulled her close and pressed his lips to hers. After a quick second, her arms wrapped around his neck and she fit against him, against his heart, like she'd been molded to him, like they were made to be together. Heat bloomed in his chest, then spread until he feared he'd combust. He ended the kiss, placed his forehead against hers.

"I'm a goner, Chloe. I've never felt this for any other woman. This is love."

She inhaled sharply and he caught her scent, fresh and sweet.

"I...I—I'm falling for you too."

❀ ❀ ❀

WHAT IRONY! TITANS SAY BUHBYE TO @SAMHARDYQB15 HOURS BEFORE ANNUAL NASHVILLE FOUNDATION BANQUET HONORS HIM.

– @FIRST&TENPODCAST ON TWITTER

❀ ❀ ❀

RUMBLINGS IN THE TITANS' CAMP. FRANCHISE QB OUT FOR THE SEASON, POSSIBLE TRADE TO LAS VEGAS. MORE ON SPORTS CENTER.

– @ESPNNEWS ON TWITTER

❀ ❀ ❀

The limo pulled into the Hotel TN's porte cochere and Chloe squeezed Sam's hand. She was going to a swanky event in downtown Nashville with her famous boyfriend who was being honored for his charity work.

"Pinch me," she murmured.

"How about I kiss you instead?" He pulled her close, pressed his lips to hers.

Before she could respond, could welcome him, accept him, the chauffeur opened the door, letting in a blast of cool air. Talk about putting a damper on things. She shivered and gathered her wrap close as she and Sam climbed out of the limo. After that kiss and the one they'd shared earlier at his condo, she'd kind of lost interest in eating. Or going out.

As if he'd read her mind, Sam followed close and put an arm around her. "Let's ditch this and go back to my place."

Tempting—and she pretended to consider it before she scoffed. "You promised me a party with Buck Mathews and I'm holding you to it."

They walked into the brightly lit lobby then followed the signs and crowd to the ballroom.

"Mr. Hardy!" someone called, and Sam guided her to a table where several young women in black skirts, white blouses, and flat shoes consulted tablets and told other uniformed staff which tables to show guests to.

"Evening, Delia." He gave a woman with a pierced nose and a pink streak in her dark hair a quick hug. "This is Chloe. Delia's my assistant."

Delia flashed them a bright smile. "Follow me." She wended her way through tables, waitstaff, and other guests to deposit them at a round table in front of the platform with the podium and microphone.

The ballroom held dozens of tables. White tablecloths, gold-rimmed plates on gold chargers, black napkins. The centerpieces were square glass vases. They were decorated with variously sized floating black and white balls and a candle on top. Black, white, and gold balloons lined the walls. Seeing Sam in his element, schmoozing Nashville movers and shakers and Titans bigwigs was a revelation.

The cocktail hour passed in a blur of names and faces. Chloe recognized a few of each. Some of the local celebrities: a combination of politicians, music royalty, and other sports superstars. Thank goodness Buck and JoJo Mathews were there. At least she knew people at the party other than just Sam. Sam did his best to keep her close by, but every so often someone would insert themselves between her and Sam and she'd find herself feeling alone and chilly. Then JoJo would turn up, pull her to their table, and hand her a glass of wine. "You'll get used to it."

Chloe shook her head. "Strangers thinking they know your boyfriend? I doubt it."

"Imagine it's your husband singing love songs and women believing he's singing to them."

Chloe stared at JoJo. "You're kidding." Because that wasn't weird. At all.

"It used to freak me out. Buck had to keep reminding me that he chose me." JoJo smiled, her gaze softening. "Like Sam chose you."

Did he choose her? Guess he did. She was chosen. His kisses left no doubt in her mind about that. The man was all in. But was she?

"Sorry about that." Sam appeared at her side and put a hand on the small of her back. Tingles darted to her neck. "It won't happen again."

They sat and an odd feeling came over her, raising goose-bumps on her arms. She glanced around. Was there a draft? Then she saw a blonde woman at a table across from them. If she could shoot daggers with her eyes, Chloe would be impaled to her chair.

She leaned close to Sam. "Who's the blonde?" She tipped her head toward the other table.

Sam looked where she indicated.

The woman in a tight red dress glared at them.

"I don't—wait..."

Chloe looked from the angry blonde back to Sam. "Your number one fan?"

"Not exactly." He turned in his chair, so his side was to the blonde and he faced Chloe. "Curvy Carla." He tipped Chloe's chin up, brushed his lips across hers. "Remember, your classy presence is supposed to discourage her. Permanently."

"Mm hmm. I like the sound of that."

Dinner was served and they sat next to the mayor of Nashville and her husband on one side and on the other was a duo who'd recently been inducted into the Grand Ole Opry. Together, they wore enough sequins to cover an entire wedding party. *They're ordinary people,* Chloe told herself. *They have friends who've known them since they were fifteen, who they did crazy stunts with, who knew all of their secrets.* Everyone was the same underneath—full of insecurities.

Except for Sam, apparently. She watched with awe during the ceremony as he swaggered with his limp across the stage to accept his award. He spoke eloquently and with passion about his foundation. About giving kids in underserved neighborhoods more opportunities for jobs, scholarships, and access to sports equipment. He talked about how he'd had a lot of advantages growing up: a family who could afford camps and coaching and cleats. How he'd worked hard, but he'd been given a head start that a lot of other gifted athletes didn't get.

After the speeches and awards, emceed by a popular game show host from Los Angeles, a band tuned up and launched into "Just in Time." Sam pulled her chair out. "May I have the pleasure?" He led her to the dance floor, slipped his arm around her and took her hand in his.

She sighed with contentment. "Does this evening have to end?"

"No," he said. "And neither do we."

CHAPTER 12

The evening turned out amazing. Sam managed to keep Bruno and Las Vegas and the Raiders out of his mind. Mostly. His speech was well received, and Delia said several new prospective donors invited her to contact them. He and Chloe danced to "What a Wonderful World." He pulled Chloe close.

"It certainly is. Since you're in it," he murmured into her ear. How much longer until he could take her back to the condo, have her alone, and kiss her silly? He moved her around the dance floor, humming the words. The song ended and moved into "Love is Here to Stay." "It's like our personal playlist tonight."

She chuckled and pulled him closer. He kept an eye out for that Carla person, but except for the death stare before dinner, she'd made herself scarce.

When the band took a break, Sam held Chloe's hand as he guided her through the crowd, talking to various people. Nashville's state representative to Congress. Music Row executives.

They wandered outside, watching people taking hot air balloon rides.

"Do you want to go up?" He nodded at the basket attached to brightly striped silks.

She shuddered. "I don't do heights."

"They're tethered the whole time."

"Thanks, but no."

"You double-dog dared me to jump off the roof into the swimming pool, but you're scared of heights?"

"It's how I deal with it. Watching others. Jean-Marc thought I was crazy too. But he enjoyed showing off, doing his extreme skiing and stuff for me." A note of melancholy crept into her voice, and Sam squeezed her hand.

They told Buck and JoJo goodnight and Sam called for the limo.

"Did you have a good time?" Sam slid into the back seat next to her.

"I can't believe there was a golf cart drive-in movie outside along with the hot air balloon rides. And this swag bag is over the top. Prada sunglasses. A Tiffany bracelet. But more importantly, do you feel properly honored?"

He pulled her close. "Not quite yet. But I have an idea how you can help."

Once they arrived back at his condo, she changed out of her princess dress into lounge pants and a long-sleeved tee, then joined him in the living room with her bag. The lights of Nashville twinkled below them.

"How about something to drink before I drive you home?" Sam handed her a glass of white wine and patted the overstuffed couch.

She settled into a corner, drew her feet up, and sipped. "From Pat Jasak as emcee to entertainment by Buck, this was an amazing night. Thank you."

"In spite of an appearance by Curvy Carla?"

"You know, I feel for her. She must think being a groupie fulfills her in some way. I think that she's just wounded and lonely." Chloe's cheeks turned red as she sipped her wine.

Sam took the glass and set it on the coffee table, then pulled her close. "I think I just fell in love with you all over again. Chloe, you're right. I need to start having that same attitude." His thumb traced a path along her jaw before he cupped her chin. His lips followed the line of her jaw, kissing her sweetly. Their slow smolder sparked into a flame, and he knew he'd go too far if he didn't pull away.

But Chloe moved first, dashing tears from her eyes.

"I'm sorry. I shouldn't—" He felt stricken and worried. He was moving too quickly. He should have known better.

She shook her head, put a palm on his chest. "No. Never be sorry. I—I liked it. I like you. In that way. I'm still shocked that I can feel these things again. For so long, I believed that the kissing, the passion, the feeling of being wanted part of my life was over, that it died with Jean-Marc."

"And you make me think about the future in a way I never have. A house. Kids."

"Me too. Jean-Marc and I never got around to kids because we were both so busy working but I want that, Sam. I do." She leaned against him and tucked her head into the crook of his neck. "I love your place. I could stay here all night."

"Well, that would be dangerous."

She sat up. "I meant—well, it is rather late."

"I'll take you home." Because if they stayed much longer— well, yeah, they should get going.

She scrambled to her feet and reached for her jacket.

Sam grabbed keys from a hook on the wall. "I do love you, Chloe. I'm all in. I'll wait until you're ready, but can you hurry it up?"

"Keep talking to me about houses and children and giving me passionate kisses and I'll be completely yours before you know it."

●●●

Once they were on the highway to Hearts Bend, the dark night and stars outside the car gave Chloe the feeling they were the only two people in the world. They were silent as the sportscar ate up the miles.

Chloe cleared her throat. "You've gotten quiet."

He smiled and glanced at her. "Yeah, sorry. I had a call from my agent this afternoon. Just thinking about our conversation. What I should do next."

"Have you prayed about it?"

"Where did that come from? Are we praying now? Going to Bible study?"

She sat silent. They'd rarely talked about faith. Maybe this wasn't the time.

"I'm sorry, that sounded rude and flip," he said.

"Mom and I—she told me the only way she got through the months after Daddy died was holding on to God's hand. I was being rude and glib and reached out a hand to Him..."

"And?"

"Sam, I felt something—someone took my hand and held it." She shivered at the memory. "I felt it as sure as I can feel this leather seat under my palm."

He gave her a quick glance before returning his gaze to the road. "I believe you. I'm just not sure faith and God are for me anymore."

"Then what about talking to your dad? He's always cared about you and your career."

"We don't have that kind of relationship anymore."

"Sam, you tell me you love me, or could love me. So please tell me what is this rift between you and your dad? I know it's about the divorce, but it seems like there's more to it than just that. You used to be close."

"Not since..."

"Not since?" Chloe prompted.

"Ah, what the heck. I never told anyone this." He drummed his fingers on the gear shift knob. "Not since I walked in on him and Janice when I was fifteen."

"Oh, Sam." Dismay filled her. What must that have been like? How awful for him.

"Jake and I were meeting at his house then going to the batting cages. I walked into the kitchen and caught them—well, making out seems ridiculous to say, but I guess it's accurate." He shook his head as if trying to dislodge the image or erase it. "Kissing his secretary. What a cliché. So like Frank."

"I don't know what to say." She sounded as appalled as he must have felt that day.

"I stood there, frozen. Then I dropped my bat and glove and I ran." He glanced at her, shock and horror and shame and guilt flickering across his face.

"Did you tell your mom?"

"She left a couple weeks later. I dreaded telling her, so I decided not to. I agonized over it, figuring that I had to. But when I got home and saw her car pulling out, I knew. The note on the kitchen table was a formality."

"Why didn't you talk to me?"

"It was too humiliating. Within a few days, everyone at school and church knew. People patted me on the head, gave me sympathetic looks. I hated Dad."

She made a low scoff. "You just called him Dad, not Frank."

"Freudian slip."

"I think it's a heart slip. You still love him."

He glanced at her. "We both lost our fathers, just in different ways. We also lost..." He paused. "Lost our futures with them. If that makes sense."

"Totally. Dad didn't see me graduate. My uncle Vern walked me down the aisle when I married Jean-Marc. But Frank watched you play ball all through high school and college. He's proud of your pro career."

"I don't want to be like him. An adulterer. That's why I never talk to him."

"Yet you slept with women you didn't care about, one-night stands, no relationships?" She called him on it. She'd been wanting to since he first mentioned Frank's affair. "How does that make you any different?"

He sighed. "That's just it. I'm not. Or at least I wasn't. I'm trying to be a stand-up, faithful guy now. But with Frank's blood in my veins..."

"Sam, you're believing a lie. Just like you called me on my lie, I'm calling you out." She gave him a steady look, the dash lights casting a glow on his chiseled face. "Frank's been with Janice for fifteen years. Did you see the way he looked at her at the party?"

"I tried not to look at either one of them."

"He loves her. He's also not traded her in for a newer model."

"What's your point?" Sam's bitterness came through loud and clear.

"I'm not saying what your dad did was right, Sam. Not in the least. But I think your bias has kept you from something pretty special. Have you ever considered this? Your dad stayed. Your mom left."

"Sure, but Mom left because of him."

"She didn't have to leave Hearts Bend and move all the way to Charlotte."

He shrugged. "True."

"I think you should talk to your dad. If not about the past, then about your career. Mom says he's a smart businessman. He'll have good words for you."

CHAPTER 13

Saturday morning, Sam drove through the Tennessee spring morning, back to Hearts Bend. He'd had a short night after dropping off Chloe and returning to Nashville. He'd awakened early, thinking about his career choices. If he had any. Could he afford to sit out a season? Did he have to leave Nashville? The thought of a move when he finally felt connected to Hearts Bend again didn't sit right. Move when he had a business here. Move when he and Chloe were starting... something. Did he really have any choice, though? If the Titans traded him to the Raiders, he'd have to go. His Titans contract gave them the right to send him wherever they wanted. He was lucky—blessed?—that Bruno was on top of it.

He parked in front of Haven's. Coffee before his therapy at Dr. Morgan's—he'd pleaded for an extra Saturday session—was all he had time for. And maybe a stolen kiss from Chloe. She was right about one thing. He and Frank needed to talk. Maybe about the past, definitely about his career. And he would, soon. He got out of his SUV and made his way to the sidewalk.

"Sam? Is that you?"

He turned and was enveloped in a bear hug. "Gabe?" He could only mumble into a crush of navy blue velour. Sam hadn't given Gabe much thought since the Rock Mill High linebacker had decided against attending UT in favor of a smaller school where he'd see more playing time. Sam had heard that after college graduation, Gabe returned home to marry his high school sweetheart.

"Good to see you." Gabe slapped Sam on the back. "It's been too long."

"Yeah, you too. How are you?"

"Great!" Gabe pointed across the street to a minivan where a dark-haired young woman wrangled a toddler and had a baby strapped to her chest with an elaborate-looking scarf-thing. "Coaching at Rock Mill High. Who'd've thought? You remember Elena? And those are our two-year-old and baby. Hey, hon," he called. "I'll catch up with you at the fountain." She nodded and waved and directed the kid toward the pathway into the park.

"I heard you were back in town," Gabe said.

"Not really. Just helping out with Haven's. My partner and I bought it."

"You should come to my men's prayer group sometime."

Prayer group? Where did that come from? Sam didn't remember Gabe being especially religious. "I'm not a prayer group kind of guy."

Gabe searched Sam's face. "Well, you're a man. That's pretty much the only requirement. And a willingness to talk to God."

"Yeah, that's where I'm stalled, Gabe," Sam said. "I'm not much of an example of a stand-up guy. There's no legacy of honor or faithfulness in my family."

Gabe put a hand on Sam's shoulder. "So, start fresh. That's

the whole point of the Gospel. Old things go. New things come. Why don't you try my group?"

Was it that simple? Talk to God and old things went away and new things came in? Good things?

"Maybe," Sam said. "But, Gabe, can I ask you a question?"

Gabe pushed his sunglasses to his forehead. "Sure. What's up?"

"When you graduated from Middle Tennessee and decided to come back to Hearts Bend, not go for the draft. Have you ever..." He trailed off, not sure how to ask his question.

"Have I ever regretted giving up the chance at a pro career and potentially millions of dollars for a job teaching and coaching in my hometown? Marrying my high school girlfriend?"

"Something like that."

Gabe folded his arms over his barrel chest. "I wasn't going to be drafted, Sam, at least not high and not for big bucks. San Francisco was interested, but I would've been on the practice squad. Nice money but not for the abuse my body was taking." He pointed to Sam's healing knee. "Football from the time I was a ten-year-old Junior Pee Wee to four years in college. After twelve years of that, the body just wants a break."

"I'm healing. My body is ready to get back in the game. But, Gabe, no regrets? Not one?"

He looked toward the park, where his wife and children had disappeared behind the rose bushes, and his expression softened. "Not one."

"Huh."

"How about you?" Gabe pointed at Sam and raised his brows.

"Me?" Sam stifled a laugh. He regretted almost everything.

Except his performance on the field. But that was changing, wasn't it? And it wouldn't last forever anyway.

"You never think about if you'd moved back and gone into business with your dad? You'd be taking over for him soon and be one of the most respected businessmen in town. You might have a couple of rug rats to chase around. Someone to spoon with on a cold night."

Someone to spoon with sounded appealing—if she had a pixie haircut and smelled of flour and sugar. "So you have no regrets right now, but how can you be sure your marriage will go the distance?"

"You mean not divorce?"

Sam lifted a shoulder in a half shrug. "Given my folks' example, I wonder if I can make a marriage work long term."

"I don't know what happened with your parents. I just know that when things are tough, Elena and I remind ourselves that we chose each other. We made promises to each other and to God. It also helps to remember that the tough times don't last."

Sam raised his brows. "It's that easy?"

Gabe scoffed. "It's not easy at all. Sometimes it's harder than a week of running drills in ninety percent humidity. But you keep God at the center and never give up."

"Daddy! We're waiting for you!" A plaintive cry sounded from across the street.

"I better go. Think about the prayer group? Saturday mornings at the church. Seven a.m."

"Saturday mornings at the church," Sam echoed as he watched his former teammate rush across the street to hoist the kid over his shoulder.

Gabe made it sound like being married, staying married, was something you did, not something that happened to you. And what was that about keeping God at the center? Sam's family had attended church every Sunday. Frank had been an elder passing the offering plate and Mom had been at church pretty much all the time. If that wasn't keeping God at the center, what was? It hadn't done their family much good.

Chloe talked about feeling God's hand. He could use some direction about his career, that was for sure. But about relationships? He wasn't sure God cared much who Sam dated.

He shrugged and climbed the four steps. Better get his coffee and head to therapy.

⬤ ⬤ ⬤

Chloe had gotten a couple hours of sleep and then worked all day at Haven's before she had a chance to tell Mom about the banquet. Evening shadows crept across the backyard and into the kitchen window where she finished up the dinner dishes.

"Did you dance? Like at Frank's party?" Mom folded the dish towel then draped it on the hook by the fridge.

"Everything was special. We danced, feasted, and hobnobbed. Did everything except go up in a hot air balloon."

Mom sat at the table and opened her copy of the *Tennessean*, then smoothed out the paper. "This says Buck was there. Did he sing? That's not special."

"Because you can call and ask him to sing you a praise song whenever you're feeling down. To the rest of the world, he's a big deal."

Mom adjusted her glasses on her nose and kept reading. She had almost lost all of her hair, but it was slowly coming back now that she'd started taking a biotin supplement. The oncologist said the tumor was shrinking and Chloe found she could breathe easier on treatment days. Only one more dose of chemo, then a round of radiation and, God willing, Mom would be fine. "Popcorn's in the pantry. How was the mayor?"

"She's—I don't know. She's nice? She's the mayor. I said hello and goodbye. She was cordial enough, but I don't live in Nashville, so since I can't vote for her, I got the feeling she was looking past me all night."

Robin had been ecstatic at all the new followers the bakery's social media accounts gained during the day. Laura Kate scrolled through her feeds, showing Chloe the posts about last night's event and the likes and comments. Chloe noted the conspicuous absence of any tweets by one @CurvyCarla and grinned to herself.

Chloe rummaged in the pantry for the popcorn and started a bag in the microwave.

"Do you love him?" Mom leaned back in her chair, looking at Chloe over the top of her reading glasses.

"Way to cut to the chase, Mom." Chloe got a bowl out of the cupboard, uncertain she could put her feelings into words. "I might...possibly yes, but I still love Jean-Marc too."

After Chloe got the popcorn set up in the microwave, she sat in her chair again, rested her elbows on the table, and placed her chin in her hands. Then she took a deep breath before asking, "Mama, why didn't you ever remarry?"

Mom closed the newspaper, refolded it. "The easy answer is that once you've had steak, you never want to go back to hamburger."

"Daddy was prime filet, that's for sure."

Mom's smile was a shooting star, there and gone in a nanosecond.

"Are you saying there's no other steak in the world?" Jean-Marc was steak. But so was Sam.

Mom folded her hands in her lap, stared at them for a long moment before looking up and locking on Chloe. "Fear."

Chloe grimaced. That was possibly the last response she expected. "Of what?"

"Oh honey, of so, so much."

Upon hearing her name, the cat raised her head from where she was curled up on one of the kitchen chairs and gave a soft mew. Furious popping sounded from the microwave.

"What if I loved again and he died again?" Mom said. "What if I married again, and you loved him, and he left us? I couldn't risk your heart."

"That's what I said. What if Sam dies?"

Mom reached for Chloe's hand. "I was wrong. Watching you these last couple of months has taught me that." The microwave beeped its ending as Chloe's phone vibrated with an incoming call. She ignored both. "You loved Jean-Marc," Mom went on. "But you're open to the possibility of loving again. You have such a big heart. That's also what makes you a wonderful baker. You put your passion and soul into everything."

The tears that had threatened earlier erupted. "But what if by loving Sam, I—I..." Chloe drew a steadying breath. "It feels like I'm saying Jean-Marc and our life didn't mean anything." She swiped at her cheeks.

Mom's expression filled with compassion. "Chloe, no one who knows you, or Jean-Marc, would ever think that. His love is a part of you. It was a big part of what molded you into who you are now."

Chloe gave a little nod and a big sniff.

"You were with Jean-Marc nearly eight years, right? And you've known Sam over fifteen years. But let's be real. You might have had a crush on Sam back then, but the fifteen-year-old Chloe and Sam, do you really think you would have been happy together?"

Chloe's mind went to that night at the fair when he'd ditched her to make out with Missy and she gave a soft scoff.

"What about the twenty-year-old Chloe and Sam—or the

twenty-five-year-old Chloe and Sam? Would they be happy together today?"

Chloe shrugged. "Probably not. Sam was doing great in the league, and I was chasing a career in Paris. He also has issues with his dad that affect his behavior."

Mom leaned forward. "Just like your marriage to Jean-Marc is part of who you are today, Sam's past is part of who he is today. You've both grown and changed. Perhaps what you've been through is what brought you both to this point."

"What brought me to this point is death and loss. What if I marry Sam and he dies too? I'll be the Black Widow of Hearts Bend."

"Sweetheart, here's the thing. The promise you want isn't possible. The happily ever after you crave is only found in books and movies and in heaven."

Chloe's tears spilled again. She wanted Mom to tell her that everything would be okay, that God had taken her father and her husband and in return, she got a free pass for the rest of her life. That God wouldn't let go of her hand. But then Mom got cancer and was at risk of dying, as well. People liked to say God wouldn't send more than a person could bear. If that was true, once He took Daddy, God should've given Chloe acne-free teenage years and a decent singing voice. She knew that was just a platitude people spouted that was supposed to be comforting, but, to her, it really felt pointless, untrue, and discouraging.

"So, then what? I marry Sam and he dies. I'm alone again for the rest of my life? What's the point if after everything, I end up alone? What if *you* die?"

"Chloe, don't go down that rabbit hole. We have to believe and trust or our faith is useless."

"I'm not sure I even have enough faith to be useless."

"Just know that God loves you, He's always there for you,

and He will help you. He never leaves us. Remember I said I didn't date or remarry in case that man died or left us? I forgot the other half of the equation, which God reminded me of recently. When I found the lump in my breast, I couldn't help but feel that God had left me. But, Chloe, He's still with me."

"Mom, I want your faith."

"Faith takes time. It's a muscle you have to work. You can start by coming to church with me on Sunday. We've both lost our earthly fathers, but our God is a good, good Father."

"I see what you're doing, Maman." Chloe opened the microwave, removed the bag of popcorn.

"Will you come? Grab hold of that hand you felt the other day and hold on tight?"

"I'll be there. And you're going to get well and start going on dates."

"You know what," Mom said. "I like that plan. A lot. Church. Remission. Maybe a boyfriend. How about extra butter on the popcorn?"

"You don't have to ask me twice." Chloe pulled a stick of butter from the fridge. "Mom, thanks. For all the talks. For being so calm even through your chemo. For sticking with me even when life turned your world upside down."

"Don't you know, Chloe? *You* are my world." Mom walked over and lifted Chloe's chin. "Let your heart be open to God, to faith, to love. That's the one thing I regret. I clung too long to the past—to the memory of a dead man."

CHAPTER 14

*T*hursday afternoon, Chloe piped the last perfect petal on the rose decoration to place on top of one of her petit fours. She loved working in her kitchen. Well, Haven's kitchen, but more and more it was beginning to feel like her own.

The repairman from Nashville had no-showed again so Sam had pulled out his American Express Black Card and had a new stove installed earlier in the week. Chloe had been reluctant to let him take care of the oven repair but in truth, he'd been a big help. She was exhausted. The last week of going in to Valentino's kitchen at midnight—though she was grateful the owner, Ord, had allowed her access—and working all night and then most of the day at the bakery was taking a toll.

She was still managing the roof repair, which was finally underway after all the rain. But for now, she had to get ready for Sophie and Eric's cake testing.

"Laura Kate, this is ready." Chloe stepped away from the table, stretching her lower back. Stiff and sore joints from hovering over tables while kneading dough and squeezing piping bags was an occupational hazard.

Chloe's phone buzzed with a text. Vivienne. *A few minutes, chére. Please.*

Yes, yes, of course. She'd meant to call her last week, but she'd lost all track of time working fifteen-hour days. Chloe did a bit of time math—Vivienne was seven hours ahead—and replied that she'd call at five p.m. Paris time. It would be good to talk with Vivienne and Albert, to hear what they had to say, maybe just to reminisce about their only child, but to also allow Chloe to ask for a bit of space to heal. In time she knew she'd come to love remembering their only son, who had been her first true love. Her fifteen-year-old crush on Sam Hardy didn't really count.

Pulling the cake samples out of the walk-in, Chloe added a few delicate touches to show them decorating options. Sophie said they'd arrive a little after four. Then Chloe was heading home for a long, long nap. She'd leave the shop to Sam and his fans. The image of him surrounded by Rock Mill High footballers, and even some boys from surrounding schools, made her smile. He had a way about him. Like he made everyone feel seen, feel special. He doubted his ability to be a good husband and father but more and more, she saw he had more nurturing genes than any man she'd ever known. Even Jean-Marc.

Although as much as she admired and yes, loved him, that didn't mean she was a hundred percent ready to take the relationship deeper. However, the things Mom said the other night still resonated in her mind. She'd given her a lot to think about. Chloe and Sam were growing closer. They'd shared secrets they'd told no one else. Well, now Mom knew Chloe feared the next man she loved would die in some tragic way. As much as Dad and Jean-Marc hadn't intended to die, she fought a sense of abandonment.

God, where were you in those moments? Could He have saved them?

Chloe startled when she felt a large, warm palm on her head. God? When she reached up, she felt something. A finger, perhaps? The same way she had that night with Mom. Her tears gathered along with a low laugh. "Okay, God, I get it. You are always with me even when I can't see or feel You. Even when I'm not sure I really believe in You."

At that moment, Chloe instinctively knew this odd experience was unusual and it would not last. She should be grateful. She should become a Believer.

She'd just turned her chair to face the back of the office and have a conversation with God when Ruby knocked on the doorjamb. "Sophie and Eric are here. They said they's early but I know you want to get on out of here and home for some sleep. Girl, have I told you lately you're my hero?"

"Hero? No, but, um, thank you, Ruby." Chloe was touched. Truly.

"I can darn well tell you Donna wouldn't have worked all night baking at another location and then worked all the next day. If Bob couldn't get the oven fixed, she'd have just stayed home." Ruby's attention remained on Chloe with a glow of admiration, then she seemed to catch herself, blushed, and turned back for the kitchen.

Whoa! Forget a Michelin star, she'd take a Ruby-bestowed compliment instead. Too bad she had no time to soak in the praise—she had a cake testing to manage.

Sophie and Eric sampled five cakes. Three made by Chloe and two by Laura Kate. In the end, the debate came down to two. Chloe's vanilla butter cake swirled with chocolate and Laura Kate's red velvet with layers of cream cheese frosting and cherries.

"What do you think, babe?" Eric said, standing suspiciously near the red velvet.

"I think we get both. The vanilla for the cake cutting and the red velvet for the groom's cake."

"Done." He leaned to kiss her. "Now I know why I'm marrying you."

"I have excellent taste, that's why. And killer problem-solving skills." Sophie beamed the way every bride-in-love should beam.

Chloe had beamed like that once. Could she *beam* again? For Sam?

Laura Kate worked up the order and Sophie placed her down payment. Chloe headed for the office to work on the bank deposit. She'd drop it there on her way home.

Laura Kate's expression made her pause.

"I can't believe it," Laura Kate exclaimed as she gathered up the testing plates and forks. "They loved my cake."

"It was delicious, Laura Kate," Chloe said. "You're a talented baker. Time to believe in yourself. And"—she gripped the girl's shoulders—"Clean. Your. Workstation."

Laura Kate laughed. "You may be asking the impossible. I couldn't keep my room clean even with Mama helping me."

"Have you ever thought about..." Chloe hesitated. Did she want to put in Laura Kate's head that she could have a monster career in a bigger establishment? With her comedic way of baking and decorating, she could have her own television show or at the very least, a YouTube channel. "Have you ever thought about moving, getting a job with a bigger bakery or even a restaurant? I know you don't have the credentials, but I could give you a recommendation that would go a long way. Shoot, we should film you working and send it to the Food Channel."

"Oh, I love that channel. *Dining with Joy* is my favorite

show. She's hilarious. But leave Hearts Bend?" Laura Kate's faraway expression said more than any words. "I think I'd die of homesickness. But I do love the idea of travel and I love the scenes from the British baking shows. I have a whole folder of pictures of places all around France on my computer. I'll go someday. I promise."

Speaking of promises—Chloe had to return Vivienne's call. A sudden urge, a homesickness, hit her to hear her mother-in-law's voice. Chloe closed herself in the office before dialing the familiar number.

"Chloe. *Ma chérie*. How are you?" Vivienne's voice, warm and welcoming as ever.

"'Allo, Vivienne. I'm well. I'm sorry it's taken me so long to get back to you. I got a job here at home and we've been rather busy. How are you and Albert?"

"We are well. And you've a job. Oh, *ma chérie*, that makes me happy for you but, Chloe." Vivienne cleared her throat. "Albert and I want you to visit. We've something very important to discuss with you and it must be in person."

"I can't, Vivienne. Maman—"

"Could not your mother do without you for a few days? Please, Chloe, *chérie*. We have something from Jean-Marc. For you."

"From Jean-Marc? What could you possibly have from him that I don't know about?"

Vivienne was quiet for a long moment. "Jean-Marc had a surprise for you and now it is time."

"What?" What sort of surprise? Chloe pictured her handsome adventurer heading out of the house for the trip that took his life. She'd been so angry at him—a regret she'd carry to her grave—but he'd smiled his charming smile and said, "*Chère cœur*, you will love me for it in the end."

She remembered thinking, *What does that mean?* And now Vivienne held the key.

"Come, *ma chérie*, and you will see." Vivienne's voice pulled at every heartstring. And with that, Chloe knew she was going to Paris.

She'd have to check with Maman, and the bakery staff but... "I'll text you the details."

"God, are you there?" She raised her hand again, but this time felt nothing. This journey had to be done in faith. "So what do I do? Do I really just go to Paris?" An image of her daddy came to mind. He was hunched over her, his hands over hers, helping her swing a bat and hit the ball off the T. *"See, you can do it."*

Her six-year-old self had collapsed in his arms and cried because she'd done it. They'd done it. He hadn't given up on her. She was the best T-ball player that year because her daddy believed in her. If her daddy could be a loving father, even if he had disappointed her at times—welcome to the human race— then an eternal Father had to be good.

"I'm going, God, okay? Want to come with?" Chloe laughed through a wash of tears. Better get going on reservations. She needed to tell her *boss*, Sam, and make sure Mom was okay for her radiation appointment, and get through the Tuesday evening town council meeting on Donut Heaven.

Then she'd go to Paris. The swirl in her middle told her whatever awaited her in Paris with Vivienne and Albert would somehow determine her future. Of that she was certain.

🍩🍩🍩

Hearts Bend, RU ready for some salted caramel deliciousness? Donut Heaven will be serving these and more when we open!

– @DonutHeaven on Instagram

●●●

Where can you get coffee and crullers served by an NFL superstar? Haven's, that's where! Come by M/Tu/Th 3-6pm to see @SamHardyQB15 in an apron.

– @HavensBakeryHBTN on Twitter

●●●

Bruno called just as Sam pulled into Dr. Morgan's for his Monday afternoon therapy session. He'd been lost in thought, thinking about a strategy for the town council meeting tomorrow. Rick had offered to come but he'd turned him down. He didn't want to look like a brute force coming in to cause trouble.

"I think Chloe and I can play on their heartstrings."

"Hey Bruno, I'm about to go into my therapy session."

"I'll make this quick. The Raiders are serious about you. They've got a state-of-the-art training facility and the best sports medicine doc. Tailor-made for you."

"I know all about their facilities. But they're still in Vegas. I don't want to move."

"I know and I've tried with the Titans' front office, but they've gone radio silent on me. We'll know more after the draft but Sam, if the Raiders want you, I think we have to take this. I'll tell the Titans you want to go free agent and I think they'll agree."

So, just like that, he was out. The rumors and tweets had all come true. When he hung up, Sam leaned back in the car. Dad used to talk about God, about trusting Him. Chloe mentioned feeling God's hand or something. Then Gabe mentioned prayer, which was just talking to God.

"Okay, God," Sam said toward the Range Rover's roof. "Show me what to do and I'll do it." Starting with the town council meeting regarding Donut Heaven. Then about his career. Was it time to hang up his cleats? Had he been hanging on too long?

Maybe the ring he needed now was not a Super Bowl ring —but a wedding ring.

❧❧❧

TITANS TODAY ANNOUNCED THE RELEASE OF FRANCHISE STAR QUARTERBACK SAM HARDY. NO WORD FROM HARDY CAMP SO FAR.

— @MASONDELROYSPORTS ON FACEBOOK

CHAPTER 15

a midst a leaking roof, a dead and now new oven, cake testing, and a trip to Paris in the works—they all suddenly took a back seat to the town council meeting.

Tonight was the night. Haven's versus Donut Heaven. The chain donut factory had peppered their social media with discounts and deals, pictures of a clean kitchen and front counter with the employees beaming their happiness to work for "the Heaven." But Chloe had been inside a Donut Heaven years ago and well, she'd just say the other H word was more like it. It was a hot mess.

Robin had been posting all sorts of fun things on Haven's social media feeds. Their own discounts and deals, pictures of Sam behind the counter, and pictures of the various savory and sweet treats they had to offer. Little by little, she posted images from Haven's early beginnings to now. She'd raided the old leather scrapbook for the early images. Chloe loved the black and white pictures of families sitting at the counter and in the booths on Saturday mornings, the kids eating donuts and drinking chocolate milk while their parents sloshed down coffee, read the paper, and caught up on the small town's goings on. Then Robin posted a video of Laura Kate with blue frosting everywhere, and the thing went viral with over a million likes. For once, Chloe appreciated her assistant's messiness.

They'd been so fixed on the town council meeting, she had yet to tell Sam about Paris. But what was there to tell?

"My mother-in-law called, and she wants to see me. I know I need to go. It will be closure for all of us."

She'd booked her ticket for early next week and worked on a schedule for the staff. Laura Kate would be in charge of all the baking. This would test her skills, but Chloe had no choice. Unless Sam-her-boss forbade her to go. Then she'd appeal to Sam-her-boyfriend. She'd told Mom about everything over pie at Ella's.

"You must go. I'll be fine. I don't have any appointments while you're gone." Mom told her it was the right thing to do, to at least see Jean-Marc's final gift. Chloe just had to tell her boss and boyfriend.

In the kitchen, Sam was putting on his apron.

"It's not time for your shift." She started to kiss him, then paused when she saw a shadow behind his eyes. "What's wrong?"

"Nothing. Our social media posts are paying off. We need the business and the support for the meeting. I came in early to help." He tied the apron belt around his narrow waist. "The Haven's merchandise my assistant ordered is in the office. We'll hand out the hats and T-shirts to our supporters at the town council meeting. The mugs and tumblers are for sale here."

"Don't know why Bob and Donna didn't think of merchandise long ago." *Tell him about Paris.* "Do, um, you think we're ready for tonight?"

"We have the town and history on our side. Haven's is the

anchor to First Avenue. What would the town, the street be without us?"

"Exactly." She reached for a cloth to wipe down the table.

"Chloe," he said softly, peering too close. "Are you all right?"

"Yeah, sure." *Smile.* "Why? Are you? Weren't you talking to your agent soon?"

"Yeah, but..." Sam shrugged off his answer. "We're still waiting."

So, they both had secrets. She'd leave it for now. No use going into the council meeting distracted by relationship issues. If indeed there were issues. Yet, what surprise did Jean-Marc have for her in Paris? Should she invite Sam along? Or was this between her and her in-laws?

A little before seven p.m., Chloe and Sam tugged on their Haven's T-shirts and hats, gathered the boxes of donuts to share at the meeting, and headed out with Ruby. Apparently all the tweeting and posting had worked. City hall was so jammed they could barely get in the door.

"Pardon me, coming through, Haven's proprietor here," Sam said.

Chloe followed closely, only to run smack into him when he stopped short. She looked around him to see Sam's dad, Frank Hardy, huddled with a group of executive-looking folks wearing Donut Heaven pullovers.

"Frank? Dad," Sam said.

"Son, hello." Frank walked toward his son. "I hate that you're finding out this way, but you never called me back."

"Find out what?"

"I'm buying the Donut Heaven franchise. I'm the one bringing them in."

Chloe shrank back, just in case pieces of Sam's exploding

head landed on her donut box. No use wasting perfectly good pastries.

❄ ❄ ❄

Dad. Frank. Behind Donut Heaven. It had never occurred to him Frank's need to talk had to do with this.

"You do know Rick and I own Haven's," Sam said in a low whisper, the heat of the crowded room stinging his skin.

"I found out about a month ago, but not because you told me. If you had, I'd have warned you I started the Donut Heaven deal over a year ago."

"So, what do we do?"

"We let the process do its job. You present your case, we will present ours."

"Do you really want to put Haven's out of business? You and Bob have been friends for decades."

"I didn't start this venture until I knew he was retiring."

"He sold to me, knowing you were bringing in competition?"

"He knew it was a possibility, yes."

Sam glared at his dad for a moment, angry, yet knowing he, himself, was partly to blame. He never communicated with his father, actually went out of his way to hide Haven's ownership from him. What did he expect?

Art Loamier gaveled the meeting to order and the council members took their seats. Frank went to his corner and Sam to his.

"What's going on?" Chloe whispered.

"You know that old headline about Donut Heaven coming here? Frank's been behind it the entire time. He knew Bob and Donna were going to retire."

Chloe gasped. "Why that stinking, sneaky Bob."

"We have history and tradition on our side. Let's focus on our past and the present, what you and I bring to the table."

Suddenly, he and Chloe were a team, and he liked it. He'd always been a team man and there was no better teammate than a beautiful, smart, kind, and sexy woman. Her being a world-class pâtissière was just a bonus. While Art passed out agendas to his council members and whispered things behind a covered microphone, Frank went into schmooze mode.

"Drummond, congrats on shooting par last week. You were looking good."

"Amanda, I heard your boy was the high scorer in the basketball tourney last week. Is he set for college? We've got a few dollars left in the Hardy scholarship fund."

Well, two could play that game. Sam had more than a few dollars left in his fund. He was about to chat up the council himself when Art called the meeting to order.

"Let's just get to the agenda item you all want to discuss." Art scanned the room. "We've not had this many at a meeting since the Wedding Shop was threatened. All right, it's Donut Heaven versus Haven's Bakery. Donut Heaven has entered an application, sponsored by our own Frank Hardy, to open a franchise here in Hearts Bend."

The room erupted with boos, cheers, and jeers.

"Enough of that," Art said, slamming his gavel down. "Mr. Elliot from Donut Heaven will speak first."

One of the pullover-clad men strode to the podium facing the committee. He opened a file and cleared his throat. "Thank you, Mr. Loamier. On behalf of Donut Heaven, we look forward to serving hot, fresh donuts to the good people of Hearts Bend. Donut Heaven will also employ at least two dozen people, bringing jobs and economic prosperity to the community."

Someone scoffed. Art scowled.

Mr. Elliot continued, espousing the virtues of a cold, impersonal chain restaurant. He talked about Hearts Bend's need for business competition that would allow everyone in town more choices. He claimed he'd use local tradesmen for the building and maintenance, which would provide even more income to the area.

"Tourists like having a familiar brand with a consistent product available," he said, finally closing his folder and thanking the council.

Art sighed and pushed his glasses up his nose. "We're allowing ten minutes for rebuttals."

Ruby made her way to the podium. "I have a petition here signed by three hundred Hearts Bend citizens agreeing that they don't see a need for Donut Heaven to open here. They're happy with Haven's being the sole purveyor of donuts in town." She approached the committee and handed a sheaf of papers to each one. A few others gave testimony to their love of Haven's and a teacher from the high school detailed the trashy and unclean Donut Heaven she'd visited in Middleborough.

"Most disgusting place ever. The thought of Donut Heaven makes me gag."

Art ended the rebuttal session and turned the floor over to Sam.

"Thanks for this opportunity, Art, and council members. My partner and I have done some research. First of all, Mrs. King's testimony of Donut Heaven's unclean establishments is substantiated by others." Sam passed around health violations from large and small cities across the country. "Second, they do not use local tradesmen to build a new franchise. They have their own construction division. It's really how they make money. Donut Heaven is not in the bakery business so much as the real estate business. As for local jobs, these minimum-wage positions will mostly be for our local teens, which is honorable, but management and salaried positions will go to current employees who will transfer in. Above all, Donut Heaven is known to cut their prices so low, the local competition cannot compete. They shut them down and then they will double the prices—and in many instances, they have tripled their prices. You want to pay three dollars for a glazed donut? Be my guest, but Haven's prices will always be affordable. We source locally as much as possible. Almost all of our inventory comes from companies within Middle Tennessee. Not so with Donut Heaven. In fact, I'm not sure their flour is even milled in this country."

The room gasped.

"Is that true?" Art said.

"Donut Heaven is a global company. We source our inventory from the best around the world." Mr. Elliot stared steadily at Art Loamier up front.

"Ask to see his sources." Sam watched as the folks in the room shifted with unease. He was winning. It was a feeling he knew well. A feeling he needed right now. He glanced toward Chloe. Her smile hooked his heart and he decided right then and there to propose. Why not? He loved her.

Art gave the floor to rebuttal, but no one moved. Then Frank rose and approached the podium.

"Well, I didn't expect to be at further odds with my son tonight. I believe in Haven's, but I also believe in Donut Heaven. I believe in choice. In opportunity. My son's right, Donut Heaven does source from around the world, and they do have their own construction company." He gazed toward the slimy Mr. Elliot. "My colleague was remiss on that detail. But choice is the heart of the American dream. Freedom. Opportunity." Oh brother. Sam glanced toward the door, half expecting Uncle Sam to enter waving an American flag. "We love our traditions here, but we also must grow with the times. We can't live in the past." His gaze landed on Sam. "We have to recognize things are not always as they seem. Most of the downtown buildings are in disrepair, including Haven's. I happen to know the leaking roof only recently got repaired. Still, we can keep up our quaint, small-town look while still modernizing. Donut Heaven will bring in highway traffic. The more we let the town businesses grow, the more we all grow.

"I'm sure the esteemed committee members are aware of the term 'brain drain.' That refers to a community losing its younger generation to other towns that can offer more employment, higher salaries, and a better quality of life. Hearts Bend must remain competitive with Ashland City, with Huntsville, with Nashville, to keep our younger people living and working here. And the best way to do that is to bring new businesses and new jobs to town." A light applause erupted when Frank returned to his seat. He'd been eloquent and stately.

When no one else rose to speak, Art huddled with his council to take a vote, their voices rising and falling in what appeared to be good-natured debate. This was it, right here and now. Sam felt jittery, as if he should've done something more.

After a few minutes, Art hammered the gavel. "The council wants more time to investigate and review documents." The room erupted in chatter, and he banged again. "Until next week. Meeting adjourned."

CHAPTER 16

"I guess we've another week to wait." Frank met Sam and Chloe on the sidewalk outside the city hall. The air was thin, if not a bit cool, with a starlit night washing over them.

"You presented your case well," Sam said with a bit of hesitation. Chloe slipped her hand into his for support. Speaking to Frank this way was huge for Sam.

"I had a speech writer, Sam. You spoke from the heart. I think the council will lean your way." Frank clapped him on the shoulder. "In fact, I'll ensure they do."

"Don't, Frank. Let them decide for the town."

"I'm a town member, aren't I? I can give my two cents." Frank started to go but turned back to Chloe. "Don't worry about your mother while you're in France. Janice and I will take care of her."

"Oh, um, th-thank you, Frank."

"France?" Sam gazed down at her, the white of his eyes evident even in the darkness. "You're going to France?"

"Well, I'll leave you to discuss it," Frank said. "Sam, call me when you can. I'd like to talk to you about something."

Sam turned from his father, searched her face. "Chloe, what's this about France?"

"Care for a cruller and chocolate milk?" Chloe started for the bakery, trying to find the pieces of her rehearsed speech about France and Jean-Marc's surprise. When she'd set Sam up with comfort food in the corner booth, and a few petit fours for herself, she told him the whole story. Vivienne's call. The surprise. Her need to go to Paris.

"Why didn't you tell me?"

"I meant to but then we were getting ready for the town council meeting."

Sam dipped his cruller in the chocolate milk but didn't take a bite. "Sounds more like an excuse. We weren't that busy with the town council meeting. Or the bakery."

"I know...I'm sorry. I guess I wanted the right moment to tell you. It never occurred to me Mom would tell Frank. Or that he'd tell you."

Sam's smile relieved a bit of the tension. "No one would've anticipated that one."

"It feels weird to talk to you about Jean-Marc. I don't want you to think I'm comparing you to him, or that there's no room in my heart for you because of him."

"I get it. Look, babe, go." Sam took her hands in his. "But come back to me, please."

"Of course. I love my job, I love you. Mom still needs me."

He smiled, the one with the right side of his mouth tugging a little higher. "That's the first time you've said that."

Her cheeks felt warm. "I guess it is."

After a moment, he turned his gaze back to his snack. "So, what's this surprise Jean-Marc has for you?" Sam dipped his cruller again and took a bite.

"I have no idea." Chloe considered one of the petit fours but decided against them. It was too late for such rich treats.

"You have to have some idea. What were things you two wanted to do? Did you own a house? What about a car?"

"I didn't need a car. I biked to work."

"Ah, the mystery of your amazing legs, finally solved."

Chloe laughed and blushed. "We talked about buying a café in the country one day but he was way too busy with his family's company, Sport de Qualité."

"That's Jean-Marc's? I love their microfiber shirts. Huh. Well, I guess it's a mystery until you get there." Sam polished off his cruller then leveled a serious look at Chloe. "As long as we're confessing, it looks like I'm going to the Raiders."

"The Raiders? In Las Vegas?" Chloe changed her mind and reached for a petit four. News that Sam might be moving called for fortifications.

"The Titans have been shopping me, and Bruno has done his best to land me with another champion team. I don't want to go and to be honest, it hurts that the Titans are using my trading power to get more draft picks, but that's the game. I've seen it a lot over the years." He got up and moved to Chloe's side of the table. "Mostly, I don't want to be apart from you."

"But it's only for the season, right?"

"Only? Feels like an eternity. Unless—unless you were with me. Then it would be bearable."

She set the petit four back on the plate again. "Sam, a-are you proposing?"

"Maybe. What would you say if I was?"

"I-I'm not sure." She loved him, but moving to Las Vegas? What would she do with herself? And what awaited her in Paris?

"I know I said I'd give you time and I will, but Chloe, I do love you. I want to marry you." He pushed his plate away. "Ah, man. I didn't plan to ask you like this. You deserve the whole romantic thing. Maybe not a hot air balloon ride—"

"Thank you very much." She grinned. Was Sam really proposing? Were they really talking about getting married? Or was this just "what ifs?" What if he moved to Las Vegas? What if Jean-Marc left her—oh, she had no idea...the patent rights to a new ski design?

"But definitely somewhere with twinkle lights and champagne. Me on one knee—my good one." He winked and she laughed. "A ring in a box. Maybe a string quartet."

All right. This had gone on long enough. Time for a reality check. "Sam. Come on. I'm like the Black Widow. My men die."

"Chloe, please don't say that." He pressed her hand over his beating heart. "One, it's not true, but two, I'm not going to die. I'm going to live a long, long life just to prove you wrong." His kiss was quick and sure, then lingering on her lips until she could almost taste his love. It tasted like chocolate milk and sweet dough.

They were startled from the kiss by someone hammering on the paned glass window. Chloe glanced around to see Sophie standing outside the bakery, her distraught face ghostly in the streetlight, tears glistening down her cheeks.

"H-he broke up with me," she said, her voice muffled against the glass. "Er-Eric—broke up with me."

❦ ❦ ❦

Happy to see the back of @SamHardyQB15. Good luck in Vegas. #hateRaiderNation #theygetwhattheydeserve

– @No.1 TitansFan on Twitter

"Gather around everyone." Chloe began the staff meeting at five-thirty a.m. Monday morning, when Laura Kate already had flour and sugar in her hair net and dusting her hairline. Ruby was on her third cup of coffee. And Chloe ached with love of the place. Whatever Vivienne and Albert had in France would not compare. Mom suggested last night perhaps they wanted her to see Jean-Marc's final headstone. Maybe they had purchased an accompanying plot for her. But that seemed like an odd surprise. Chloe was sure graves were not what Jean-Marc had planned to give her as a surprise.

"This is our last meeting before I leave for France early tomorrow." She tapped the schedule in her hand. "I presume you reviewed this. Everyone will have to work a bit more, but you can do it. Rick has approved the overtime. You can have some extra cash for your Christmas savings accounts."

"But why are you going to France?" Ruby said, her eyes wide with a bit of sadness. "What on earth for?"

"My in-laws need me to come. They said something about a surprise but either way, I think we all need closure. Perhaps we'll talk about Jean-Marc and laugh, cry, and go away feeling the grief has loosened its grip."

"What does Sam say?" Ruby again with her bold inquisition.

"What can he say? Of course, as my boss, he—"

"Forget boss, he loves you."

"Yes, but he's also a kind man and letting me do what I need to do. Is that okay with you, Ruby?"

"Well, no, but I guess it'll have to be." She waved the schedule at Chloe. "I'm doing all the banking?"

"I've shown you how. You can handle it."

"What about me? The schedule says I'm doing all the

baking." The schedule trembled in Laura Kate's thin hand. "Chloe, I'm not you. I-I can't."

"Yes, you can. And no, you're not me. In some ways, you're better. You know where my recipes are if you forget something. We're a bakery, not saving lives."

"That's what you think," Ruby said with a huff.

"If something doesn't get done, no big deal. Well, except for the special orders."

"And the Triple Chocolate Fudge Cookie. I tell you, I still hear rumblings of an insurrection."

"Ruby," Chloe said, "I'm beginning to think you're the one starting the rumblings."

"Oh, look at the time. I'd better get the coffee started."

Yeah, just as she thought. Ruby was the sweetest kind of troublemaker.

"Are you sure I can do this?" Laura Kate said.

"I am. And oh, sad news. Eric broke up with Sophie."

"What? I thought they were so in love."

"Me too. Apparently, the wedding cake testing put the fear of commitment in him, and he said he wasn't ready for the ole 'ball and chain.'"

"I'd like to ball and chain him." Laura Kate tacked the schedule to the bulletin board and punched the air with her chocolate-frosted fist.

"Get in line behind Sam. He asked Sophie if she wanted him to talk to Eric, but she said no. If he doesn't want her, she doesn't want him guilted into going through with it."

Oh, love. Why was it so glorious yet so provoking and painful?

Chloe had known a great love with Jean-Marc. Could she have it again with Sam? And so soon?

"Chloe, do you mind if I work on the TCFC while you're gone?"

"Please. Save us from Ruby the Rebel. Oh, Laura Kate, see if you can't get Robin to come in on time for the next week. Early would be better, if you can talk her into it."

"Will do, boss."

By noon, she'd done all the banking and caught up on all the invoices and ordering. Chloe announced to Ruby and Laura Kate she was heading home. As she exited the kitchen door, she ran smack dab into Robin...coming into work...early.

I'll be, there is a God.

❦❦❦

Hardy Insurance was a spectacular office building. Modern with wide windows, concrete floors, and wood accents. Sam could see the appeal of Donut Heaven to a man like his dad.

Meredith greeted him as he approached the executive office. "Go on in. He's expecting you."

Sam hesitated, hand on the knob, then went in. He'd gone to his therapy appointment, which went well, then ate a bite of lunch with Chloe before she went home to pack. He was taking her to his place for dinner then to the airport for a departure just after midnight. He had a few hours to kill so he'd rung Frank. After all, he'd been wanting to talk. Besides, Chloe was right. Maybe his dad would have advice about the move to the Raiders.

"Come in, come in." Frank led Sam to a lounge area that overlooked downtown Hearts Bend. The décor smacked of Janice's taste. Sam liked it. "Coffee?"

"Sure, that'd be nice. Cream, no sugar."

Frank returned to the couch with two cups and perched on the edge of the adjacent chair.

"I had wanted to give you a part of the Donut Heaven franchise. That's why I kept calling. But I'm guessing that's not why you're here. I read sports news, Sam. Is it true? The Titans are letting you go?"

"They want Fields out of Ohio State. One injury and they're looking to find a new franchise quarterback."

"How's your knee?"

"Good. Dr. Morgan is starting to believe I'll be ready for camp but, Frank, should I be loyal to a team that's not loyal to me?"

"Follow the money, Sam. They can get Fields, who's a good quarterback, for less than they pay you and his legs are fresher, so to speak."

Sam laughed. "True. But the Raiders?" He stood and paced to the window where he could see the downtown shops. It might be his imagination, but the dark Book Nook window seemed to echo Sophie's broken heart. He turned back to Frank. "Vegas?"

"Play there and live here."

"Sounds like a nice rhyme but doesn't work so well in real life. I'll have to be there seven, eight months out of twelve. Hey, where do you see this Donut Heaven going up?"

Frank joined him at the window. "See that lot to the south of the bank? I bought it a few years ago and Donut Heaven reached out, offered the franchise to me."

"Do you really want a chain restaurant here?"

"Not after hearing your speech the other night. Then Janice made me look at Haven's nostalgic social media posts. I talked to Art. Said if he could persuade the council to side with Haven's, I'll do something else with the lot."

"Th-thanks, Frank. I mean it."

"Now, what do you do about the Raiders? How bad do you want that ring? Can you get to a Super Bowl with them? What about the Falcons or Dolphins?"

"Bruno says the Raiders are my best option. Yes, I can get to the Super Bowl with them. Maybe not this year but next year."

"You don't sound excited." Frank sipped his coffee and rocked back on his heels, a father standing next to his son, looking out over the town.

"Been wondering if I want the wrong ring."

"Wrong ring? What do you mean?"

"Maybe I'd rather have a wedding ring."

"Wedding ring?" Frank nearly spewed his coffee. "What? Who? Don't tell me that Curvy girl."

Sam downed his swallow of coffee with a choke. "No, not Curvy Carla. Chloe, Frank. I'm in love with Chloe. Chloe Beason, er, LaRue."

"Meredith's girl." Frank clapped him on the back. "Well done. Nice choice."

"She's off to France today. Of course, you knew that before I did."

"I had a feeling I'd let the cat out of the bag the other night."

"Her in-laws have something for her. Not sure what that means, or what the future holds there, but I think she loves me too. Well, I know she does but getting over her husband's death will take time. I'm in no hurry. And, side note, I don't think she's thrilled about Vegas either."

"If I know you, Sammy, you'll make it work. And I recommend it—marriage."

"Do you?" Sam faced his father, drawing from a shallow well of courage. "Then why did you cheat on Mom? Why did you get divorced?"

"Ah, well, that..." Frank refilled his coffee and returned to his chair. Sam followed, perching on the edge of the leather sofa. "I didn't toss your mother out, Sam. She left."

"Because you were having an affair with Janice. I saw you kissing her."

"You know, we've been wondering for fifteen years if you saw us. I guessed so by the way you treated me, but I didn't want to bring it up in case your bitterness was related just to the divorce. Then Janice told me Chloe hinted at something during my birthday party... Sam, I'm sorry. I should've talked to you like a man. At fifteen, you'd have understood, I think. At least more than leaving you in the dark."

"I came into their house, and you were hugging Janice. Then you kissed her. Two weeks later, Mom left for Charleston."

"You asked me why and I never told you."

"I can only imagine it was because she didn't want to live in a town with her cheating husband." Sam regarded his father for a moment, then went on in a low tone. "What hurt the most is then I realized you weren't the man I thought you were. Not the dad I knew. You betrayed everything you said you believed in. Our family. Your faith. My friendship with Jake was never the same."

"The night you saw me with Janice was the night your mother told me she was leaving. I stopped by Janice and Bill's to deliver some papers and I was so upset I told her everything. She hugged me and that led to the kiss. We both regretted it the moment it happened. Believe me, neither one of us liked the fact she was my secretary. Did you know she quit when she realized she had feelings for me? She and Bill were having troubles too. We didn't start a relationship until we were both divorced. I'm just stating the facts. Not making excuses."

"No, I hear you. Mom said she was leaving?" Sam stood, then sat down. This messed with everything he'd believed for fifteen years. "Why didn't you tell me?"

"I wanted you to believe the best of her. You knew things

weren't always great between us, that we'd been in counseling for over a year. What we didn't want you to see was that we weren't going to make it. Your mom wanted out way more than me. She'd been talking to a *friend* in Charleston for months. Your mom was on her way out the door six months before she left."

"She told me she moved back to Charleston because Gramps and Grandma needed her."

"Right. I told her you needed her, but she was enamored with this guy from her old high school. Didn't last. Do you talk to your mother much?"

"Now and then. She sends me people who want to meet the Titans quarterback. I think it's her way of relating to me."

Frank laughed. "Now I've never done that..."

"No, you haven't."

"As for my faith, you're right. I lost my way for a while. I wasn't in a good place with God when your mother and I had our troubles. But Janice and I are members of the Sunday faithful these days." Dad reached across and touched Sam's hand. "Don't base your hope in love and God on me. Base them on Him alone. Talk to Him. Trust in Him. Especially if you're serious about Chloe."

Sam was on his feet, walking toward his father, who stood, meeting him in a bear hug. "Dad, I'm sorry, so sorry. I've judged you all these years and it was Mom too." The sting of tears surprised him. "Forgive me for being such a jerk."

"Of course, of course, and please, I know I failed you. I'm sorry for my part, Sammy, I truly am."

And just like that, the truth set him free.

Dad invited him to dinner the next week. Sam promised to call and arrange a time. But as he walked out to his car, he knew he had one more call to make. One more truth to be told.

He'd have a lot to talk to Chloe about over dinner tonight.

Settled behind the wheel of his Range Rover, Sam started the car then told Siri, "Call Mom, iPhone."

He was going to ask for her side of the story, for the truth, and to stop sending him people who loved the Titans. He was going to be a Raider for the next season of his life. But, if at all possible, he'd just like to be her son again, not her famous NFL quarterback.

CHAPTER 17

*I*f Chloe had held any trepidation about returning to France, they vanished the moment she landed in her old homeland. The mid-day sun was just breaking through the vanishing rain clouds as her driver took her to her in-laws' home in the Bastille neighborhood where she'd worked, where she'd lived with and loved Jean-Marc.

The reunion had been tender with tears, sweet with laughter and memories, cozy with one of Vivienne's delicious dinners followed by coffee on their back porch. However, when Chloe asked about the surprise she'd flown four thousand miles to receive, they said, *"Tomorrow morning,* ma chère."

She'd texted Sam just before collapsing in her bed from jet lag. *All is well. Love you.*

She slept long and hard and now, Wednesday morning, after a breakfast of café au lait and croissants, she was riding in Albert's Mercedes down a familiar road. She, Vivienne, and Albert chatted of nothing much as the driver navigated them out of the chaos of the city traffic and into the suburbs. As the cityscape faded into countryside, Chloe lowered her window and breathed in the fresh air of Deux Jardins. She loved this little town.

This was where she and Jean-Marc were going to—

"Vivienne, Albert, the café? Is that the surprise?" She pressed her hand on her father-in-law's shoulder. He peered at her over his dark-rimmed glasses and smiled. "The café I loved? No, please tell me he did not buy the café?"

The driver turned the car into a graveled drive and circled a small, white-stoned building. The café. Her dream. Their dream. Jean-Marc had believed in her enough to buy her a building. That must be where their savings had gone.

Her memory of their last argument, in the bedroom of their Paris flat, still haunted her. Jean-Marc's stoic expression as he asked if she was certain about not accompanying him to Zermatt, even though he was the one reneging. He'd promised to help her with the Moveable Feast. *"Just stay and work. Work until your arms are covered by burns and your fingers are calloused. We both know you'll never allow yourself to believe you're enough. But you are, chère cœur. You are more than enough."* Then he'd made that cryptic comment about how she'd love him more after the trip, picked up his duffel, and left.

"We are here, *mon amour*. Café LaRue." Vivienne placed a set of keys in Chloe's hand. "We are only calling it Café LaRue for now. You may name it whatever you like."

"No, no, that's the name." Chloe nearly stumbled getting out of the car. "We were going to call it Café LaRue." The white stone glowed in the morning sunlight, a juxtaposition to the stained and broken roof tiles and very dead garden. But it was beautiful. Glorious. It was home.

"The cottage goes with it." Albert pointed to the structure down the road with flowered window boxes. "The former owner still lives there for now. He's renting from us. It's in good shape so all your money can go into the café."

"Money?" She stared at her father-in-law. "I don't have any money."

"No, *ma chére*, but we do. Jean-Marc wanted this for you and so do we."

"I don't know...what...? I can't." Chloe held up the keys. "I'm not really your daughter-in-law anymore. And I think I'm in love with another man." Think? Yes, she was in love with Sam. "I can't accept this. It's too much."

"Darling, you can, and you will," Vivienne said. "Of course you're in love with another man. You've French blood now and we French always find love." Vivienne kissed Chloe's cheeks. "Jean-Marc planned to give this to you, but life and death had other plans. We know he'd want us to do this for you. It's all yours. You cannot deny us."

The tears were impossible to battle.

A car pulled in next to them. "*'Allo*," a feminine voice called from the vehicle. Walking toward them with the same sway she'd employed at Jean-Marc's funeral was the blonde. The mystery woman.

"Beatrice, come, come, meet Chloe," Vivienne said. "Chloe, this is Beatrice Dupont. She and Jean-Marc were working together on this project when he died. She wanted to know if she should continue to acquire the project or let it go. We told her to get it."

"I'm grateful." And ashamed. Of course, Jean-Marc had not cheated on her. "But why are you just now telling me? It's been nearly a year." Chloe glanced toward the café and felt peace. So much peace. And to her surprise, the soft touch of a large hand on her shoulder.

Lord, what do I do now?

"That is our fault, Chloe," Albert said. "In our grief, we didn't really understand what Beatrice was telling us at the funeral. She finally got in touch with us again a few months ago and we investigated the purchase. Then we knew we must tell you."

"Shall we go inside and see where you will one day serve delicious croissants and fresh roasted café?" Vivienne extended her arms to Chloe, drawing her close and walking with her inside the stone building.

It was beautiful, if not a bit beat up with dull hardwood floors, stained glass windows, and high-pitched ceilings with rough wood beams. The kitchen was enormous but in need of a total overhaul. Out back was a garden. Given the right care, it would be a lovely place for tables and chairs, for weddings and garden parties.

Chloe wiped a fresh wash of tears from her cheeks. "I—I just don't know what to say."

"Say you love it, *ma chérie*," Albert said. "We've no expectations. We shall love if you keep it and stay, bring your new man. Should you want to go, we will be sad but understand."

Beatrice handed Chloe a folder. She opened it to find a stack of legal-looking forms. "I can read recipes in French, but this?"

Vivienne gestured to Beatrice, who leaned forward and pointed at the top paper. "This is a copy of the deed to the property. *Je suis agent immobilier*—that is, how you say...real estate agent. I negotiated the purchase on behalf of Jean-Marc and worked with the *notaire* in his absence."

"I heard you at his graveside." She turned to Beatrice, who on true inspection, did not look like an adulteress. "You said, *'petit chalet'* and *'affaire de cœur.'*"

"*Oui.* He loved you so. He told me when you were newly married he made an extravagant purchase he should not have, and he bitterly regretted it. He wanted to make another extravagant purchase, this one for you. The house was for you and your children." Beatrice's words were appropriate to the occasion and her tone kind. "He was so excited to share the news with you at your Moveable Feast."

"The Moveable Feast? But he went to Zermatt instead of the restaurant event."

"*Non*, Chloe," Vivienne said. "He insisted the ski test be early so he could fly back to Paris and be with you."

Chloe sat down hard in the nearest chair, a rusted wrought iron thing that had once been painted red, and tried to take it all in. She'd been so angry—and so wrong.

"Is that why he crashed?" Her eyes flooded over as she looked up at Albert. "He was in a hurry, rushing?"

Albert's own sorrow showed in his eyes. "He crashed because the skis were faulty. A degree off on the sidecut in the design. Another degree during fabrication. We are the ones to bear the guilt."

"Non, *mon amour*." Vivienne reached for her husband's hand. "We agreed we'd not blame ourselves. Jean-Marc would not be pleased."

Tears sprang to Chloe's eyes. Dear, darling Jean-Marc. Of course, he wasn't having an affair. That was her imagination running wild with the loose reins of anger and the steel bit of grief in her teeth. "I'm not sure I can accept it." A wave of love and longing and loss washed over her.

Albert patted her hands. "You can and you must," he said in a gravelly voice. "It was Jean-Marc's focus and sole project the last months of his life." He cleared his throat. "Vivienne is correct. If you'd rather not stay and run it, we understand. We will purchase it from you and hire someone."

So many emotions swirled through her. Love. Regret. Anticipation. Her tears spilled over like water breaching a dam, slow to get going, but once they started... Her beloved Jean-Marc had planned it all. Their perfect life.

But Sam was her future. Wasn't he? Chloe walked the café while Albert, Vivienne, and Beatrice stepped outside.

"Jean-Marc, darling, I love you so much for this. But I'm in Hearts Bend now and there's the matter of Sam Hardy." Chloe whispered to Jean-Marc as she strolled along the walls, a finger trailing the rough stones. "What should I do? What would you want me to do?" How could she create a future with one hand grasping Sam's and the other holding onto Jean-Marc? Yet she wanted this café more than anything. She could almost smell the freshly baked croissants coming from the oven, almost hear the chatter of the locals as they sat on the patio or in the garden. Even more, she felt God's hand on her, and she knew. She knew.

This was exactly where she needed to be. Café LaRue was her home.

CHAPTER 18

The therapy, exercises and evaluations had helped Sam keep his mind occupied and not brooding on Chloe back in Paris for the last few days. Perched on his couch with an ice pack on his knee Friday morning, Sam reviewed the health checkup Dr. Morgan had sent to the Raiders. Despite his positive progress, there was a hint of hesitation in her notes.

"...range of motion...tenderness..." and some other doctorly words.

Nevertheless, it was official. He was gone from the Titans. Tossing the report aside, Sam determined any tentative words the good doctor wrote on his progress would all be moot when he visited Vegas. He'd show them he was well on his way to being one hundred percent. He had no doubt he'd be on the field in the fall. Just that he'd be wearing black and silver instead of Titans blue, red, silver, and white.

Sam shifted in his seat and adjusted the ice pack. He'd never played for the opposition before. He was always a "be true to your school" guy. He'd grown up cherishing the "home team" and reviling his rivals. Soon enough he'd don the jersey of "the rivals." Even now, Bruno was in the kitchen on his phone, finalizing some things with the Raiders' front office.

An interesting aside about his knee... Since he'd aired out things with Dad, he'd had less pain and in general, the cares of his life didn't seem to be as burdensome. Proving Dr. Morgan was right about that one thing. He'd talked to Dad at least three times since their True Confessions session and talked to Mom twice. She'd confirmed Dad's details of their divorce and apologized to Sam in tears. Now he wrestled with the sting of regret for being bitter for so long. For his assumptions. For not seeking the truth. Even at fifteen, he'd known there had to be more to the story.

Yet what he wanted more than anything was to talk to Chloe, to see her, read the expression on her face as she talked about the lovely surprise that had awaited her in France. A café. From her dead husband. If any man wanted to pull one last heroic deed before his demise—if he could predict such a thing—it would be to fulfill his wife's lifelong dream before buying the big one.

How could Sam compete? There was no game plan, no play, no scramble that could outdo what Jean-Marc had done. Bravo. Sam concluded it wasn't even honorable to try. Reaching for his phone, Sam reviewed the images Chloe had texted him over the last two days. Beautiful scenes of a sun-soaked French countryside, snapshots of her standing in front of the café with her arms wide, head back, happiness all but leaping off the screen. The place needed a major overhaul, but even football-minded Sam could see the potential.

He'd managed one phone call in the time she'd been away. *"This was our dream. Jean-Marc surprised me with it. Can you believe it?"* The excitement in Chloe's voice was so palpable, Sam felt it.

"Amazing... cottage... gardens... weddings... parties... Christmas... so romantic..."

Well, he believed that was the gist of their conversation. Every other word was French, and he'd taken Spanish in high school.

In other news, the town council decided against Donut Heaven, so his sweet little Haven's was safe. He'd been excited to convey the news to Chloe, but it was pretty anticlimactic after her news.

"Hurray for hometown politics. You must be so excited, Sam."

You. Not *"I'm so excited."* He'd become a singular entity to her. A "me and you" instead of the familiar us.

Flipping through Chloe's pictures one last time, he looked for a hint of hesitation, some insecurity about resuming a life in France, taking over a huge renovation, and returning to a dream she'd had with a dead man.

Choose me, Chloe. Choose me.

"You know what you have to do, don't you?" Bruno walked toward Sam with two cold Diet Cokes and handed one to Sam. By his tone, Sam knew his agent and friend wasn't talking about the Raiders.

"Of course, I know." Sam sighed and popped the top of his soda. He'd confided everything to Bruno over dinner last night. "I have to let her go. The café is her dream, her 'ring' so to speak."

"Well said. After all, that's why you're taking the Raiders' deal. To win a Super Bowl, which is what you've always wanted."

"Two dreams driving two people apart," Sam said, not bothering to cloak the sadness resonating from his heart. "I'm willing to try a long-distance relationship from Hearts Bend to Vegas, but Paris to Vegas?" The time difference alone would make it impossible to have a relationship. Besides, if she owned the café, the pretty little town of Deux Jardins would be her home. Had Chloe mentioned something about her mother moving there? If that happened, she'd never come back to Tennessee.

"I tried it once," Bruno said. "Didn't work. The big thing here is to realize you've come to the place where you want to move on in life, do some adulting, fall in love, get married, have a family."

More than anything. The urge was even stronger after he'd patched things up with Dad and Janice and Mom. He knew he could be a good, faithful husband and father. The desire beat in him almost more than his thirst for the ring. And he wanted all of that with Chloe. He loved her. Which was exactly why he had to let her go.

"If you love something, let it go..."

He'd been talking to God a bit more since Chloe flew to France. Some of the guys on the Titans had a prayer meeting on Friday morning so he thought he'd go there before heading down to Hearts Bend to spend his Friday at Haven's. And there was Gabe's Saturday gathering, too.

"The Raiders want a meeting next week." Bruno scrolled through his iPad calendar. "When do you want to go?"

"Any time but Monday. I'm at the bakery that day. The guys from the Rock Mill football team come in and we talk shop, toss the ball around in the alley." Which he'd realized lately how much he loved. Maybe he'd coach one day.

"Careful of your knee." Bruno clapped him on the shoulder. "Sam, I'm sorry about Chloe. But just wait, see what God might do."

Bruno rarely mentioned God to Sam though he knew him to be a man of faith based on his own backstory. But at this moment, his agent uttered the words Sam needed most.

"But I still have to let her go."

"I think so. If she really wants a French café, hanging onto her will only cause resentment."

Late in the morning, long after Bruno left, Sam sent a text. He'd tried to call her but when she didn't answer, he battled an intense restlessness. Another benefit of clearing the air with his parents? He couldn't hold things in anymore.

Hope you're having fun in France. The pictures are amazing. Been thinking, and I'm behind you and your dream, your own French countryside café. Go for it. We'll find someone to manage Haven's though I'm sure she, or he, won't be anything like you. I'm off to meet with the Raiders next week. Guess we're both pursuing our dreams. I wish you all the best, Chloe. Honest.

⚫⚫⚫

When Sam showed up at the bakery later that afternoon, the place was packed and Ruby tossed an apron at him the moment he darkened the back alley door. A drop of disappointment hit him as he entered the kitchen. No Chloe. She'd not responded to his text and the more time that ticked on, the more he regretted sending it. *A text? Really, Hardy? You didn't learn your lesson the first time?*

"What's going on?" He did a double take when he passed Laura Kate bent over the oven. She was covered in a fine white powder and shook her head as she pulled out a cookie sheet and set it on the stainless-steel table.

"W4C," Ruby said. "We're running around here like a one-armed paper hanger. Can you man the cash register?" She pushed through the double doors to the front.

He followed her to the register. "Sure, but what's W4C?" He smiled at the young woman in front of him who blushed when she recognized him.

"I'd like a W4C," she said with a slight batting of her lashes.

"Ruby." Sam leaned toward her as she passed by with a pot of coffee in hand. "What's a W4C?"

"Sweet girl," she said to the young customer. "The W4C line is over there. A fresh batch will be ready in ten minutes. Sam, take her order and give her a number, yeah, right there from that basket. When she gets her cookie, she pays."

"Okay, but would someone please tell me what the heck W4C is?"

Every warm body in the bakery shouted, "White Chocolate Cookies and Cream Cookie."

"Laura Kate was playing around this week with a different sort of cookie and well, that one struck gold," Ruby said. "Word got out it was the new TCFC and orders started flooding in."

"Word got out, did it?" Sam gave Ruby the *knowing* eye.

Ruby fielded his look and raised him a chin as she flitted toward the dining room. "Well, *someone* had to quell the coming insurrection."

For the next thirty minutes, he took nothing but W4C orders both in person and on the phone. Which required more concentration than running the RPO—run/pass/option offense. When Laura Kate, covered in even more frosting and flour, brought a fresh batch of W4C to the display case, the customers surged forward. Sam stole one for himself before cashing out everyone's order. After all, he needed to know what his bakery was selling. One bite and he was in heaven. A light golden brown, coated with miniature chocolate chips and cookie crumbs, still-warm cookie melted in his mouth. "Laura Kate, this is amazing."

She ducked her head with an "aw, shucks" kick at the floor. "Who doesn't like white chocolate, cookies and cream candy, and chocolate sandwich cookies? They had to make an amazing cookie."

"Back in the kitchen, Laura Kate," Ruby barked like she owned the place. "More cookies. Sam, we can't bake them fast enough. Trust me, the TCFC was *never* this popular."

"Really? Tell me what makes this one so popular." Sam leaned close, almost invading her personal space.

"Well, I might have, or someone might have, I'm not sure, said that this recipe was devised by one hometown quarterback and it was his most favorite cookie of all time. Maybe. I can't be sure. I just heard a rumor."

Sam laughed and roped Ruby into a Titan hug. "Remind me to give you a raise."

By the time they flipped the door sign to *Closed*, they'd sold four hundred cookies. Sam felt like he'd been hit by the front seven of a stellar defensive line.

Ruby was cooling herself in the walk-in with the door open. Laura Kate wore so much flour and sugar she needed to be hosed off outside. And Robin flopped into a chair, waving her apron to cool her red face.

"I declare, what are we going to do next week?" Ruby said. "We can't keep this up. Sam, when does Chloe get home? We need her."

"Not sure...anyway, I think we're going to limit how many W4C orders we manage. Isn't that what Bob and Donna did with the TCFC?" Sam used his I'm-the-boss voice. "When we run out, we run out."

"You want an insurrection?" Ruby said.

"No, and we won't have one if you stop spreading stories in the grocery store."

Ruby harrumphed. "Where's the fun in that?"

"Here, y'all, I saved four cookies, so we each get one." Laura Kate passed a plate of cookies around their weary circle.

Sam poured everyone a glass of milk and they ate in beautiful, contented silence until Ruby brought up Chloe again.

"So, what was the big surprise in France?"

"A café." Sam drained the last of his milk, wishing there was one more cookie. He needed comfort food right about now. "Her husband bought it for her as a surprise."

"But isn't he dead?" Robin said.

"Yes, and there's a story behind why she just now found out, something about his parents not knowing and a blonde real estate agent—or whatever they are in France—but either way, Chloe has her dream. A French countryside café."

"But what about you? She loves you." Ruby closed the walk-in door and took a chair from the office to sit next to Sam.

"It's pretty hard to compete with a dead man, Ruby. Besides, I'm moving to Las Vegas to join the Raiders. She doesn't want to go there. She's already told me."

"What? You're leaving too?" Laura Kate's sincere question touched him. "We love having you around here."

"I love it here too. But I have a Super Bowl championship to chase, and I don't think I'm done playing ball." He'd loved the game for so long he wasn't sure he knew who Sam Hardy was without it.

"If you ask me, I'd rather have Chloe than any Super Bowl championship." Ruby never shied away from sharing her opinion. "Sam, you got a room full of trophies, I bet. And do you look at them? Wear the rings? They'd just be collecting dust. Family, people, and relationships, now those are life's real trophies."

"Maybe, but I told her to take the café. I don't want to stand in her way and—"

"What?" Ruby flicked him on the forehead. *Flicked* him. "Are you really so dumb and dull? You do exploits on the field and fumble in real life. Sam, go after her. Tell her you love her.

If you have to sacrifice a Super Bowl ring for a wedding ring, then do it. She'll be with you long after the league will, which, by the way, won't give you children or grandchildren, or keep you warm at night when you're old and cold. Sammy, don't you know, one fine day, yes one fine day, you'll realize that loving Chloe LaRue was the best decision you ever made?" Ruby sat back in her chair and crossed her arms. "That's my story and I'm sticking to it."

Suddenly, Sam was on his feet. She was right. One hundred percent right. She'd even echoed his own thoughts on which ring he really wanted on his finger. He wanted Chloe's ring, which represented the greatest prize of all. Love.

"Ruby, you're a genius. Remind me to give you a raise." Sam grabbed Ruby's face and smacked her on the forehead with a big sloppy kiss.

"Is that the same raise as before or are we talking two raises now?"

"Yes, whatever, I've got to go." Sam dashed for the door and then dashed back to Ruby and kissed her again. "You are the fount of all wisdom, despite stirrings of insurrection. I love you." Another dash for the door, where he paused with his arms raised in victory. Bruno was right. He knew what he had to do. "I'm going to France, ladies. Wish me luck!"

CHAPTER 19

Saturday morning sun broke through the drawn curtains in Chloe's second story bedroom at the LaRue's sprawling estate. Making sports equipment gave them a generous life. She'd been so tired last night she'd turned off her phone and gone to bed after dinner. She'd never been good with jet lag, and this trip seemed to be making her more weary than usual. Sometime in the night she dreamed of Sam. He was drifting farther and farther away, and she couldn't quite reach him. Now in the light of day, she realized her heart had been speaking to her in the night. What was she to do about Sam? Would he move to France? No, no. He had a job with the Raiders. He had his dreams and she had hers.

They'd talked once, but she'd been so excited about the café he didn't say much. Though he'd texted he loved all the pictures she'd sent him. Still, where were they in their love affair? They'd confessed their love, but Chloe had made it clear she wasn't ready to move on. Yet. Maybe the café was the reason. That her heart was still connected to Jean-Marc and she knew he'd not said his final words. Knew they still had unfinished business. Literally. Knew she had to resolve feeling like the Black Widow of Hearts Bend.

Reaching for her phone, she saw a flurry of texts from Robin.

Robin: *Look at all the lines for the W4C, Laura Kate's cookie! It's a hit. She invented it this week.*

Chloe: *Wow! W4C?*

Robin: *White Chocolate Cookies and Cream Cookie. It's the new TCFC. Ruby might have told everyone it was Sam Hardy's own recipe and his favorite cookie.*

Oh Ruby, you rascal. So, Haven's had their new TCFC. Good for Laura Kate. And if they'd found the next big cookie hit without Chloe, wasn't that a sign that she was no longer needed at Haven's? That she was free to accept Jean-Marc's gift?

The next message was from Sam. Her heart grew a protective shell as the words sank in. A long, singular message in which he once again called things off. *Hope you're having fun in France... Go for it... I'm off to meet with the Raiders next week... Guess we're both pursuing our dreams... Wish you all the best... Honest.*

Her tears collected as she read the message over and over, sad and angry, hurt, yet wondering if he wasn't just ripping off the bandage and saying what needed to be said. Despite their affection for one another, their love, their destinies had taken dramatically different turns. In the cozy safety of Hearts Bend, it was easy to pretend they could be the boy and girl next door, the all-American couple who'd secretly loved each other all through high school. But that wasn't their reality, was it?

The café surprise couldn't have come at a better time. Mom was nearing the end of her treatments. Laura Kate had invented the W4C. The town council had saved Haven's from Donut Heaven. While she had to get back to France as soon as possible—she and Albert were meeting with an architect about the café remodel—she'd take time in Hearts Bend to make sure everything was shipshape before she moved here.

Back to France. A wave of wonder washed over her. Was she actually going backward? Would she sink into a world of grief again, working the café without Jean-Marc?

Chloe fell back on her bed, tears slipping down her cheeks. "Sam, I needed to talk to you, but you broke up with me in a text. Again."

She tossed her phone to the floor, buried her face in her pillow, and cried.

⚅ ⚅ ⚅

An hour later, showered and dressed, her questions and sorrow in check, Chloe followed the aroma of coffee and croissants to the LaRues' kitchen. She paused to give Fezzik, their Great Dane, a rub behind the ears. He sighed and settled back onto his giant pillow bed. At the coffee bar, she poured herself a cup and set a buttery pastry on a plate.

"Bonjour," she said with her best smile.

"What troubles you, Chloe?" Albert saw right through her. Jean-Marc had been the same. She could hide nothing from him.

"The man I love, the one I told you about, sent me a text."

"I don't like the sound of this story, *ma chére*," Vivienne said, stretching her hand out to Chloe.

"He says I should follow my dream as he's following his." Tears she'd been determined to hold in surfaced and spilled over. "I was so excited, I didn't think what it meant for us. I suppose in the romance of it all I thought he'd say, 'Forget the football championship, I'll move to France.'" She laughed softly and reached for the tissue Vivienne offered. "I miss him, but I

217

guess I have to move on. After all, we've only really been back in touch for a few months. How can true love bloom in two months?"

"True love blooms the moment it finds the right sun, Chloe." Albert was the poet of the LaRue clan. "I knew the moment I set eyes on Vivienne."

"I, however, did not know, and he chased me for two years."

"Ah, two of the most heartbreaking, joyous, *très chaotique* years of my life." Albert blew a kiss at his wife who pretended to accept it and place it to her chest.

"Chloe, you must follow your heart," Vivienne said. "Poor darling, Jean-Marc's surprise has broken your heart again."

"To be honest, Vivienne," Chloe said, "I've never felt more loved. But yes, Sam's message hurt more than I expected. I guess I didn't know how much I loved him until right now."

Suddenly, the sunlight shifted through the windows and a ray of golden light washed over Chloe and she settled into an unusual peace. The answer would come. She must believe.

Albert folded his paper and set it aside. "Shall we still meet with the architect? If so, I must change. We'll leave in an hour."

"I'll be ready to go when you say." So this was it. Meet the architect and Chloe was in, all in.

Albert had just set his coffee cup in the dishwasher when the doorbell chimes played through the house. After a moment, the maid appeared.

"For you, mademoiselle." She nodded at Chloe. "Visiteur."

"A visitor? For me?" Chloe pushed away from the table with a glance at her in-laws. "Albert, is the architect coming here?"

"No, we are to meet at his office."

Chloe went through the arched kitchen doorway toward the grand room and stopped cold when she saw the handsome, broad, American footballer Sam Hardy. He looked sheepish, unsure, and like he'd sat up all night on a long flight from Nashville.

"Surprise," he said quietly, his humble posture the antithesis of his player persona.

"Wha—what are you doing here?" Chloe reached for the nearest chair to support her trembling legs.

"I came to see you. Got the last seat on a flight from Nashville to New York, New York to Paris. No first class. Middle seat all the way. Last row, over the engine."

Chloe touched her fingers to her lips as a quivering laugh escaped. "Six-foot-four, bad knee Sam Hardy crunched up in the middle seat of an overnight flight. You had to be miserable."

"I was and it had nothing to do with the seat." He stepped toward her. "I ached in here." He touched his chest. "I had to see you. There I was, working the W4C rush—that's our new cookie sensation, by the way—"

"Robin texted. Way to go, Laura Kate."

"And all I knew was that you weren't there. Then Ruby had to pummel me with her advice when we were all exhausted, sitting around after we closed, and I knew...I love you, Chloe. I can't be a Raider quarterback without you. That stupid Super Bowl ring will collect dust. But you and I will never collect dust. I'll make sure of it."

"You texted I should take the café, follow my dream."

"We both know I'm an idiot when it comes to texting. I'm sorry. I was assuming, just like I did with my parents, which has a new and happy ending, and—"

"You're talking to your dad?"

"And my mom. We're not one big happy family again, but I know the truth. I'd been wrong for fifteen years and, Chloe, I don't want to be wrong for another fifteen years. The only ring I want is your ring. Our ring." Right in the LaRues' living room, Sam dropped to one knee and pulled a ring from his jeans pocket. "There's still no twinkle lights and no string quartet. And I'm probably a jerk doing this in Jean-Marc's parents' house—"

Chloe choked back a sob.

"But I'm on one knee and I have a ring. Marry me, please, right here, right now. Be my wife."

Chloe bubbled then with a laugh before the tears took over. "Yes, yes, I'll marry you." She flew into his arms, knocking him down before he could stand. They tumbled over the thick carpet patterned with a French pastoral scene. "I love you, Sam. I love you."

"I didn't have time to get a ring, but this is for now—" Sam slipped his college national championship ring onto her finger. "Ruby was right, it was dusty and tarnished. I never wear it. Chloe, please hear me. I'm committed to you. Not my career, not my dreams. It's you and me from now on."

His kiss was rich and full, passionate and unashamed to be holding her on the floor of her former husband's parents' home. He was in, all in—she felt it in his beating heart under the palm of her hand.

Fezzik gave a low growl and Chloe looked up from Sam's embrace. "Hush, Fezzik. He's a good one."

They stood and the giant dog gave a sniff before returning to his bed. As she led Sam to meet Albert and Vivienne, Sam's hand rested on the small of her back. But when Chloe turned to him, he was reaching to shake Albert's hand.

She smiled. The hand she'd felt belonged to God, her approving Father.

CHAPTER 20

*W*hen Chloe first left Paris, if someone had told her she'd be back a few months later, standing in her former in-laws' guest room preparing for her second spring wedding in France, wearing the close-fitting, cream-colored gown that Vivienne had worn when she married Albert, she'd have laughed. Loud and long. Yet today everything felt right and divine. In some way, wearing this dress, life and love had come full circle. The blush satin and tulle skirt swished as she moved, and in less than an hour, she'd be Sam Hardy's wife.

His romantic proposal and suggestion to get married in France had bogged them down in wedding details. It turned out two foreigners couldn't just run down to the courthouse and get married in France. But Vivienne and Albert used their well-earned influence to work some LaRue magic and found a way for Chloe and Sam to avoid the red tape. She and Sam had visited the Deux Jardins *mairie*—city hall—yesterday, signed the forms, been issued their family record book, or *livret de famille*, and been legally married by the mayor. Today was their real wedding.

"My beautiful girl," Mom said as she clipped a crystal-and-silver comb behind Chloe's ear. A silver vine circled around her head and the crystals twinkled in the light streaming through the window. "You've found love again."

"Yes, and you're next."

Mom blushed and said, "We'll see." Her oncologist had declared her done with treatment, and likely cancer-free. She'd need scans and tests to make it official, but everyone was optimistic. And Chloe determined Mom would have more than a lonely widow's life.

"Welcome to the family." Janice hugged her and pressed a handkerchief into her hand. "This was my grandmother's."

The tears today were generous and sweet. Once the date was set, Mom, Frank, and Janice had flown over, and they'd spent the past week touring Paris and Deux Jardins, inspecting the café, and talking about the future.

Sam missed his meeting with the Raiders but he didn't seem at all worried. *"I'll meet with them when I get back."*

Since the café renovations would take time, they decided Chloe would return to Hearts Bend and Haven's. Sam would decide about Vegas after his visit. Yet more and more he seemed less enthralled with the game that had captured him for over two decades. His knee was healing well and he thought he'd be able to manage a few dances at their two very small receptions.

Sophie, still grieving her breakup with Eric, stepped up to help manage Haven's while Chloe and Sam were gone.

"If I can run a bookstore, I can run the bakery. It's no problem, promise. Just give me first dibs on some W4C for my shop."

Done.

Still, there were some feelings of anticipation. She made

Sam promise not to die. For at least fifty years. But he made her promise to let go of fear and trust God. She was nearly a decade older than when she'd married Jean-Marc, so in love, so lost in the fairy tale, believing they'd live happily ever after. Even though Chloe knew no one's future was guaranteed, she would live each day to the fullest.

"Are you ready?" Albert knocked on the door and then peeked inside. "The driver is here. Oh, Chloe, you are *si beau*."

"Goodness, is it time?" She hugged her mother. "I'm suddenly nervous."

"Sam is right for you, darling. We're all here for you."

Sam waited for her on the steps of the Deux Jardins stone chapel. "Ready?" he said.

"Ready."

He didn't say she looked beautiful, but he didn't have to— she saw it in his glistening eyes.

Vivienne handed her a bouquet before she hurried inside the chapel. "The best of everything, my dear beautiful daughter."

Daughter. Yes, she'd always be Vivienne and Albert's daughter.

Deep inside the church, the organist began Pachelbel's Canon in D, and Sam offered his arm.

"Man, Chloe..." He slapped one hand over his heart. "I'm the most blessed man on the earth today. Thank you for marrying me."

"Save it, Titan man. See how you feel in a year."

Sam laughed. "Backatcha, babe."

"That was one fine day when I walked into Haven's, looking for a job, and found you. Shall we get married, start our new life?"

"Hardy on three." Sam stuck out his free hand and Chloe clapped hers over his. "One, two, three... Hardy."

❦ ❦ ❦

"Wait." A week and a half later, Sam stopped Chloe at the threshold of his Nashville loft and scooped her into his arms.

They'd honeymooned on the Riviera for five days—a gift from the LaRues—then worked on the plans for the Deux Jardins café another week. There was lots to be done, which didn't leave much time for decisions. In the quiet candlelight after making love, they'd talked of their future, of God, and what mattered in life. The children they'd someday write down in their *livret de famille*.

"I don't think either of us are good at the God thing, but let's pursue it together. I'm serious, Chloe. I think we need Him."

"I know we do."

"Welcome home, Mrs. Hardy." Sam kissed her, firm and hungry, then trailed kisses down her neck.

"Welcome home, Mr. Hardy." Chloe slipped from his arms. "When is your call with the Raiders?"

Sam checked his watch. "Two hours." He grabbed Chloe's hands and tugged her toward his room.

"Got any ideas on what we can do until then?" she said, laughing.

"I might." He drew her to himself for a lavish kiss. "Are you happy, Mrs. H?"

"Very, Mr. H. Very."

EPILOGUE

$\mathscr{F}$unny how it was when a girl and a guy gave the reins of their lives over to God, to trust His hand. After their May wedding in France, Chloe and Sam settled into an easy, newlywed routine. They bought a recently renovated house in Hearts Bend. On the day they signed papers, the Raiders called to say they were turning Sam down due to his knee. They didn't like their doctor's report or how he'd looked on the day he worked out with the team.

Guess what? He didn't care. He said he was actually relieved, and Chloe knew then and there, God was indeed in heaven. Not that she doubted much these days.

They talked of having kids, but decided to wait a year. See how the near future worked out. Then one July morning when Chloe was at the bakery, getting the morning pastries mixed and in the oven, it hit her. The answer.

Laura Kate to Deux Jardins. She'd be perfect. Minus her messiness, but she was trying and getting a little better. She'd become an excellent baker and her W4C creation had been written up in the local paper as well as a national culinary magazine. Sam knew someone who knew someone, but it was a true and genuine article.

"Laura Kate," she'd said when the girl arrived to start the donuts, "how would you like to move to Deux Jardins and run Café LaRue? We have about six months until the renovations are done, so I can train you properly. I'll go over and help you hire a staff and stay with you through the opening but—" The girl gaped at her, mouth open, eyes wide.

"Yes, yes, yes." She flew at Chloe and wrapped her in an enormous hug. "I was hoping you'd ask because I was too scared to ask but look—" She pulled her phone from her pocket and opened an app. "I've been learning French, you know, just in case." Sam thought it was the best idea since sliced bread, and the LaRues promised to look out for Chloe's protégée.

Mid-July rolled around, and Sam resigned himself to retiring. The Raiders' rejection scared off any other interested teams. The seemingly brusque castoff was something he wrestled with in the night. Chloe prayed for him through the night as he paced the living room crying out to God for help.

Then just before July camp, the Titans called. They wanted him back. Fields had torn his Achilles during drills and was out for the season.

"How's the knee?" Bruce said.

"Ninety percent," Sam said, honest and upfront.

"Good enough."

Bruno negotiated a great deal. Sam Hardy had willingly, heartily given up his dream of a Super Bowl ring for love and a wedding ring. Yet here he was now on the field in Miami this February Sunday playing in...

The Super Bowl.

Chloe sat huddled with the other players' wives, Mom with

her new beau Tom Worley, Janice and Frank, Sam's mom Annabeth, Sophie and her new boyfriend, Alex.

"Come on, Sam." Chloe cupped her hand over her lips and asked God for a bit of Titan help. It was fourth and four on the ten-yard line. Two minutes left in the fourth quarter. The Titans were down by six to the Tampa Bay Buccaneers. This was potentially the final play for them. If they failed to get the first down or score, the Buccaneers would take over on downs and their quarterback would take a knee, letting the clock run out.

Sam looked to the sidelines, then called the play. Chloe could hear his calls in the stands.

"Blue fifteen, fifteen, fifteen..."

She smiled. She knew that play. The fifteens indicated a play Sam had drawn up with the coordinator. If executed correctly, it would catch the Buccaneers' defense completely off guard.

Sam had the ball. He dropped back to pass.

Come on, babe, come on.

Suddenly he took off running. The defense scrambled. He got the first down. Chloe rose to her feet.

"Come on, Sammy!" she screamed.

He was still running. Five-yard line. The two... Touchdown!

The Miami stadium exploded, the cheers so loud, Chloe had to cover her ears. Or maybe it was just the sound of her own screaming and screeching.

Frank boldly hugged everyone who would be hugged, announcing, "That's my boy! Way to go, Sammy."

The extra point kick sailed through the goal posts and just like that, the Titans were ahead by one. With a minute and a half on the clock, the Buccaneers tried for a comeback, but the Titans' defense was having none of it. Marco Martelli had two more sacks in the last thirty seconds. As confetti rained down on the field and the players celebrated, Sam pushed through the throng of players and media personnel, scanning the bleachers.

"Chloe," he called. "Chloe."

She waved from her seat and when Sam spotted her, he jumped over the barrier and climbed up. Wrapping her against him so tight, he whispered in her ear as they swayed side to side. "I love you, babe, I love you."

"I know, Hardy, I know. I love you too."

So far, their happily ever after was off to a good start. A very good start.

* * *

MOST LIKED/TWEETED PICTURES OF SUPER BOWL CHAMPIONS TN TITANS INCLUDE @SAMHARDYQB15 LAYING A SMOKING HOT SMOOCHEROO ON HIS WIFE AFTER THE WIN. TAP THE BIO LINK FOR MORE.

— @PEOPLEMAG ON INSTAGRAM

* * *

CONGRATS @SAMHARDYQB15 AND @MRSHARDYOF-HAVENSHBTN ON A GREAT WIN! #LOOKINGFORASINGLEN-FLPLAYER #JUSTKIDDING #LOOKINGFORTRUELOVE

— @CURVYCARLA ON TWITTER

* * *

THANKS FOR THE WELL WISHES @CURVYCARLA! I HIGHLY RECOMMEND A BAKERY WITH CRULLERS TO FIND #TRUELOVE. I CAN POINT YOU TOWARD A GREAT ONE IN FRANCE! #CAFELARUE #TRUELOVEFOREVER

– @MRSHARDYOFHAVENSHBTN ON TWITTER

AUTHORS' NOTE

Ah... a wedding in Paris. The Eiffel Tower or the Arc de Triomphe in the background. What could be more romantic?

Unfortunately, putting together a wedding in France for non-citizens is nearly impossible. There are no strings to pull to cut the red tape.

In real life, Chloe and Sam would not have been able to get married in Deux Jardins. But we couldn't resist the thought of the romantic village as a backdrop for their special day, so we used some poetic license to make it happen for them.

COOKIE RECIPE

Want to make the cookie that inspired the W4C—complete with white chocolate chips, miniature semi sweet chips, crushed Oreos, and chopped-up Hershey's Cookies & Cream candy bars?

Due to copyright, we can't reprint the recipe, but we sure can share! Go to Baking with Blondie (bakingwithblondie.com) and search the website for the Cookies & Cream Cookies.

You won't be sorry. Enjoy!

CONNECT WITH SUNRISE

Thank you so much for reading *One Fine Day*. We hope you enjoyed the story. If you did, would you be willing to do us a favor and leave a review? It doesn't have to be long—just a few words to help other readers know what they're getting. (But no spoilers! We don't want to wreck the fun!) Thank you again for reading!

We'd love to hear from you—not only about this story, but about any characters or stories you'd like to read in the future. Contact us at www.sunrisepublishing.com/contact.

We also have a monthly update that contains sneak peeks, reviews, upcoming releases, and fun stuff for our reader friends. Sign up at www.sunrisepublishing.com.

OTHER HEARTS BEND NOVELS

Hearts Bend Collection

One Fine Day

You'll Be Mine

Hearts Bend Novels by Rachel Hauck

The Wedding Chapel

The Wedding Shop

The Wedding Dress Christmas

To Save a King

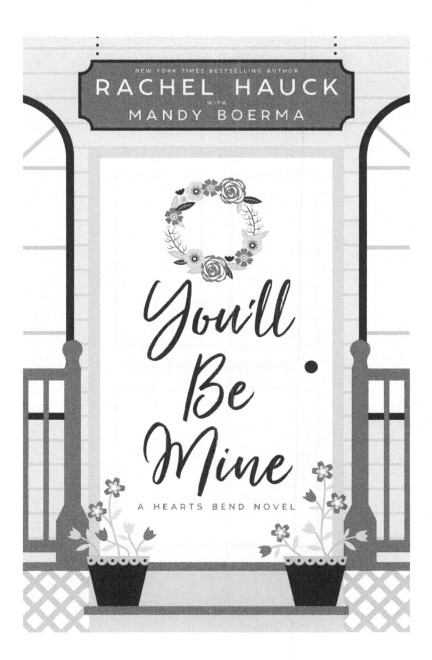

NEW YORK TIMES BESTSELLING AUTHOR

RACHEL HAUCK

WITH

MANDY BOERMA

You'll Be Mine

A HEARTS BEND NOVEL

Turn the page for a sneak peek of the next Hearts Bend novel, *You'll Be Mine* ...

Cupcakes, coffee, and closing a huge deal, all before lunchtime. What more could a girl want?

New shoes? Absolutely.

The cherry red Prada pumps Cami wore today were her splash of color to close the deal with Emerson—the largest property Akron Development acquired in the last two years, in Nashville, Tennessee where the main office is located. All negotiated by Camellia Jackson, the boss's daughter, thank you very much, with zero, zip, nada help from him.

Cami exited the elevator on the second floor from the top to a round of applause.

"Way to go, Cami!"

"Chip off the ol' block!"

"On fire, girl!"

A shrill whistle pierced the air, breaking through the symphony of office sounds—keyboards clicking, voices humming, and printers printing. Had to be Maddy Patterson, who coached her daughter's softball team. Yep, when Cami looked around, Maddy's fingers were on her lips, forming another loud whistle.

Cami bowed and curtsied. Was she glowing? She felt like she was. "Thank you all. I couldn't have done it without the amazing team here at Akron."

Maddy whistled again as Cami made her way to her office, soaking in all the attention. Make no mistake, she'd worked hard for this one. Really hard. Because being the boss's daughter afforded her nothing.

"Love the shoes! Jimmy?" This from Astrid, Cami's personal assistant who stood by her office ready to trade Cami's Gucci purse and attaché for an iPad and a Perrier. Soothing jazz piped through a speaker hidden behind a silk plant in the corner. Astrid always played music, insisting she needed to cover the noise outside their office that filtered in when the door was open, which was always.

"Prada. And nothing says success like red shoes."

Cami's shoes were her *thing* outside of closing deals for her father's company. Which was her number one thing. She strived for his approval. Don't judge. At least she could admit it.

"I'd love to talk shoes and shopping but..." Astrid said with a hesitation in her voice. "Brant wants to see you."

Cami stared at her assistant. "You're kidding." Dad, aka Brant, was always busy when she closed deals. It took days, sometimes weeks, for him to congratulate her on a deal.

While her colleagues had his approval, praise, and delight, atta boys, atta girls, slaps on the back, celebratory steak dinners, plaques for their walls, goofy trophies for their desks, Cami received a passing congratulations and eventually, sometimes, her steak dinner.

When it came to his dear ole daughter, Brant Jackson's

words were few. Sometimes she wondered if it pained him to really praise her.

"Not kidding. He buzzed down right before you came in," Astrid said.

Cami started for the door. "Do you know what it's about?"

"Haven't a clue."

The duo walked to the elevator together. Astrid whispered a *good luck* then turned back to their office space. Good luck? Why would she need it? She'd just closed a huge deal. Was he actually calling her up to his penthouse office to congratulate her?

Brant was sitting at his desk when Cami knocked lightly on his open office door. "You wanted to see me?"

"Cami," he said, standing. "Come in, come in."

For years, her relationship with Dad seemed to be a tug of war. Which one would show some sort of affection first? As her father, Cami felt it was his responsibility. Especially when she was a teen, especially after Mom died. But she learned quickly she had to extend the olive branch. Which eventually made her angry. Which made her quit trying.

However, he knew she'd closed the Emerson deal, so was he bending first?

"I'm flying down to Palm Beach this afternoon." Dad moved to the chair at the small glass-top table in the corner of his office. "Roger Davis finally agreed to meet about his ocean-front property. I was going to take you for your steak dinner, but I'll need to reschedule."

She struggled to mask her surprise. He was going to take her to dinner?

"I couldn't go tonight anyway, I made plans with Annalise." Her sister was her best friend and counselor.

When Dad cancelled Cami's steak dinner after her second,

or was it third, big acquisition, Annalise threw her a surprise dinner. Her husband, Steve, sizzled steaks on the grill along with corn on the cob. Annalise made Mom's green bean casserole and homemade apple cake and invited half a dozen of their childhood friends. They were the picture perfect, happily in love couple.

It'd been the best steak dinner ever. Cami smiled remembering.

"To Cami Jackson, Nashville's next great businesswoman."

In her seven years on the job, Cami worked harder than anyone else to get to the top. And now, here she sat, in the boss's grand, top floor office.

"I had dinner with your sister and Steve last night," Dad said. "Look, we'll reschedule your congratulatory dinner." His fixed smile was part father, part boss.

She wanted to say she'd not hold her breath but refrained. With Dad, Brant, it was always something. A golf game. Another business deal. Or just the general excuse of "too busy." He'd not solidified anything with her for tonight even though he knew from the staff meetings and her emails, as well as her weekly report, she was closing the deal.

"So, Roger?" Cami said. "You finally wore him down. Congratulations." She shifted her stance, trying to get comfortable in Dad's stiff, formal office.

His expansive cherry desk sat in front of the floor-to-ceiling windows overlooking the Cumberland River, which was vastly different than her view that looked over the downtown Nashville streets. A small sitting area of black leather pieces sat in the far corner and were more aesthetically pleasing than functionally comfortable.

On the other side of the office was a glass and metal conference table with black leather chairs. The beige walls were, well...beige. And empty. Devoid of art and nothing of color.

If it wasn't for the large pane windows overlooking the river, the place would be a desert for any creative mind.

"We both knew he'd cave sooner or later." Dad pointed to a pink box from Sweet Tooth Bakery on the small table. He pulled out a chair and sat, gesturing for Cami to follow suit. "Jeremy ordered your congratulatory cupcakes." He smiled as if the treats were a perfectly suitable substitute for a celebratory steak dinner with the boss and founder of the company. "He asked for the chocolate ones you like."

"Thank you." Really, she'd have to remember to thank Dad's assistant on her way out. The cupcake tradition was usually for the staff meeting. This private celebration surprised and touched her.

Over the years, she'd adjusted to their cordial, non-affectionate father-daughter relationship, and it worked well for Akron Development. It was how things were between them since Mom died.

"Is that why you called me up here?" Cami opened the pink lid to reveal two double fudge chocolate cupcakes.

She pulled one out and reached for the napkins next to the box, then slid the box toward her dad.

Sun filtered through the windows, giving the dull office some brightness as Cami sank her teeth into the delectable treat. Calories didn't count on closing day. Especially with a multi-million-dollar property.

"I'm going ahead with the new office in Indianapolis." Dad took a small bite of his cupcake and returned it to the box before he reached for a napkin. "Indianapolis is too hot a market to delay any longer." His heavy, steady gaze landed on her. "I want you to head it up."

Cami stared at him, lip deep in chocolate cake and frosting. "Hmmphph?" She chewed with a napkin over her mouth, swallowing, trying not to choke. "What?"

"You're opening the Indy office." Dad moved to his desk to retrieve a large green folder and brought it back to Cami and sat down again. "While you closed on your deal, I closed on office space. Here's the information. It's a blank slate so you can build it out however you want. You'll find the name of a recommended contractor and the budget for the remodel. I want the work done and the office up and running by September first, so you've got a lot to do."

"Wait, wait, what?" September first? Less than three months away. "Dad, I thought we were not going to risk the capital right now."

"I looked at the data. We need to go now. I'm starting to feel we're already too late. Are you in? Because if you're not—" Dad reached for the folder. "I'll see if Geoffrey—"

She stopped his hand before he could take the folder. "Can you give me a second to wrap my head around this? You didn't think to at least ask me first?" She was on her feet. "I have a life here, you know." Not much of one but he didn't need to know. "Friends, Annalise." Could she live four hours from her sister? "I just moved into my condo a few months ago. I finally got my soaker tub last week. I have a view of the river."

Her shoe closet was the size of a small bedroom, mostly because it *was* the spare bedroom. She'd spent months designing and decorating, picking the colors, the fixtures. She finally had *her home.*

"You can sell it for a profit. Downtown lofts are up fifteen percent." Was it always about numbers with him? "Or you can lease it if you want. But you're heading up Indy." Dad rose up, stretching to the six foot three that used to make her feel safe and protected.

"And if I refuse?" The emotion flowing through her made her voice quiver and she resented it.

"Cami, you've been telling me for two years you want a

pathway to promotion. You want to take on more responsibility. You want to take over the company one day. Don't tell me you didn't mean it."

"I meant it." No doubt Indianapolis was the opportunity she needed to advance, so why did it feel like her father was sending her away?

From his desk, Dad's landline buzzed and he circled around to answer it, giving Cami a moment to compose herself. After a five-word conversation with Jeremy, he returned to their little table of chocolate cupcakes and surprises.

But the short interlude gave her time to think, take her emotions in command. The city *was* ripe for expansion. It *was* a fantastic move for the company, and if she'd get her head on straight, a huge stepping-stone for her.

"What's it going to be, Cami? You can refuse, of course, or resign, but yes, Indy is yours. You'll be promoted to director. If things go well, vice president after two years." Dad leaned toward her. "This is what you wanted, wasn't it?"

"Yes." Cami cleared her voice. "Yes, thank you, it is." When Dad retired, there would be no doubt in anyone's mind that she'd earned his office through her own merit. She could do this...spend a few years in Indy then head back down to Nashville. "All right." She sat back in her chair and opened the green folder. "Give me the details."

Dad relaxed with an exhale and smiled. "I bought a refurbished warehouse in the center of the business district. Take what office space you need then rent out the rest. Build out your space first then oversee the rest. Give yourself two years to complete the build-out. But you, Cami, I'm serious, be ready by the first of September. Get Astrid to start posting jobs for the positions you want to fill. Make a list of potential Akron folks who might like to transfer up north."

Really? Who'd want to leave Nashville?

"You should talk to her about going with you." Dad peeked into the pink box. "I think you'll need her." He considered the rest of the cupcake then closed the lid.

This was why he was so great in business, in life, in everything. Discipline. When they passed around cupcakes in the staff meeting or gathered for the quarterly office potluck, Brant Jackson proudly proclaimed he only weighed ten pounds more than in his high school wrestling days.

But when it came to Cami, his disciplined life, emotions, went too far.

"Maybe," she said. "Astrid's been going on and on about Boyfriend proposing." He had a real name which Cami couldn't recall at the moment. "I'm not sure she'll want to go."

"Hasn't she been dating him for a while?" Dad made a face. "If he's not proposed by now, he probably won't."

"Well I'm not going to tell her that, Dad." With him, business always came first. Even over family. Over his wife and daughters. But if Astrid had a chance for a happily ever after, even with a sloth for a boyfriend, Cami wasn't going to stand in her way.

"Someone should. Get her to go with you, Cami. She's one of the best. If I didn't have Jeremy, I'd steal Astrid from you." Dad pointed to the folder again. "The real estates agent sent some apartments for you to review."

Cami flipped through the top pages, all apartment listings. Already she could tell they wouldn't compare to her beautiful downtown loft, the one she'd customized for herself.

She read the name on the real estates agent listing. Max Caldwell.

"I-I'll call today." September first would be here way too fast.

"Good. Glad you're on board, Cami." Dad stood, indicating

the conversation was coming to a close. "I saw on the project board you're working the Landmark Shopping Complex. I saw Jared Landry the other day and he said you'd approached him about it. Excellent property, Cami, but I want you focused on the Indy office. You won't have time for a Landmark kind of deal."

Cami stood, reaching for the cupcake box. More than half of hers remained. But then she glanced at her lean father and changed her mind. "Dad, do you lecture Geoffrey or Mark on how to manage their lives *and* their jobs? Or just me?"

Dad regarded her with something she interpreted as respect. And she'd take it. "Good point. You've proven yourself. Do what you feel you must but, Cami, my advice is to focus on Indy."

He was right. Of course, he was the great Brant Jackson. Already details of the massive project had started swirling in her head. She had a lot to do in two and a half months.

"Can I ask why September first?"

"The city gave us a huge tax break if we open by the third quarter. The contractor's bid goes to August thirtieth. He can finish the build-out but if we don't get on it, give him enough time, he can't guarantee when he can complete the work. He has another job September first. That's why we have a two-year goal on opening the rest of the property."

"Then I have work to do." The sweetness of the cupcake soured as she walked toward the door. Then for some odd reason, she got a bit of *grr* in her gut and she spun around. "You need artwork in here, Dad. Why don't you let me acquire some for you before I go?"

"That's not necessary, Cami."

"But it is necessary. How do you work in this uninspired space?"

Dad tapped his temple. "I got all I need in here."

She sighed, eyed the pink box one more time, then bid her father a good trip. "Tell Roger hi for me."

By the time she made it back to her office, her head was pounding with details, her red shoes pinched her toes, and she felt completely void of the cheering and accolades from thirty minutes ago.

ACKNOWLEDGMENTS

From Carrie:

It's true that it takes a village to launch a debut novelist into the world and I required an entire municipality.

I've been part of more writing classes and critique groups than anyone should admit to. I'm forcing myself to limit my thanks to those who've been in my life as I've worked on this book.

First, I must thank Elnora King and her family. Elnora opened her home to classes for years and I learned more from her than I can say. Thank you to Jeff and Sally King and Brad and Mary King for sharing your mom with us. I miss her every week.

Other craft and critique partners I value: Bethany Goble and Sheri Humphreys. Phyllis Brown, Terell Byrd, Elizabeth Hiett, Twyla Smith, and Toni Weymouth. My breakfast group: Kim Bagato, Shawna Bryant, Penny Childers, and Kelly Hollman. You are all wonderful writers!

The teaching I received through Novel Academy and My Book Therapy has been outstanding. Thank you to the staff there! I also need to thank my prayer huddlers: Jeanne, Erin, Penny, and Elly. Janie, Lisa, and MaryAnn. Thank you for the prayers. They kept me going on so many days when I doubted I could face another blank page.

My Spa Girls: Abbie, Carol, Debbie, Nancy. Friends for more years than I care to say publicly. Thank you for the prayers and texts and notes. I love you all.

Huge thank you to my Golden Heart Dreamweaver sisters. Y'all are the best cheerleaders and encouragers around. Not to mention very fine writers.

When I started this journey with Sunrise, I never expected to find three new sisters: Mandy Boerma, Carrie Vinnedge, and Carrie Weston, I'm so grateful God brought us together. I can't imagine doing any of this without you.

The rest of the Sunrise team: Lindsay Harrel, Rel Mollet, Kate Angelo, and our amazing Susan May Warren. You are all rock stars!

A special thanks to my agent, Janet Kobobel Grant of Books and Such Literary Agency. You've been my dream agent since I first dipped a toe into the publishing industry. Thank you for seeing some potential and signing me. I looooove being a Bookie!

Rachel Hauck: You're a beautiful person inside and out. Thank you for your patience in teaching, guiding, and mentoring me.

My parents: Deanna, Dale, Darlene, and Bernie. One birthed me and has been there since the beginning. (Thanks, Mom!) The rest of you came into my life at just the time I needed you. You've always been cheerleaders and encouragers. Thank you.

My family: David: The love of my life. The reason I know there are happily ever afters and I want to write them all. Daughter Amber and son-in-law Martin, daughter Taryn and son-in-law Landon: Thank you for not thinking I was crazy (or at least not saying it out loud) when your mother said she was going to write romance novels. My grandchildren: Evelyn, Gavin, Charlotte, June, Zachary, and Ellinor. I love you to the moon and back.

Thank you, Jesus, for saving me when I was lost. I don't know where I'd be without You. *Soli Deo gloria.*

And a note from Rachel:

Thank you Carrie for all your hard work!

ABOUT THE AUTHORS

New York Times, USA Today & Wall Street Journal Bestselling author **Rachel Hauck** writes from sunny central Florida. A RITA finalist and winner of Romantic Times Inspirational Novel of the Year, and Career Achievement Award, she writes vivid characters dealing with real life issues. Readers have fallen in love with the quaint and loveable small town of Hearts Bend, TN introduced in the NYT bestselling *The Wedding Dress,* which launched her Wedding Collection novels. Visit her at www.rachelhauck.com.

Carrie Padgett thinks nuts take up room where chocolate ought to be. She also believes in faith, families, fun, and happily ever afters. She lives in Central California where she writes contemporary women's fiction with sweet romance, humor, and sass. Visit her at www.carriepadgett.com.